PRAISE FOR
LADY ALEXANDRA'S LOVER

"Ms. Hardt has a way of writing that makes me forget I'm reading a book. It's more like slipping into a world she created and getting lost for a while."
~Tiger Lily, Whipped Cream Reviews

"Helen writes these books with such grace and finesse that you feel as though you've been transported back in time and are walking among the characters. You feel every bit of passion, anguish, and love emanating from the pages. It envelops you and leaves you grasping at the hopes that these two wonderfully in love couples get to have the HEA they both deserve."
~Bare Naked Words

LADY
ALEXANDRA'S
LOVER

A Sex and the Season Novel

HELEN HARDT

WATERHOUSE PRESS

LADY
ALEXANDRA'S
LOVER

A Sex and the Season Novel

HELEN HARDT

In memory of
William Charles Belcher
1936 - 2015
Rest in peace, Daddy.

CONFESSIONS OF LADY PRUDENCE

by Madame O

My Dearest Amelia,

Forgive me for not having written in several weeks, but I had terrible sickness on the ship home. I miss you so, and I especially miss all the fun and frolic we shared whilst I visited you on holiday in the Americas.

I was no sooner back in our London townhome when Auntie Beatrice insisted that I begin art lessons. Amelia, I can't draw a straight line to save my own soul. Art lessons? Truly? I dreaded the very thought. An hour several times per week listening to some old codger preach the virtues of light and dark hardly excited me, and I possess the artistic talent of a tomato. But Auntie would not be swayed. So yesterday, I began.

My instructor, rather than the foul old lech I imagined, is a young Frenchman. I nearly swooned when I saw him, Amelia, so beautiful is he. Dark hair and simmering brown eyes...and the way he looked at me... My quim started pulsing just from his gaze upon me.

"You must be Lady Prudence," he said with a smile.

I let out a sigh. "I am."

"It is a pleasure." He took my hand and kissed it. "I am Christophe Bertrand."

Oh, Amelia, he is a delicacy. How my stomach fluttered when he brushed his lips over my hand. I thought perhaps

I could learn something after all. He set up two easels and placed canvases upon them. We spent the next hour learning and mixing color, until he finally turned to me.

"Forgive me, my lady, but I find I can no longer ignore your beauty."

My cheeks heated to blazing, Amelia. I am quite sure they were redder than the crimson paint on the palette.

"Monsieur Bertrand... Our lesson..."

He took my hand and kissed it again, this time letting his lips linger just a touch longer. A surge charged straight to my cunny, and a slight moan escaped my lips.

"My lady, beauty such as yours is a rare gift. Please, if you would allow me to paint you—"

"Paint me?" I stood, aghast.

He wanted to paint me? I'd been so hoping he might want to kiss me. Truly kiss me, the way you did, Amelia, and the way Broderick and Miles did when the four of us were together. What wonderful times we had!

"Yes, my lady. Your azure eyes, your raven hair, your lips the color of the rarest ruby—you are stunning. If you would allow it, I will find some way to compensate you for your time. I'm a man of modest means, but I could make your lessons gratis."

"My aunt is paying for the lessons," said I.

"Perhaps if I spoke with her—"

"No!" I screamed.

Can you imagine? Prudish Auntie Beatrice allowing me to pose for this young man? It would never happen. And suddenly, Amelia, I wanted him to paint me. I wanted it more than my next breath of fresh air. More even than a kiss from him.

"Monsieur Bertrand"—I smiled coquettishly, or so I hoped—"I would be happy to pose for you. Gratis."

"Outstanding!" His grin lit up his face. "When may we begin?"

"How about now?"

"Well, I do have some time presently," he said. "Perhaps we could go out of doors. The afternoon sunlight would highlight your lovely fair complexion."

"No." I touched his arm lightly. Such sparks I felt! "You will paint me here, in the parlor." I walked to the door and turned the key in the lock. "And you will paint me nude."

CHAPTER ONE

Brighton Estate, Wiltshire, England July, 1853

"I'm going to sleep with Mr. Landon."

Lady Sophie MacIntyre abruptly straightened her back and dropped her crocheting to the floor with a soft thud. "Excuse me?"

"There's not a thing wrong with your hearing, Sophie dear." Lady Alexandra MacIntyre smiled. "I said I'm going to sleep with Mr. Landon."

Sophie picked up her crocheting and let out a sigh. "I'm not in the slightest mood for one of your jokes, Ally."

"Who is joking?"

"For goodness' sake. You don't expect me to believe—"

Alexandra stood, held up a hand to stop her sister's words, and placed her own knitting in the basket next to her. She wasn't joking. She'd been waiting months now for Mr. Nathan Landon to propose marriage to her, and she was damned tired of his foolish trifling. "I certainly do expect you to believe it. I've allowed him so many liberties I'm beginning to feel like I've already lost my virginity. Yet nothing. No promises from him, not even a bloody 'I love you.'"

"Have you considered," Sophie said, "that perhaps it's because you've allowed him so many liberties that he's not taking you more seriously?"

"Don't be silly. I haven't allowed him liberties to get him to propose marriage. I've allowed him the liberties because I wanted to."

"Ally..."

"Have you never been curious, sister dear?"

Sophie's cheeks reddened. "I'm as curious as anyone, but I know my place."

"You and Van Arden never—"

"Of course not!" Sophie said hotly. "Not even a kiss."

"You're missing out on life's pleasures, then."

"I've no interest in—"

"Oh, Sophie, please spare me the self-righteous drivel. You just admitted to curiosity. We're all interested. Lily and Rose both slept with their husbands before marriage. And while it might have been behavior to expect from Lily, it was not from Rose. Yet she did it."

"Still, Ally, if it's marriage you're after, perhaps you should not have let him have so many liberties."

"And you think he would have proposed by now if I hadn't allowed the kissing?"

"I think it's a distinct possibility."

Ally rolled her eyes. No man in the world would marry a woman just to get into her drawers. There were places one could go to get *that*. And with Mr. Landon's money, he could have as much as he wanted. "I disagree, dear, but it's quite a moot point. I've allowed the liberties, and I can't take them back. Nor do I want to. I enjoyed it."

"And now you think to give him the ultimate liberty?"

"Yes."

"Whatever for?"

Ally smiled deviously. "So you can catch us, of course."

★ ★ ★ ★

Lord Evan Xavier entered his father's mansion on the Brighton Estate, handing his riding gloves to the butler.

"I trust your ride was pleasant, my lord?"

"Yes, thank you, Graves. Are my stepsisters at home?"

"Ladies Sophie and Alexandra are in the front parlor."

"Thank you." Evan turned and headed up the long staircase to the second level, his goal to get as far away from the front parlor as possible. He didn't want to deal with his stepsisters at the moment, especially Alexandra, who had lately turned into the very bane of his existence.

Their newly wedded parents had left for the continent nearly a month ago, and while they were abroad, the girls were Evan's responsibility. His father, David, the Earl of Brighton, and his new stepmother, Iris, the girls' mother, were desperately in love with each other, and Evan didn't expect them home anytime soon. He normally enjoyed having the estate to himself when his father was away, but now... Well, he was no longer alone.

He found sanctuary in his own suite of rooms on the third level. The girls would never dream of setting foot there. He dismissed Redmond, his valet, and stripped off his riding clothes himself. After cleaning up, he lay on his bed and closed his eyes. Only a bloody hour until dinnertime...

★ ★ ★ ★

"Catch you?" Sophie said, her green eyes wide. "Have you lost your mind?"

"Of course not. You catch us, and you tell our new stepfather, the esteemed Earl of Brighton, and he will force Mr. Landon to do right by me." Ally smiled. The plan was brilliant.

No one would think for a moment that her sweet and prudish older sister had made up the tale. And their new stepfather had already proven himself to be vastly overprotective.

"Absolutely not." Sophie vehemently shook her head. "I'll not take part in this ridiculous scheme."

"But you must, Sophie. Everyone will know you're telling the truth."

"This is a truth I want no part of. Please reconsider, Ally. You'll be ruined."

"Do you think I care about being ruined? I want to be married, and Mr. Landon is my choice."

"Do you love him?"

"What does that matter?"

"It's the only thing that matters. Just ask Lily or Rose."

"Lily and Rose both made fine matches," Ally said, "and I'm thrilled for them. But I'm not going to wait around forever. I want Mr. Landon."

"You want his million pounds."

"I've made no secret of that. But I do care for him. He's kind, and he makes me laugh."

"But do you love him?"

"Yes, I think I might." It wasn't exactly a lie. Ally enjoyed his conversation and his kisses, and she loved him as one might love a friend.

"Then you don't. Both Lily and Rose say you'll know when you're in love with a man."

"Perhaps Lily and Rose are wrong. Did you ever consider that?"

"No."

Honestly, Ally hadn't considered it either. "Then perhaps Mr. Landon is my true love after all, even though I don't feel the fireworks that Lily and Rose felt. After all, that crone at the Midsummer Festival said my true love was closer than I knew."

"First of all, I don't believe any old crone knows anything," Sophie said. "But even if she does, what makes you think she's talking about Mr. Landon?"

"Who else in the world could she be talking about?"

Sophie sighed. "I'm sorry. I won't take part in your scheme. I cannot, in good conscience."

Her sister's reaction didn't surprise Ally in the least. But no worry. She'd simply go to London on her own, find someone else to help her, and seduce Mr. Landon into taking her to bed. How difficult could it be?

She turned toward the parlor door when it opened.

"My ladies," Graves said, "dinner is served."

"Thank you, Graves." Sophie stood. "Will Lord Evan be joining us?"

"Yes, my lady. He returned a little less than an hour past."

"Lovely," Sophie said.

Yes, lovely. That was all Ally needed—her stuffy new stepbrother hindering her every movement. Well, she was going to London, no matter what he had to say about it.

Ally took her place at the small table in the informal dining room. Taking meals with only her sister and her new stepbrother for the past month had become tedious. Sophie hardly said a word unless Ally or Evan engaged her, and Evan rarely engaged either one of them. He still wasn't quite comfortable with their parents' marriage, and he made no secret of it.

When Evan entered, Ally's heart lurched. She couldn't help it. As much as he tried her patience, he was a beautiful man. A former oarsman at school, he was big and muscular, with blondish hair and warm brown eyes. His high cheekbones, slender nose, and broad jawline formed near masculine perfection. He resembled his father, and Ally had no trouble imagining her mother being swept away by the earl twenty years ago, even though she'd been married at the time. Married, of course, to the girls' tyrant of a father who'd abused all three of them and left them penniless due to his negligence and reckless spending.

"Good evening, Sophie, Alexandra," Evan said, taking his seat at the head of the table.

"Good evening, E-Evan." Sophie blushed.

Ally couldn't help smiling. Sophie still had issue with using Evan's Christian name. Always true to convention, her sister. Timid and shy to a fault, Sophie often stammered around new people—though Evan was hardly new in their lives. Before their parents had married a month ago, he'd been courting their cousin Lady Rose Jameson. But Rose had loved another and was now married to Cameron Price-Adams, the Earl of Thornton and heir to a marquessate.

"Yes, good evening," Ally said.

"I trust your day passed pleasantly," Evan said.

"Yes, of course. And yours?" Ally asked.

"Pleasant indeed."

Of all the insufferable small talk! As if he gave a care about their day. About as much as she cared about his.

"I'm going to London." There. That would get his attention.

Evan looked up from his soup. "I beg pardon?"

"Ally..." Sophie began.

"I said I'm going to London. I have a dear friend whom I would like to visit, and she is excited to receive me."

Evan cleared his throat. "And who is this friend, might I ask?"

Ally smiled, thinking quickly. "Miss...Prudence...Spofford. She is expecting my visit. I'll be leaving on the morrow."

Evan looked to Sophie. "And I suppose you will go with her?"

Sophie shook her head. "No, my lor— er, Evan. I have no plans to accompany her."

"Then I'm afraid it's out of the question. You cannot travel alone."

"Nonsense. I'm twenty-one years old. The coachman will be with me. He will see me safely to the rail. And Prudence is expecting me."

"No," Evan said flatly.

"No?" Alexandra raised her eyebrows.

"You heard me. No."

"Since when do you have authority over me?"

"Since my father and your mother left you under my protection. You're my responsibility while they're gone, and I won't have you gallivanting all over London unchaperoned."

"I'm of age, Evan. I can go to London if I want. And I'm leaving tomorrow."

"Ally," Sophie said, "I do wish you would reconsider. The railway is still new. Perhaps traveling by coach would be safer."

"No," Evan said.

"You don't trust our coachmen?" Ally asked.

"Yes, yes, of course I trust our coachmen."

"Then what is the problem?"

"I don't trust *you*." He pushed away his plate and stood, summoning a footman. "I'm no longer hungry. Please clear my place."

Ally's skin tightened. How dare he? "You don't even know me. How can you possibly say you don't trust me?"

Evan closed his eyes for a moment, and then opened them. "Forgive me. I misspoke. I have no reason not to trust you. However, you may not go to London unaccompanied."

"Well, I'm going," Ally said hotly. "And you have no right to stop me."

"Very well." Evan sat back down, a look of defeat on his chiseled features. "Then I have no choice but to go with you."

CONFESSIONS OF LADY PRUDENCE

by Madame O

Christophe's eyes nearly popped out of his head, Amelia! His fiery gaze well-nigh melted my garments right off my body.

"My lady..."

"If you could help me with my gown, sir," I said, "I would be most appreciative."

"I'm not sure this is proper..."

"Goodness, how can you paint me nude if I don't disrobe?" I turned around. "Since there is no maid present, and I don't intend to summon one, I need you to unfasten me and unlace my corset."

He cleared his throat. "Yes, my lady."

When he had unbuttoned my dress, he slipped it over my shoulders and it fell to the floor. He unlaced my corset, and I gulped in a breath of precious air as he removed it. I stood before him in my chemise and drawers. I turned and let my chemise drop to the floor atop my dress and petticoats.

"My lady..."

I held out my already throbbing breasts. "What do you think, Monsieur Bertrand? Do you like my bubbies?"

His cheeks pinked. "Ah...they're...lovely, my lady."

"What color do you think will do my nipples justice? Rose? Light brown?"

He shook his head. "A brownish red, perhaps."

I fingered my nipples slowly, and then pinched them

both between my thumbs and forefingers. Tingling sensations arrowed to my pussy. "Now what color, sir?"

"Brick red, my lady. Lord..."

"What is it?" I asked innocently.

"You. You're so..."

I inched forward. "Would you like to pinch my nipples, Monsieur Bertrand? I'd like it if you would."

I placed his hands on my breasts. He sucked in a sharp breath.

"Don't be afraid, sir."

"I'm not afraid, but this—"

I laid my finger over his soft pink lips. "We are alone. The door is locked. My auntie sleeps during the afternoon, and no servant will dare disturb us. Now pinch my nipples, sir."

He squeezed them lightly, and oh, Amelia, my cunny throbbed! Remember how we used to pinch each other's nipples and suck them? I do so love to have someone play with my diddeys.

"Harder," I whispered. "Pinch them harder."

He briefly tugged on them and then let them both go. I whimpered at the loss of his touch. How I wanted more!

"Would you like to suck my nipples, sir?" I entwined my fingers through his silky dark hair and pulled his head forward. "Please. Kiss them. Suck them."

He let out a shaky breath and lowered his lips to one turgid bud. Oh, how I wanted to reach into my drawers and between my legs and rub my cunny! I was already wet with cream slickening my thighs.

He kissed my nipple lightly, and then more passionately, until he finally sucked it between his lips and tugged.

"Oh, sir! That feels wonderful."

He continued sucking whilst he found my other nipple with his fingers and pinched it hard.

"Oh!" How I longed to touch my pussy and bring about the lovely climax you taught me, Amelia.

He swirled his tongue around my nipple, licked it, kissed it, sucked it, continuing to pinch and tug at the other one. The sweet smacking of his mouth echoed against my hot skin. When I could bear it no longer, I untied my drawers, let them fall to the ground, and touched my slick pussy lips. I steered clear of the magic button. I did not want to explode yet. But the warmth of my own cream against my fingers nearly drove me mad.

When I'd had all I could take, I threaded my fingers through his soft hair and pulled him toward me. His mouth crushed to mine and we kissed, our tongues twirling, swirling, dueling, until we were both nearly void of breath.

I gasped and broke away. "My cunt," I said. "Please, sir. Lick my cunt."

CHAPTER TWO

Sitting across from Evan in a coach all day wasn't the worst to ever befall Alexandra. Gazing at his handsome face and wonderful body was certainly no hardship. His grey traveling suit accentuated his thunderous broad shoulders to the point that Ally feared the seams might rip if he flexed those amazing muscles. He was a glorious sight.

But listening to him? That she could do without. He didn't speak much, but when he did, she tuned him out—or tried to— by hiding behind a novel. They had hours to go, for Evan had decided to take the coach all the way to London rather than go by rail.

"It looks to storm," he'd said, "and the rail won't be safe."

"For goodness' sake," Ally had replied, "I've traveled during many storms and had no problems at all."

"Not by rail, you haven't."

True. She couldn't argue. She'd rarely traveled by rail. Having grown up in near poverty, she wasn't accustomed to such. In her mind, the rail would be safer, as they weren't dependent on horses, who could spook at any time.

Evan had refuted that concern as well. "My team is well trained and will do fine. Besides, if the weather gets too unruly, we will simply stop for the night for lodging."

Of course. Lodging. Something else she wasn't used to. Lodging cost money, which she'd never had in abundance. Money matters seemed to be over now that her mother had married the earl, but Ally couldn't be a burden forever. If her current plan worked out—and she had no doubt it would—money would no longer be a worry to her. With Mr. Landon's millions at her disposal, she could take care of herself and Sophie both. Spinsterhood was probably in her sister's future. Ally loved Sophie dearly, but given her timidity and adherence to convention, the poor dear was likely never to marry. Ally had every intention of taking care of her older sister and making a home for her. She could be a doting auntie—the picture suited Sophie well.

Ally looked up from her book at Evan's handsome face. The rain was pelting the roof of the carriage now, but Evan didn't seem concerned. Good. Neither would she be concerned then. The horses were doing fine, and the coachman hadn't said two words since they left.

Evan. Ally smiled to herself. While the idea of spending time with him hardly enamored her, her scheme couldn't have worked out better. Evan would be the perfect person to catch her and Mr. Landon in the act. His sense of honor would work in her favor. He'd demand that Mr. Landon do right by her. He might even call him out. Evan had a temper, though he kept it well disguised most of the time. He'd come close to calling out her cousin-in-law Cameron a month previously, when Rose had chosen him over Evan.

Yes, he might be insufferable, but the more she considered her circumstances, the more she was sure everything was progressing perfectly.

When a jolt of thunder crashed through the air, Ally jerked forward and nearly fell into Evan's lap.

He took her arm and steadied her back into her seat. "Are you all right?"

She nodded. "Of course. But are you sure we should be continuing? This is a bad storm."

"John will let us know if we should be concerned, Alexandra. Trust me, I've driven through far worse."

Ally nodded and gulped down a swallow. "You may call me Ally. Everyone does."

Evan nodded and turned back to the newspaper he was perusing.

Well, then. That was that. Ally returned to her novel and tried reading the page she'd been on for the last half hour. When she'd finally absorbed the words, she closed her eyes and tried to drown out the whomping of the rain on the carriage roof.

Her eyes shot open as she was catapulted into Evan's lap.

"John! John!" Evan was yelling. "What's going on?"

The carriage was bumping along the road—or not the road—and Ally's heart thudded right along with it. Icy fear gripped her.

"What's happening?" she yelled, trying to gather her wits. She'd been half-asleep and now... What was going on?

"I don't know," Evan said. "Calm down, Alexandra." He held her tightly.

Still, she shivered.

"It's Thor," came the coachman's voice. "I think lightning struck him. And Odin—"

Ally let out a blood-curdling scream as she was jammed against the side of the carriage, blacking out.

★ ★ ★ ★

"Alexandra. Alexandra!" Evan shook the woman gently, and then not so gently, gripping her shoulders like a vise.

"Wake up! Please!"

She'd been thrown against the side of the carriage when it toppled, but she was breathing, and he thanked God for that. Poor John had been thrown much farther outside and hadn't fared as well. A good man, John, and he deserved better in life than to have it ended because a horse got struck by lightning. What were the chances? Thor was comatose. Poor beast. Evan's heart broke for the horse, but he could do nothing. His first priority was Alexandra.

They'd driven off the road and into the countryside. John had clearly lost control of the horses. The road was no longer visible, no doubt only because of the rain and fog. At least Evan hoped that was the case.

No sooner had Evan unharnessed Odin than he galloped away, whinnying. The poor thing was petrified. Evan hoped the horse could find shelter when he calmed down.

Evan had laid Alexandra in the shelter of the toppled coach. His head hurt, and he felt a bit woozy, but all in all he was in decent shape. Alexandra didn't appear to be hurt. Perhaps she just had the wind knocked out of her. His father would never forgive him if something happened to either of Iris's girls.

At least she was somewhat protected from the pelting rain. He continued to try to rouse her while watching for anyone else to come down the road to help them. Minutes ticked by and no one came. Most had more sense than to come out in this mess.

The storm had come out of nowhere. What had started as the gentle pitter-patter of rain had turned violent in what seemed like no time at all.

"Alexandra, please wake up." He shook her again.

Even with her hair and clothes in disarray and wet from the rain, the woman was a beautiful sight. Her chestnut hair, having come loose from its bun, fell in waves against her tan traveling clothes.

"Please," he said again, his heart pounding. "You've got to be all right."

Her ruby-red lips twitched.

"Alexandra? Can you hear me?"

Her eyes fluttered open. "Wha— What happened?"

"A carriage accident. Are you all right? Do you hurt?"

She gulped. "I... I believe I'm... I don't know."

Confusion. Well, of course, that was inevitable. "We need to find some shelter. Can you get up? Can you walk?" He stood to help her.

When she put his hand in hers, a tingle shot through him. Odd, and definitely no time for that now. He pulled her to her feet, and she fell against his soaked clothes.

"Who? What are we doing here?"

"It's me, Evan, and we've had an accident. One of the horses was struck by lightning. Come now, we need to go. Can you walk?"

"Yes, Evan. I will try."

Her strength humbled him. She was no pampered daughter of an aristocrat, even though she was indeed born the daughter of a Scottish earl. From the little he knew, her father had been abusive to her, her sister, and her mother for most of their lives and had left them in near poverty.

She sank against him as they walked toward the road, or at least his best guess as to which way the road was. The fog was thick as night, and the rain still pelted them like stinging needles. They weren't too far out of Wiltshire yet. Surely they could find shelter somewhere.

Alexandra grew steadier, though she still gripped his arm as she rallied forward, never once complaining. Her will fascinated him. But then, she had grown up with a tyrant. No doubt her will had come in handy.

After what seemed like several hours, an image emerged in the distance. A shed, perhaps? Or a cabin? Evan wasn't sure. The ground under his feet was soggy, and he didn't know whether he'd ever found the road. They could be anywhere.

His heart thudded against his sternum. He had to find safety. Alexandra was his responsibility, and he would not let his father down. If only she hadn't insisted on going to London. Why hadn't he put his foot down? He could have dissuaded her. His brother was in London, and Evan had control of the estate while his father was gone. The servants answered to him and no other. This trip had not had to happen.

So why had he relented and said he'd go with her? He enjoyed London, yes, but no valid reason existed for him to be there other than to accompany her.

Had he *wanted* to accompany her?

She probably had plans to meet up with her paramour, Mr. Nathan Landon. Landon was a good bloke but a renowned skirt chaser, never serious as far as Evan could see. What Alexandra saw in him Evan didn't know. Surely she wasn't expecting a proposal of marriage. Why, Landon had a girl in every port.

A stab of jealousy hit Evan hard in the gut. She was his stepsister, for God's sake, and a bloody pain in the arse, as well. Landon could damn well have her. Though she did deserve better...

"Alexandra," he said, "there's a building in the distance.

Do you see it?"

"Looks like a cabin," she said, "but right now anything is better than this. Do you suppose anyone is at home?"

Though the fog was thick, daylight was still upon them, so Evan couldn't tell if a light was on in the small dwelling. They continued to trudge, Alexandra holding her own like a champion. He was proud of her.

When they finally reached the small building, Evan knocked on the door.

"For goodness' sake, you'll have to knock louder than that," Alexandra said. "No one will hear you during this downpour."

He nodded and pounded on the door. Nothing. Gaining hope, he turned the knob and the door opened. Thank God!

It was small, just one room, and clearly it had been vacant for quite some time. It was probably an old tenant or hired hand's home on one of the neighboring estates. But the estates were vast. They could easily be isolated.

No time to worry about that at the moment. Once the storm passed, he would figure out where they were and walk to get help. For now, they could at least dry off and rest a bit.

They walked into the small dwelling. It was sparse, of course. A bed with a worn comforter sat in the far corner, and a small table and chairs, a bureau, and a slipper tub completed the picture. A few cupboards lined the walls. Certainly far from the elegance they were used to, but they would make do.

He helped Alexandra to one of the chairs. "How are you feeling? Do you hurt anywhere?"

"Kind of a dull ache all over," she said, "but I think I'll be fine. It's not the worst I've been through."

Evan's heart lurched. What might she have meant by that?

"What happened to the coachman?" she continued. "And

what of the horses?"

"Old John was thrown from the carriage. I couldn't do anything for him."

Alexandra's eyes widened and her lips trembled. She clutched her hands together. "No! How horrible. We must have been extremely lucky then."

Evan nodded. "Being in the coach saved our lives. And it's still a miracle neither of us was hurt more than we are. I've a few bruises that I can already feel, but I'm all right. I'm so glad you are all right as well."

"Yes. And the horses?"

"Thor, who got struck, was near dead. I cut Odin loose, and he went running off."

"The poor dears." She sighed. "I don't suppose there are any spare garments here. We must get out of these wet clothes before we both catch our deaths."

Evan looked around. She was right. He found only a few sets of bed linens folded inside one of the cupboards. "These will have to do." He handed a set to her.

"Well, I guess we can be Greek today then."

Evan furrowed his brow. "Greek?"

"We'll wear togas, silly, like the Greeks." She smiled wearily, her pretty face pale. She stood, gasping softly.

"What? Do you hurt?"

"Just a touch. I'm fine, really." She lifted her lips in a saucy grin. "You'll have to unfasten me."

CONFESSIONS OF LADY PRUDENCE

by Madame O

Christophe widened his brown eyes. "Your cunt, my lady?"

I smiled the most wicked smile I could summon. "My cunt, sir. Surely you've heard the term?"

"But from a lady of the peerage..."

I pulled him toward the gold brocade settee, sat upon it, and spread my legs wide to his view.

"My sweet cunt, Monsieur Bertrand. It's aching for your lips and tongue. Lick it, and I promise you will be handsomely rewarded."

"To taste your sweet nectar is reward enough, my lady." He bent to the task. "Ah, yes, let me see that lovely quim. So beautiful."

Amelia, as he swiped his tongue across my pussy, I tingled all over. His lips were magical, tantalizing me to new heights in sensation. Soon his finger was inside me, stroking my wet channel, as he lapped at my tight bud. He sucked it, licked it, all the while sliding his tongue around my quim.

Within minutes, I burst into climax, nearly flying to the heavens and back. Still he licked me as I flew again and again, until I begged him to stop.

"Please, sir, I cannot go on. I must have your cock inside my aching pussy!"

"Your wish is my command, my lady." Though still fully dressed, he unfastened his trousers and let them fall to his ankles. With one swift thrust, he plunged his cock inside me.

The sweet fullness, Amelia. He was quite big, larger than Broderick or Miles, and though my virginity has long been gone, I confess I felt like I was being taken for the first time. So hard were his thrusts, so large his member, that I screamed in joyful agony.

Thank goodness, Amelia, that Auntie is as deaf as a stone and the servants would never dare barge in. I expect I was making quite a ruckus. He fucked me with hard, long strokes, and soon I came again, and then again.

When I could take it no longer, I begged him to release. He withdrew his cock and furiously pumped it in his fist. Soon his seed spurted like a milky fountain onto my belly.

"Oh, sir," I said, "that was the most lovely fucking I've had in some time. I do so look forward to our next art lesson."

Dearest Amelia, I must take my leave now, as I have errands to attend to. And then on the morrow, another art lesson with Monsieur Bertrand.

Until then, I am affectionately yours,

Prudence

CHAPTER THREE

Alexandra couldn't stifle a soft chuckle, though it ached in her belly. The accident had clearly taken its toll on her body. Stiff and conventional Evan would never dare unfasten her garments, but what choice did he have? They needed to get out of their sopping clothes or risk catching cold. Plus she was uncomfortable as the dickens with her many layers clinging to her skin in a soggy mess.

"Come now," she said, "surely you've undressed a woman before."

Evan breathed in deeply and seemed to hold it for a few moments before he spoke. "Whether I've undressed a woman is certainly no concern of yours."

"It would certainly be helpful if you had, because then you won't have any problem now. And Evan, I must be free of these clothes. I'm dreadfully uncomfortable."

He nodded. "Of course. Turn around."

She complied, and he gingerly unfastened her outfit.

"You'll need to loosen my corset strings."

He breathed in again. "Of course."

Once she was sufficiently able to disrobe, she turned to face him. "You'll need to look the other way until I tell you otherwise."

Though the thought of Evan seeing her nude gave her little shivers, she knew it wouldn't happen. He was a gentleman through and through. No need to peek over her shoulder to make sure he wasn't looking. Besides, if she didn't peek, she could delude herself that perhaps he *was* stealing a look.

She hastily discarded her wet clothes and wrapped herself in a makeshift toga. "You can turn around now." She draped her wet clothes over two of the chairs.

Evan didn't quite meet her gaze as he picked up another set of linens. He cleared his throat. "I guess I need to tell you to turn around now."

The task proved more difficult than Ally imagined. Evan stood, his blond hair dripping wet and plastered against the beautiful contours of his cheeks. His wet clothes were pasted to the muscular lines of his magnificent body. To watch him peel them from his tan maleness...

Goodness, Ally! "Of course," she said, and turned toward the bed.

The bed.

Dear Lord, only one bed graced this sparse room. Well, they'd deal with that later. For now, the issue was food. She was suddenly famished. The basket of sandwiches had been left in the coach. Her mind fuzzy, she hadn't thought of it when they'd started walking. Evidently, Evan hadn't either.

Certainly someone would come along soon and find them. In the meantime, at least they had plenty of water. The downpour continued, the pounding on the roof drumming in her head. If only she had a headache powder. She ached all over from the accident, and bruises were emerging on her arms and legs. Thankfully, they'd been spared serious injuries. The poor coachman could not say the same.

Ally pulled what hairpins remained from her wet hair and finger combed the long tresses as best she could. What a mess.

"You may turn around now," Evan said.

Ally did...and gasped. The man resembled a Greek statue come to life. So large was his frame that he'd wrapped the linen only around his waist. His golden chest was bared to her view. Light brown hairs grew around his copper-coin nipples. His tresses, still matted with moisture, adhered to his neck and shoulders. The white linen covered what she knew must be a fine looking derriere and thighs. And in between those thighs...

She mustn't think of it! He was her stepbrother, and she had no use for him at all, other than a fine bauble to look at. And he was fine indeed...

She cleared her throat softly. "Evan, do you think there might be something around here to eat?"

"I don't know, though I'm rather hungry myself."

Ally walked to the small cupboards surrounding the wood stove and peeked in. Nothing. "Drat. Anything sounds good to me. Even blood pudding."

Evan let out a little laugh. "Not your favorite, I take it?"

"I can't abide it. Perhaps it's the dark color. Or that it's made from pig's blood. I don't know. All I know is it's all we had some days during my childhood, and I've truly learned to abhor it."

"I don't mind it myself. A bit tangy, I think."

She shook her head. "Try eating nothing but that black sausage plus oatmeal porridge for days on end. Trust me, you'd learn to despise it. I choked it down. It was either that or go hungry."

Evan walked closer to her. "It was that bad for you?"

"You don't know the half of it."

"I only know what my father has told me." He helped her to a chair and sat down opposite her at the table. "I'd like to know more, if you're willing to share."

"Why would you want to know? I'm not interested in your pity." And she wasn't. She had her pride, which was why she'd never go without again, even if it meant marrying a man she might not be in love with.

"For God's sake, Alexandra, I'm not offering you pity. I'd like to get to know my new stepmother better is all."

"Then speak to her about it," Ally said dryly. "It's nothing I wish to relive." She rose, and then sat back down. "Why the sudden interest in my mother? You certainly weren't in favor of the wedding."

"I just thought they were rushing."

"Is that truly the only reason you were against it?"

He shook his head and sighed. "I was very close to my own mother, so it's difficult to see someone take her place."

"Yes, I understand. Well, I can try to understand. I wasn't close to my own father at all. In fact, I'm glad the bastard is dead."

Evan widened his eyes.

"Don't look so shocked. He was a tyrant."

"I thought you didn't want to discuss your past."

"I don't. What we're discussing is why you were so against the marriage, and why you want to know about my mother now."

"I'm interested. She's my father's wife."

"Yes, she is. And I do believe the problem you first had when they announced their impending nuptials had to do with your estate, come to think of it. You think my mother is after your father's money."

"I never said that."

"You don't have to say it. It was written all over your face then, and it still is now. That's why you're interested in our past. You want to know just how destitute we really were and are. You want to know how much of your father's money my mother wants."

"Alexandra—"

"Ally, damn it! I detest Alexandra." She was named for her father. So was Sophie. Angus Alexander Sophocles MacIntyre. Her dreaded name and her sister's would always remind her of *him*. They'd both paid the price for not being boys.

Evan swallowed and let out a breath. "Alexandra, I don't think your mother is after my father's money. It's clear how much she loves him, and he her."

Ally sighed. The truth was her mother had no interest in the earl's money, though surely it was a wonderful fringe benefit. Her mother was in love, and had been for twenty years. She was now married to the love of her life. No, Iris hadn't married for money, either time. She was forced into marriage with the girls' father when she was twenty-five years old, and she married David because she loved him.

It was Ally who was marrying for money. Perhaps this conversation was hitting a bit too close to home. She bit back her words. No need to be so defensive.

"You don't have to worry," she said. "Your father has assured us that there is plenty to go around and that neither your future nor your siblings' will be affected by this marriage."

"Yes, I've come to realize that."

"You're not entitled to anything anyway, as a second son."

Evan pursed his full lips.

Oh, no. She'd hit a nerve.

"By law, that is correct."

"What will you do, then, when your father passes on and your brother inherits the earldom?"

"For God's sake, I'm an able-bodied man, not a nitwit. I'll be fine. That I promise you." He stood. "I'm bone tired. The sun has set. I'm going to lie down."

As soon as Evan said the words, fatigue hit Ally like a freight train and she let out a yawn. "Yes, I am also exhausted."

"You take the bed. I'll spread some linens on the floor."

A gentleman to a fault. But the bed was large enough for both of them, and no reason existed for him to be uncomfortable. They were both bruised and battered and deserved a good night's rest, even if it was to be on an old lumpy mattress.

"There is no need for that. We can both lie on the bed."

"It would not be proper."

"Under these circumstances, it is certainly proper. You're tired and hurt. The hard floor will not be good for your injuries."

Ally strode to the bed and lay down, moving to the far side to make room for Evan. She turned to face the wall and closed her eyes.

After a few moments, the bed shifted with Evan's weight.

Now, how would she sleep a wink with a handsome man next to her?

★ ★ ★ ★

Sleeping turned out not to be an issue after all. Ally woke to a cold drop of water on her forehead. "Oh!" She sat up and looked toward the ceiling. A leak! And right over the bed, no less.

She looked down and gasped. Her breasts were exposed! The toga had loosened off her shoulder during the night. She turned. Evan was gone. She hastily reattached her toga and stretched, moving away from the leak in the roof. She'd have to move the bed forward a bit to escape the leak. But could she do it herself?

She braced herself to push the bed slightly when Evan entered, a mass of unruly wetness in his riding outfit.

Ally's cheeks warmed. Surely he must have seen her breasts when he got up this morning. The thought intrigued her, and her nipples tightened against the linen.

Well, nothing to be done now.

"What are you doing?" he asked.

"Moving the bed a bit. There's a leak that was dripping on me."

He looked up. "I see. Not a huge problem. I'll move it and then find a basin to catch the water. I'm honestly surprised there's only one leak in this old shack. By the way, there's a privy about fifty yards behind the house."

She did need to see to her necessities. But she could hardly walk outside in the downpour in her toga. She'd have to dress.

"Were your clothes dry this morning?" she asked.

"Still moist, but I had to go out and see about food."

Her stomach jumped. "And?"

"Nothing. There are rabbits and fowl around, but they're all in hiding with the storm, and I've nothing to kill them with anyway."

Her heart sank as her tummy rumbled. Blood pudding was sounding even better this morning.

"I did gather some fresh water for you." He went to the door and lugged in the slipper tub. "There's a dipper on the table."

Fresh water did sound good. She was parched. After she'd quenched her thirst, she looked at her clothing. Still quite wet.

"Is there anyone around here?"

"Not that I could see. We're quite isolated, and the fog hasn't yet lifted. I thought to try to find our valises, but in the fog I honestly don't know which way to go, and they could have been thrown anywhere. They're likely ruined by now anyway."

"Well, I hardly see the point in putting these wet garments back on to go to the privy and get them wetter. I'll simply wear my drawers and chemise. They'll dry quickly."

"Alexandra..."

"For goodness' sake, you just said no one is around. Look the other way if it blemishes your eyes."

She hurriedly donned her drawers and chemise and headed out to the privy. She took care of necessities and returned drenched, her thin garments clinging to her and leaving nothing to the imagination.

Evan had changed back into his toga and was building a fire in the stove. "Not much wood in here, and I'd be hard-pressed to find anything dry to make a fire with out of doors until this rain lets up." He turned, and his cheeks turned crimson. "Er...Alexandra..."

"Look away, why don't you? Did you expect me to stay dry? It's a veritable swamp out there."

He turned and grunted.

"And for the last time, please call me Ally." She discarded her sopping underclothes, shook off as best she could, dried with another linen, and replaced her toga. "You may turn around now."

Evan sat down at the table. "Please, sit."

Ally joined him.

"We need to decide what to do," Evan said. "Once this rain lets up, I'll go for help. It can't last much longer."

"You will not leave me here alone! I'll go with you."

"That's silly. You're perfectly safe here, and you will just slow me down. With the fog, I can't even tell where the main road is, and I have no idea how far the carriage was off the road. It may be a day or two before I find help."

"And you'll leave me here to starve to death? No thank you."

Evan furrowed his brow. "This does create a dilemma. I don't want to leave you here, Alexandra, believe me. Your safety is my first priority. But my best chance of keeping you safe is to go for help alone. I can travel faster that way and get back here to you sooner. I can't risk your safety by taking you out with me."

"And why is this solely your decision?"

"Because I am charged with your protection, damn it!" He pounded his fist on the table.

His brown eyes lit on fire. Something hit Ally like a brick in the gut. This was real. Here was the real Evan that he kept hidden underneath his stiff convention. His splendid looks were suddenly all the more captivating. This was a man who wouldn't back down in a fight, who would kiss a woman senseless, who would...

She shivered and warmed—an odd sensation to feel such opposite temperatures at once. Her nipples hardened against the linen.

Ally wanted to see more.

"I most certainly will go with you," she said. "I'm perfectly used to going without, and I'm not some pampered proper lady. I'll not slow you down. I promise you that."

He sighed and raked his fingers through his soaking hair. "Very well, then. At least you'll be with me and I'll be able to keep you safe. I didn't relish the thought of leaving you here."

"What in the world ever gave you the idea you could control me, Evan?" She smiled sweetly.

He shook his head. "God only knows."

Ally couldn't help giving him a sly smile. "What do we do now? We've nothing to read, no cards... I don't even have my blasted knitting."

Evan let out a chuckle. "You don't seem the knitting type."

"I'm not. I abhor it. But with Lily and Rose both in the family way, I'm knitting baby booties. It's what's expected."

"Frankly, you don't seem the type to ever do what's expected."

She smiled again. "I'll take that as a compliment." Then, "I know what we can do. Let's play truth."

Evan raised his eyebrows. "Truth? What is that?"

"A game Sophie and I used to play with Lily and Rose when we were younger. You can ask anyone anything, and they have to tell the truth. If they refuse, they have to do something you tell them to do."

"What fun is that?"

"It's loads of fun, actually. And we've nothing but time on our hands. I need something to take my mind off food."

"Very well, then." He adjusted his toga. "Ask away."

"Hmm. All right." What to ask? Or rather, what did she have the nerve to ask? What she wanted to ask would be frowned upon in mixed company. "Tell me about your mother."

"That's not a question, Alexandra."

"Ally, please. And touché. What was your mother like?"

"For God's sake, where are the parameters? My mother was a complex individual. I could write an entire book about her."

"Give me the abridged version."

"Why are you so interested in my mother?"

"Sorry, it's not your turn. You must answer my question first, and then I shall answer yours."

"Of all the blasted— Fine. My mother was a lovely woman. Her name was Maureen. She thought herself plain of face, but I thought she was lovely. Her hair was light brown, about the same color as yours, actually, and she had warm brown eyes. I favor my father, as you know, but people say I have her eyes."

"Did she love your father?"

"Yes, I believe she did."

"But he was never in love with her, was he?"

Evan shook his head, his brown eyes cast downward. "No, he was not. It was an arranged marriage. My mother deserved better."

"I doubt love is all it's cracked up to be," Ally said. "More important things exist than an emotion that can cause as much pain as happiness."

"Like what?"

"Is that your question?"

"All right. Call it my question, then. What is more important than love?"

"Oh, little things like knowing you might be fed, for one. My God, I'm famished. Having enough so you're not a burden on anyone else. Silly things like that."

"How can you say that when you just saw both your cousins fall in love?"

"Sorry, it's my turn to ask a question. I just answered yours."

"Rubbish. I answered several of yours."

Ally laughed. "It's not my fault you don't understand the

rules of the game. I answer one question, and then I get to ask you one."

"Lord... All right. Go ahead."

"Were you in love with Rose?"

"I don't think that's any of your concern."

"Very well. You shall do something. Hmm." She rubbed her chin. "I'm thinking I should like to see what's under that linen..."

"Alexandra!"

"Then answer, Evan."

"Fine. No, I was not in love with Rose. Nor she with me."

"Have you ever been in love?"

"No." He pounded the table. "Damn! That's two questions."

Ally laughed again. "Yes, you're going to have to pay more attention now, aren't you?"

He lifted his lips into a lopsided grin. Good, he was unwinding a bit. Such a beautiful man shouldn't always be so stuffy.

"My turn, then," he said. "Did your father strike your mother?"

Ally's body heated, and she clenched her hands into fists. Angus MacIntyre, the Earl of Longarry, had done far more than strike her mother. "I'm not going to answer that."

"The game was your idea, Alexandra."

"I know. And it was a foolish one."

"You don't strike me as a woman who backs down from a challenge."

"I'm not." She stood. "Give me my action, then. What must I do?"

"You'd better watch yourself," he said slyly. "I may actually drop my toga and force you to look."

"You think that would deter me?" She scoffed. "I nearly made you take the dratted thing off a moment ago."

"Yes, you did. But you were bluffing, I'd bet. I don't think you're nearly as experienced as you'd like me to believe you are."

She sat down with a huff. "Yes, my father struck my mother. Now why do you want to know?"

"Fair question. I want to know because your mother, you, and your sister are part of my life now. I care about all of you."

"What does it matter, though? The man is dead, thank God. It's not like you can call him out."

"No. But my father cares very deeply for your mother. He's in love with her. He told me your father was abusive, and that it makes him sick inside to think of it. He wants to make it up to her and give her the life she deserves."

"He seems to be doing that just fine, so why all the questions?"

He paused a moment and stroked the light night beard on his jawline. "Not your turn, Alexandra." He gazed at her, his brown eyes ablaze, as if he could see her innermost thoughts. "No man should ever strike a woman. Any man who does is nothing but a bully and a coward."

"Frankly, I couldn't agree more." That was the truth of it. "Your question, please?"

He reached forward and lightly brushed his fingers over hers. "Did your father ever strike you?"

CONFESSIONS OF LADY PRUDENCE

by Madame O

Dearest Amelia,

I've had my second art lesson with Monsieur Christophe Bertrand, and it was even more engaging than the first. If you're looking to dabble in something new, might I suggest art? Perhaps there are instructors as fascinating as Christophe in the Americas. I hope so, for your sake, my dear.

My pussy is still hammering as I write this, only an hour past my lesson. Today we worked on charcoal drawing, and he gave me the most fascinating subject—his cock!

It is a work of art, dear Amelia, long and thick and perfectly marbled with two violet veins meandering around it and springing from a bush of onyx curls. He was erect when he produced it, and I couldn't help myself. I dropped to my knees and licked the tip. The salty drop of liquid tantalized my tongue, and I so longed to take his entire length to the back of my throat.

He pulled me to my feet, however. "My lady, as much as I would love your ruby lips around my member, we must first have our lesson. I promise you may suck my cock to your heart's content after we finish."

He wanted me, Amelia. I could see it in his lovely dark eyes. But he is a gentleman of honor, and he must first do what he is being paid by Auntie Bea for—teach me art.

I drew several charcoal drawings of his beautiful shaft.

When our hour was complete, he pushed me back down to my knees.

"And now, my lady, you may suck my cock."

My lips were on him in a flash, and I slid my tongue up and down his thick member. He plunged into my mouth, and soon my quim began throbbing in time with his thrusts. If only I had disrobed beforehand! How I wanted that thick cock inside me.

"Sir," I gasped, letting his cock fall from my mouth, "I must have your cock in my cunt. Please!"

"You got yours last time, my lady," said he. "Today I want that lovely mouth around me."

How could I say no? He had given me such pleasure during our previous engagement. I continued my assault on him, laving the underside of his swollen cock and kissing and licking the knobby head before I took him deeply once more.

"My lady," he said, breathless, "I fear I'm going to come!"

I nodded, unable to speak with my lips around his thickness. He plunged and grasped the sides of my head, spurting his cream into the back of my throat. I feared I might gag, but held strong, and when he withdrew, I smiled.

He pulled me to my feet and kissed me thoroughly, and Amelia, as our tongues mingled together and I tasted his essence, I could no longer bear it. My quim ached for his tongue, his fingers, his cock...but I was still fully clothed! I couldn't even reach between my legs to sooth my ache.

Christophe finally broke the kiss, and I took a much-needed breath.

"That was wonderful." He smiled. "And now, my lady, you shall have your reward."

CHAPTER FOUR

Though Evan's light touch made her nerves sizzle, Ally drew her hand away. "Show me whatever you have under your toga, then. I'll not answer your question."

"I'm sorry," he said softly.

"Sorry about what? About what you've got under your toga? I doubt that's anything to be sorry about."

"Stop joking, Alexandra."

"Who is joking?"

"I'm sorry," he said again, "that your father struck you."

So much for keeping her little secret. She was probably an open book. She'd gotten used to the beatings long ago, and now, over two years had passed without any. It had been a wonderful respite. Never again would a man strike her. She'd kill anyone who tried. She'd kill anyone who touched her mother or sister as well. The situation had been rougher on both of them, especially Mama. She'd tried to hide it, but Ally always knew. Sophie, who was two years older, took the brunt of the earl's anger that wasn't heaped on their mother until Alexandra put a stop to it. Larger and less fearful, Alexandra began provoking her father on purpose so he steered away from Sophie. Timid, shy little Sophie, who was still sweet and good despite the experience. Not Ally. She'd toughened up. To hell with love. She was marrying Mr. Landon. He was nice enough. He wouldn't beat her, and if he ever tried... Well, he would wish he hadn't.

She had no desire to relive any of her experiences with her father. But dratted Evan couldn't let it go. "Why do you care?" she asked.

"Because I care about you. You're mine to protect now—"

"Hold on one minute!" Her ire rose. "I'm no one's to protect, least of all yours. I can take care of myself."

"You can, can you? What if I'd allowed you to travel to London alone? Where would you be now?"

"I would have taken the rail, like I'd planned."

"And you'd have been derailed in this storm. You'd most likely be severely injured or worse, dead, right now."

Ally bit her lip. He was no doubt right. It irked her, but she needed him. And she was glad he was here. "I guess it's my turn."

"All right. What is your question?"

"Have you ever been to a brothel?"

Evan stood. "Pardon?"

"You heard me."

"I'm not answering that. Men and women of our station don't discuss such things."

"Bloody hell, we're dressed in bed linens, Evan. Why stand on ceremony now?"

"I'm not answering." He fidgeted with his toga.

"No, no!" Ally looked away. She wanted to see it, but the thought scared her senseless. Evan was so handsome, and so well put together... "I'll ask another question."

"Fine." He sat, his lips curving into a saucy grin. "Ask your question."

"Just so you know, I've inferred by your reluctance to answer my previous question that the correct response is affirmative."

He said nothing, but his nostrils flared. Just a touch, but she noticed. And then the perfect question came to her, darted into her mind as if someone had flipped a switch. She'd take care of that saucy grin with seven little harmless words.

"Did you see my breasts this morning?"

★ ★ ★ ★

"I beg your pardon, my lady?"

Sophie looked up from her novel. "Yes, Graves?" she said to the Brighton butler.

"I'm sorry to disturb you, but a wire just came in from the caretaker at the London townhome. Lord Evan and Lady Alexandra did not arrive yesterday as planned."

Sophie frowned, worry chewing at her gut. "What could have happened?"

"They were waylaid by the storm, no doubt. They most likely stopped at an inn for the night."

"Wouldn't Lord Evan have sent word to London?"

"Not necessarily. The lines could have been down. Or perhaps he didn't think of it. Lord Evan is a bachelor. Bachelors sometimes forget that others might like to know their whereabouts."

"I'd say that's true of my sister, but Lord Evan seems so... responsible."

"I'm sure there's nothing to worry about, my lady."

Sophie nodded. "If you say so, Graves."

"Of course. Luncheon will be served in about ten minutes."

"Thank you. I'll be there promptly."

Graves left the room.

Sophie's nerves jumped. Where were Ally and Evan?

Mama and the earl were on their wedding trip, as were Rose and her new husband, Cameron. Lily, being in the family way, was at the Lybrook estate fairly nearby, but the duke was in Scotland on estate business.

She had no one to turn to.

Well, best get to luncheon. Though she was certain she would not be able to swallow a bite.

★ ★ ★ ★

Evan gulped.

Yes, he'd seen her beautiful rosy mounds. He'd required all his strength and power of will not to fan his fingers over the peachy skin, the lovely rosebud nipple... He'd risen and run outside for a quick shower in the rain to cool his simmering arousal.

The woman was his stepsister, not to mention a genuine pain in his arse. She was beautiful though, with a body that would tempt even a monk. She was tall, which fit his large frame well. He'd gotten a glimpse of her shapely legs yesterday when they peeked out from her toga. Long and slender, they could wrap all the way around him as he...

No, no, no!

"Are you going to answer?"

He'd have to bluff again. She'd stopped him the last time. Perhaps she would again. "I'll show you what's under my toga. Or do whatever else you'd like."

She lifted her lips into a saucy grin. Lord, she was tempting. Her light brown eyes sparkled with mischief.

"Hmm. I've tired of that. Clearly you don't want to show me what lies thereunder. I shall think of something else."

He stood. "I'm going to have a dipper of water. I'll be waiting with bated breath for your challenge."

The water cooled his parched throat, but unfortunately did nothing for his erection that threatened to poke through the linen. Damn it all. He shouldn't have stood up. Fortunately, his back was to Alexandra as he dipped water from the slipper tub. Once he was reasonably certain his arousal wasn't visible, he set the dipper down and quickly moved back to his chair.

"Still thinking, are you?"

She smiled, her cheeks rosy. "Yes, yes. I'm thinking."

"May I ask you another question in the meantime?"

"Of course. Do go ahead."

She fidgeted with her fingers on the table. Was she happy not to have to think of another challenge for him? It certainly seemed so. His stomach rumbled. First time he'd thought of food in a while. Her game had at least been good for that. Would this damned rain never stop? He had to get out to find some kind of sustenance for them, and then he had to get help.

"How often did you go hungry as a child?"

She bit her lip. Dear Lord, he wanted to suck that lower lip between his own and...

"Why must you drudge on and on about my childhood?"

"Sorry." He smiled. "You said I could ask another question, so I'm not answering yours."

"For goodness' sake." She rose, walked around the table, and stood directly in front of him. "We never starved, all right? But we certainly never had six-course meals with footmen serving them. Mother insisted we have a tutor, Miss O'Hara, but we couldn't keep her for long. We had two servants near the end—a housekeeper who doubled as a maid for my mother, and Millicent, a maid who served my sister and me. You've no doubt seen her. She's still my maid today. I wouldn't trade her for anything. Now may we end this discourse on my past? Please?"

Her cheeks were fiery red, her eyes ablaze with gold flecks. His cock nudged the linen.

"Very well. No more questions about your childhood. And I'll ask for no more questions about my experiences with the fairer sex, including whether I've been to a brothel."

"Goodness. Deal." Then her lips turned up. "I've thought of a challenge for you."

He sucked in a breath. It would be a killer, for sure. He nodded.

"I want you to kiss me."

CONFESSIONS OF LADY PRUDENCE

by Madame O

Amelia, Christophe left me tongue-tied. I needed him so badly at that moment. My quim was pulsing faster than my heart. But instead, he pulled up his britches and buttoned them, hiding from my view the glory of his manhood.

"Sir, you said—"

"Worry not, my lady." He pulled a watch out of his pocket and looked upon it. "Your reward should be arriving—"

A knock on the parlor door interrupted him. With luck, we were no longer in dishabille. I strode to the door and unlocked it. Auntie's butler, Jensen, stood outside.

"My lady, a Mr. Joshua Peck to see you?"

"I'm afraid I'm not acquainted with such a gentleman, Jensen."

Christophe strode toward me. "Mr. Peck is a colleague of mine, sir. I've asked him to sit in on Lady Prudence's lesson."

"Very well, if it's all right with Lady Prudence?"

I had no idea what to expect, but I nodded. Somehow, my reward was wrapped up in this newcomer. I hoped he was as pleasing to the eye as Christophe.

Oh, was he! Light where Christophe was dark, Mr. Peck had silvery-blond hair and sparkling blue eyes. Slightly taller than his friend, Peck strode in with purpose, his rugged musculature apparent beneath his street clothes.

"Mr. Joshua Peck," Jensen announced, and then closed

the door behind him.

I turned the key in the lock once more and faced the two men.

"Lady Prudence, this is my good friend, Mr. Joshua Peck. Josh, Lady Prudence Spofford."

"I'm charmed." Joshua took my hand and brushed his lips lightly over it.

"Lady Prudence has the sweetest cunny I've tasted in quite some time," Christophe said, "and she's quite good at sucking cock, as well."

I warmed all over, Amelia. Such bold words! They made me tingle, and flutters coursed through my body, landing between my legs.

Joshua raked his blue gaze over me, and I could swear he could see me nude beneath my garments.

"I'm delighted to hear that, old chap," Joshua said. "I hope you two will allow me to join in your festivities."

"That is why I invited you"—Christophe bowed to me—"if the lady will allow it?"

I couldn't wait to find out what they had in mind...

CHAPTER FIVE

Ally shocked even herself when the words escaped her lips. She'd been bold enough asking if he'd seen her breasts, and his blushing and stammering convinced her that he had. The thought excited her, and her nipples rubbed against the soft linen, longing for...something. She wasn't quite sure what.

Oh, no use lying to herself. She was quite sure what she longed for. His mouth on her nipples, sucking, kissing...

She'd kissed two men in her life—Theodore Wentworth, who was a slobbering fool, and Mr. Landon, whose kisses were much more acceptable. Other than some lovely nibbles to her exposed décolleté above her gown, that was as far as she'd gone. She had every intention of sleeping with him and trapping him into marriage, but if she could get some experience first, she'd be better able to satisfy him and make sure he could never live without her. She'd done her share of reading, and Lily and Rose had been forthcoming about their experiences, but all Ally knew was theory. No practice.

Who better to teach her than this fine-looking man before her? In truth, he was finer than Mr. Landon. He was nearly as fine as men came with his large muscular build and artist's dream facial features. She burned when he looked at her with those blazing brown eyes.

Evan cleared his throat. "You want me to kiss you?"

She swallowed, nodding. "Yes." Her voice was not much more than a whisper.

"Alexandra, that would not be proper."

"Why on earth not?"

"Well, you're my stepsister, for one."

"Who cares? We're not related, and we only just met a few months ago. It's not like we grew up thinking of each other as brother and sister. A couple of months ago, you could have just as easily been courting me as much as Rose. Would you kiss me if our parents hadn't rediscovered each other a month ago?"

"That's another question..."

"Oh, drat it all!" Ally was growing weary of the stupid rules to this stupid game. "Are you going to kiss me or not?"

"I will not. This game is over."

Ally's insides churned. The hell it was! "I've answered all of your questions, Evan, truthfully. Even the ones I wasn't thrilled to answer, which is more than you've done. You're not being fair."

"Why would you want to kiss me?" he asked, his voice cracking.

Those words slammed into her. What could she say? She couldn't very well tell him she wanted to practice for her seduction of Mr. Landon. Then again, why not? That was much more acceptable than telling him she found him an utterly splendid specimen, which she did.

"Practice," she said.

"Something tells me you've had plenty of practice."

Rage boiled inside her veins. Who did he think he was? And only minutes ago he'd accused her of not having nearly the experience she'd like him to think she did. "I do not see why you feel the need to insult me."

"You insulted me. You asked if I'd visited a brothel. If I'd looked at your..."

"My breasts, Evan. They're right here, in front of you, covered only by thin linen. And I didn't ask if you'd deliberately looked at them. I asked if you'd seen them." She strode back to her chair and sat.

"You are a handful, Alexandra," he said.

"You have no idea." She let out a sigh. "I suppose this game is over. I guess I should have expected as much from you. You're nothing but a coward, after all."

She jumped when he pounded his fist on the table.

"No one calls me a coward and lives to tell about it."

"Oh? Is that a threat?"

"Not a threat, only a fact. You stand there, high and mighty with only linen covering your ample charms. Do you think it's easy for a man to resist you? Most others would have torn those rags off of you by now and taken what you're flaunting whether you wanted to give it or not. I'll not be called a coward for being a gentleman. It's not fair." He stood. "I ought to take you right here, right now, right in that bed we shared last night. It would show you."

Her whole body tingled, her blood turning to hot ambrosia. She shouldn't taunt him. She knew she shouldn't. But something fueled the desire budding within her.

"You wouldn't, Evan. You're too much of a gentleman, as you said."

He moved closer to her.

She gulped. His arousal was apparent under the linen, jutting forward as if at attention. He wanted her. She'd never seen the male anatomy in person, but she'd done her share of reading illicit literature. He was ready. And by God, so was she.

"Do not take this any further, Alexandra," he warned, his eyes ablaze, "or you *will* be sorry."

Oh, she'd never be sorry. Her passion grew as the tickle between her legs became unbearable. To have him, to truly have him...this beautiful man...

"All I asked for was a kiss," she said softly.

"You want a kiss?" He forced her to her feet.

"Y-Yes."

He crushed his mouth to hers.

Ally never considered refusing. She was petrified, no doubt, but she wanted this. His lips were warm and unexpectedly soft. He nibbled at her mouth and enticed her lips to open.

And then—she was lost. Wentworth's kiss had been disgusting, Mr. Landon's enjoyable, but this—this was something new entirely. As Evan's tongue swirled around hers, her legs trembled beneath her. He gripped her shoulders and pulled her closer. How she ached to drive into him, to deepen the kiss, but fear overrode her desire. Perhaps she wasn't as ready for marital relations as she'd thought.

She pulled away.

But his strength was unmatched. "Kiss me back, Alexandra," he whispered against her chin. "You wanted this, and now so do I."

Lord. Her knees weakened, and she nearly collapsed in a puddle on the dusty wooden floor. Her toga had loosened, and only time would tell how soon her body would be exposed. She no longer had any will to resist. She wanted this man. Evan Xavier. The most amazing man she'd ever laid eyes on. And he wanted *her*.

He cupped both of her cheeks and gazed into her eyes. "Please."

"Oh my God," she whispered. "What have we started?"

He smiled. "I don't know, sweet, but I really want to finish it." He lowered his lips to hers once again.

As their tongues tangled together, she slid her hands upward, his muscular arms and shoulders sleek and hard under her fingertips. She toyed with the roughness of his night beard, the strength of his jawline.

Her breasts crushed against his chest, her nipples rubbing against something soft, creating friction. Pleasure surged through her. *Lord!* Her linen had fallen, and they were crushed together—bare chest to bare chest!

Her nipples tightened into hard nubs.

He trailed his lips across her cheek, down her neck, and to her ear, tracing it with his tongue, nipping the soft lobe. "My God, you're lovely."

She let out a soft breath. His words tantalized her, plummeted straight to her core, filling her with passion and longing.

"You smell like juicy berries," he said. "Lord, you are driving me mad." He inhaled as he kissed her cheek, her neck.

His erection pressed into her belly, hard and enticing. Boldly, she grasped it with her right hand.

Evan gasped. "Alexandra..."

"Ally. Please."

He gazed into her eyes. "No. Alexandra. It fits you. It's beautiful, just like you are."

And suddenly her hated name became beautiful. It was no longer her father's middle name, but her own special name. Evan had made it her own. She would never forget him for that.

Under his appreciative gaze, she was Alexandra, and she felt beautiful. She let go of his erection and clasped her arms around his neck, her lips finding his. She kissed him with all the beauty, desire, and gratitude surging through her at that moment.

Unrestrained passion took her over, and she thrust her hips against him, the strength of his arousal apparent against her belly. She imagined him inside her, filling her, pleasuring her with that muscular body. She had never wanted Mr. Landon or anyone else like this. Her fear abated, she ached only for completion with Evan.

He broke away. "This isn't right," he said.

Her heart lurched. "How can this not be right?" She cupped his cheek. "Evan, I'm feeling so...so..."

"I know. As am I. But I can't violate you in this way."

"Who says you're violating me? I'm a willing participant."

"God, I want you so much." He raked his fingers through his hair. "But—"

"Have you thought about what might happen if no one finds us?"

He stepped back slightly. "What? Where is this coming from? As soon as the rain abates, I'm going for help. I thought you wanted to come with me."

"Evan, the rain hasn't subsided in over twenty-four hours. We've no food, no provisions. What if—" Oh, it was too terrible to think of... "What if this is all we have? This...*thing* between us? Ever?"

He curved his lips upward. "You're being a bit melodramatic, I'd say."

She smiled back at him. "Melodramatic? Or persuasive?"

"Lord, how am I supposed to resist you?"

"Perhaps you're not supposed to." She tangled her fingers in his unruly tresses. "Please, Evan. Show me the ways of love. Teach me..."

He clamped his mouth on hers, taking her to new heights

with a gut-wrenching kiss. They kissed frantically, desperately, as though the world were ending. When he finally broke off and they both inhaled, he cupped her breasts in both his large hands.

"So beautiful," he said. "Lovely nipples, Alexandra. Tell me, has anyone touched them before?"

"Only me." She clasped a hand to her mouth. "Oh!"

"Don't be embarrassed, sweet. The thought of you touching yourself arouses me." He thumbed both of her erect nubs.

Chills coursed through her, and she squeezed her thighs together. "Please, Evan." She wanted his mouth on her nipples, but she didn't know how to ask for it.

But he knew. He lowered his head and took one nipple between his full pink lips.

Ally nearly shattered.

Oh, how he knew how to pleasure her! This small contact with him excited her more than all the thoughts of bedding Mr. Landon had. That was to serve a purpose. This, with Evan, was purely for physical satisfaction.

And she had no doubt that she'd be satisfied in the end.

He twirled his tongue around her nipple and gently sucked it, tugging lightly. His fingers found the other one and circled it. Her areola puckered at his touch, and when he lightly pinched the nipple, she nearly lost her footing.

"So lovely," he said against her breast. "You are beautiful, Alexandra." He rose and gazed into her eyes.

"Oh, so are you," she said, her breathing unsteady. She slid her hands down his arms to his waist, where the toga still covered him. "Please. Let me see you." She whisked the sheet away, and it fell to the floor in a white heap.

His cock stood straight out, beautiful and majestic, springing from a patch of light brown curls. She fought the urge to reach for it.

"Do I pass muster?" he asked.

"Oh my, yes."

He reached between her legs. "I bet you're beautiful down here too."

She weakened, and her core pulsed rapidly. His words nearly sent her into oblivion. She'd experienced climax before, at her own hand, but to actually have a splendid man make her feel that way...

In one quick movement, he lifted her and carried her to the bed, gently laying her down.

"Spread your legs for me, sweet," he said.

No hesitation at all. She was ready. She spread her thighs and let him gaze upon her most private parts.

"Yes, beautiful. So pink and wet." He stroked her moist folds, spreading her juices over her vulva.

"My God, Evan." She leaned back into the limp pillow, her head sinking into nothingness.

He continued to stroke her, and in the next moment, one of his long, thick fingers filled her channel.

"Oh!"

"I'm sorry. Does that hurt?"

"God, no. It's wonderful."

"Mmm, yes, it is." Slowly he moved the finger in and out of her, creating a delicious wave of friction and wanting.

"Taste me, please, Evan. I must feel your mouth on that... part of me."

She closed her eyes, and soon his soft lips grazed the insides of her thigh, his stubble delicately scratching her. He licked her folds—oh, the sensation!—and thrust his tongue into her entrance. Had anything ever felt so heavenly? Not in this lifetime. Nor would it ever, Ally was certain.

"Oh my!"

His fingers were on her nipple, tugging and pinching.

Pure bliss! The actual act couldn't possibly be any better than this.

Evan found the tight nub of her sex and licked it, still fingering her, until she writhed on the ragged comforter.

"Yes, yes!" she cried, as she exploded into climax, flying, soaring...

He continued to finger her, softly and gently, through the waves of euphoria. When she finally opened her eyes, his dark gaze was upon her.

"Do you have any idea how beautiful you look right now?"

She warmed under his admiration. She never imagined she'd feel the most beautiful in her life with her legs spread and a man's finger inside her.

She reached for him and he came to her, lying next to her and embracing her.

"Please, Evan," she said.

"Please, what?"

"Please...make love to me."

CONFESSIONS OF LADY PRUDENCE

by Madame O

Amelia, you can't imagine how fast my heart was pounding as I looked from Christophe to Joshua, and back again. Two beautiful men focused on my pleasure! How often I dreamed of having Broderick and Miles to myself whilst in the Americas. Not that I minded our foursomes, but to have them focused solely on me...such a fantasy!

And now it would become a reality.

"I'd like to eat your sweet pussy," Christophe said, "while you suck on Joshua's cock."

Sounded delightful to me. "Which of you handsome gentlemen would care to help me undress?"

Christophe turned me and unfastened my gown while Joshua faced me and cupped my cheeks.

"If you'll allow me a kiss, my lady." He lowered his lips.

Oh, such a kiss, Amelia! Perhaps even better than Christophe. He pushed his tongue deep into my mouth. He tasted of peppermint and tobacco...so enticing! I couldn't get enough. Meanwhile, Christophe rid me of my gown and corset and then reached under my chemise and wrapped his arms around me, fondling my breasts. Rough fingers pinched first one nipple, and then the other.

I deepened the kiss as Christophe played with my diddeys. My knees grew weak and my cunny grew wet. I broke Joshua's kiss and took in a breath.

"Please," I said, "I'll continue to undress." I rid myself of the chemise and drawers and stood nude, the two handsome men still fully clothed.

I turned and fidgeted with Joshua's buckle and trousers, pushing them down past his knees as quickly as I could.

"My, we are in a hurry." Joshua smiled.

"Oh, she enjoys her pleasure." Christophe lay down on the floor, still fully clothed. "Come, my lady. Sit on my face so I can taste that sweet quim."

My pussy dripped in anticipation, Amelia, so wet was I. I squatted over Christophe's lips, whilst Joshua stood facing me, his hard cock beckoning from a nest of the lightest blond curls.

As I took his swollen member into my mouth, Christophe started working on my cunt. Soon I was writhing over him, grinding against his mouth as I pleasured Joshua with my own.

"Yes, my lady. Take my cock. Take all of me!" Joshua plunged into my mouth, his cock grazing the back of my throat.

And still Christophe ate me, my heart pounding. I was near climax, but I needed a cock so badly.

I pulled away from Joshua and let his cock fall from my mouth. "Please, dear sirs. I need to be fucked. Which one of you will fuck me?"

Christophe was still fully clothed, but Joshua gripped me under my arm and pulled me away from Christophe's probing tongue. He turned me and set me on my hands and knees, and in an instant, he pushed his thick member into my cunt.

I cried out in pleasure as he pounded me, fucked me, pushed that hard cock into my tight depths. Climax overtook me, and I soared to nirvana.

"My lady! My lady!" Joshua cried with one last thrust, and then he pulled out, and his warm cream spurted over my bum and back.

We three fell in a heap together, all of us breathing rapidly.

"Thank you for a wonderful afternoon, good sirs," said I. "I think next time it is I who shall have a reward for you."

And now, dear Amelia, I must close...and come up with a suitable reward for the kind sirs who showed me such pleasure.

I remain yours, affectionately,

Prudence

CHAPTER SIX

Evan let out a sigh. As much as he wanted her, he had to keep his head rational. "It's one thing to give you pleasure with my mouth, Alexandra," Evan said. "It's something else altogether to take your virginity—to ruin you."

"For goodness' sake, you're not taking anything. I'm giving it."

Lord, she wasn't helping. He'd had enough women to know that they got as aroused as men did. He had no doubt she wanted this. His fear was for her regret, which would come later. She could not take this back.

"You need to think about this."

"I'm tired of thinking, Evan. I just want to *do* for once, without considering all the dratted consequences. I want you. I want you to make love to me."

He wasn't made of iron! He bent toward her and kissed her. Her mouth was so sweet and inviting, warm and smooth. He could kiss her forever and never grow tired of it, and here they were, both naked, both aroused. Alone in the world...

"Are you sure?" he said against her soft lips.

"Very sure. Take me. Please."

He thrust into her.

"Oh!" she gasped.

"I'm so sorry. But it's best to get it done quickly. The pain will subside."

"Yes, yes, I know. Oh my!"

The urge to withdraw and thrust back in overpowered him. He felt like a wild boar in rut, unable to control his actions, devolving to his very basest instincts.

Yet he held himself still, letting her get used to the fullness. "Tell me when you're ready, sweet."

"I'm fine. Truly. I know it's uncomfortable the first time. I was expecting it."

Sweat dripped from his brow. He could hold off no longer. He withdrew and plunged back in.

Sweet heaven, she felt like she'd been perfectly cast to hold him, the tightness and suction so exquisite he could have spent with the first thrust. He breathed in deeply, concentrating. When he felt slightly more in control, he pulled out and thrust back in once more.

"Better?" he asked.

"Yes, yes. It doesn't hurt so much. It just feels...full."

"Normal."

"But I craved it so, Evan. Shouldn't it do more than hurt? Or feel full?"

He chuckled against her smooth neck. "Don't worry, sweet. It will." He thrust once more, wincing to keep from losing it. He had to keep going, had to make it good for her.

He kissed her lips lightly and pinched one of her nipples. And another thrust.

She gasped. *Yes, there she goes. She's starting to feel what it's truly about.* He withdrew, thrust, withdrew, thrust.

"Oh, yes!" she gasped.

"Good, sweet?"

"Oh, Evan. It's so...so... When you push down you hit that lovely spot... Oh!"

Hold on, old man. Keep it going. It's good for her. Make it last.

But as much as he wanted to keep going, he could bear it no longer. He thrust mightily and spent inside her welcoming pussy with a loud groan.

He collapsed atop her but quickly moved. His weight would be too much for her to bear. She was hardly frail, but he was a big man. Though it pained him, he pulled out and slid to the side, lying beside her.

"I hope I didn't hurt you too badly."

"No, no," she sighed. "It was wonderful."

"No regrets?"

"Not a one. You?"

He smiled. "No man alive would regret that. You're absolutely lovely."

He rose, tore off a small piece from one of the linens, and moistened it in rainwater from the slipper tub.

"Here," he said when he returned, "let me take care of you."

"Goodness, it's cold."

"Yes, I'm sorry about that." He wiped the small smudges of blood from her. "There. Are you in any pain?"

"Not really. I just feel deliciously used."

He discarded the rag and lay back down beside her. She curled into his arms and snuggled against his shoulder. He closed his eyes and smiled. He couldn't remember ever feeling quite so content.

★ ★ ★ ★

"My lady," Graves said to Sophie. "I'm afraid Lord Evan and Lady Alexandra have not yet arrived in London. I just got word from a wire."

"Not yet?" Sophie gasped. Now she really was worried. The rain had ended, and who knew what the weather was like in London? Evan surely would have sent a wire ahead to let the caretaker know if they were to be detained any longer.

"Do you wish to send anyone out to look for them?"

"Whom would I send? Lord Brighton and my mother are gone."

"Some of the servants would be happy to assist."

Sophie chewed on her lip. "Darkness has fallen."

"Yes. I suspect they'd wait to start in the morning."

She nodded, her nerves jumping. "Yes, Graves. Please have them leave at first light.

★ ★ ★ ★

Ally walked briskly toward the informal parlor in the Lybrook mansion. Sophie and Rose were napping, and Lily was gone on her wedding trip. It was nearly teatime, and Ally was famished for a scone with lemon curd. She halted when her mother's soft voice wafted out the door.

"Yes," Iris, Ally's mother, said, "but it's difficult to tell David everything."

"You should try," another voice said. Auntie Lucy—Miss Lucinda Landon, her mother's best childhood friend.

"It's so horrid, Lucy," Iris said. "He might think less of me. The things I let Longarry do..."

"None of this is your fault," Lucy said.

"You wouldn't think it if you knew."

"You can tell me if you'd like. Sometimes it helps to talk. I promise you'll be no different to me one way or the other."

"I... I know what my daughters must think of me. They think me weak. And I was. But I did it— I let him do whatever he wanted to me... I was..." She exploded into sobs.

A few moments passed as Iris sniffled and wept.

"What, Iris?"

"H-He, he said if I didn't succumb, he would turn to the girls. He would r-rape them."

In the foyer, Ally's heart leaped into her throat. Her father was evil, but even she hadn't imagined such...corruption.

Lucy gasped. "My God."

"I... I couldn't let that happen."

"Of course you couldn't."

"He had all the power by law. There was nothing... I was so helpless..."

"I know, my dear."

"And even that wasn't enough. He beat them badly, Lucy. Ally took the brunt of it. She provoked him. Sophie and I tried talking to her about it, but she was determined. She has such strength, Lucy."

"Yes, she does. Both of your daughters are lovely. It's a tribute to you, Iris, that they are so well adjusted despite what you all lived through."

"I should have done more..."

And then more sobs, muffled.

Sobs Ally had heard many times before...

★ ★ ★ ★

Alexandra awoke with a jolt.

Not a dream, but a memory of a conversation she'd heard between her mother and Auntie Lucy over a month ago. She calmed her rapid breathing as shame overwhelmed her. In the past, she'd often thought her mother weak for submitting to her father. She'd had no idea that he'd threatened...

Her mother had protected her and Sophie, just like Ally had protected her sister. Ally and her mother were more alike than Ally had ever known.

Once her heart rate returned to normal, she looked around. Darkness had descended. Something odd met her ears. She couldn't quite put her finger on it until... Silence. The rain had finally stopped!

Her stomach gurgled. She'd gone nearly thirty-six hours without sustenance. She rose, wrapping herself in one of the discarded linens, and drank a dipper of water from the tub. What must the hour be? She had no idea. Evan breathed softly on the bed. She hated to wake him up. Where might his pocket watch be? She checked his garments. Nothing.

Well, what did it matter? When the sun rose, they could go for help. Thank goodness.

Evan was probably dying of thirst. She refilled the dipper and brought it to him. "Evan." She nudged him.

His eyes fluttered open. "Yes, sweet?"

"I brought you some water."

"You're an angel." He sat up and drained the dipper. "How are you feeling?"

"A tad achy, but fine. And I have some wonderful news. The rain has stopped."

He smiled. "So that's what sounds strange. Nothing."

"I had the exact same reaction." She returned his smile.

"I'll leave at first light," he said.

"*We'll* leave at first light." She punched him lightly on his upper arm.

"Very well. We will indeed."

"I'm so very hungry, Evan. The water was refreshing, but it's far from enough."

"I know. We'll be all right. Now that the rain has stopped, I can go out and look for something to eat."

"In the dark? All I'd do is worry about you. We don't have a lantern or torch. How would you see? Plus you said yourself you've nothing to kill a rabbit or bird with."

He sighed. "That is true enough. We'll have to wait, I guess."

"It's been so long since we've eaten anything. I feel so weak."

"You'll be all right. We have water. That's the most important thing, and tomorrow we'll get out of here."

"Let's pray the rain doesn't start up again."

"Even if it does, we're leaving. What stopped us was the fog, not the rain."

She lay down next to him. "Thank you for..."

"No need to thank me. In case you hadn't noticed, I enjoyed it immensely." He kissed her upper arm.

"I never even imagined... I mean, I'm hardly innocent. I've been reading...*literature* for ages."

"Literature?" He smiled.

"Well, perhaps not literature in the finest sense..."

"How on earth would such a lovely young lady get her hands on such things?"

She laughed. "Oh, you'd be surprised. My maid, Millicent? She had quite the collection. Mother and Sophie never knew, of course, but she shared it with me. Well, she did after I stumbled upon it and demanded to know where it came from or I would tell Mother. I read about Fanny Hill and Justine.

And then there were the papers..."

"You little rascal!"

"I suppose I had my moments. But I had to have something fun to do to exist in that environment."

His features softened. "I'm sorry you had to go through that."

"I don't like to talk about it." But for some reason, her mouth stayed open, words tumbling out of it to this kind man who had given her such a lovely gift. "When Sophie and I were young, we used to hear Mother crying at night. Father would come home drunk and do God knows what to her."

"Alexandra..."

"Once, I got up and went to her bedroom. My father was on top of her, and he turned to me and ordered me out or I'd be beaten with a broom handle. I couldn't have been more than five or six at the time. Sophie was two years older." The memories crashed into her, the anger, the fear, the hopelessness, the invisible worms crawling over her skin. She brushed them away.

"You don't have to say any more."

But she wanted to. She *needed* to. "Do I have your confidence?"

"Of course. Always."

"She tried to fight back, I found out. I overheard her talking to Auntie Lucy about it after she and your father announced their engagement. My father beat her and told her if she didn't succumb to his desires, he would turn to Sophie and me." Tears clogged Ally's throat. "I'd always thought she had a weak spirit. I was so wrong. I feel terrible about that."

"My God, your father never—"

"No, no, thank God. What I thought was her weak spirit

was her protecting both Sophie and me. The man was horrible. I've no doubt he would have raped us if she'd refused him. The beatings were bad enough."

"My God..."

The sting as the belt hit her bottom. The cane on her shoulders. The slaps and punches to her cheeks and nose. The blood... She winced. "I took more of it than Sophie. He started on her when she began blossoming into a woman. I was nearly as tall as she at that time. She was such a little thing. And so timid. It killed me to see her get beaten and to hear her sobs. So I began deliberately provoking him. And he turned on me."

"My God. You did that to protect your sister?"

She sniffed. "Yes." How good it felt to say the words! The pain she'd endured had been nothing compared to the cries of her older sister. They'd cut at her heart like a jackknife. She'd stopped hearing her mother cry after a while. That had been hard enough to bear. But her shy, sweet sister? No. She hadn't been able to take it.

Who knew Evan would be the one she confided in? Just days ago she'd thought of him as a stuffy aristocrat interested only in convention. "I don't know why I'm telling you all of this."

He lightly stroked her arm. "Keep going, if you'd like. I've nothing better to do than listen. Well, I suppose there's something, but you need to rest." He smiled.

She couldn't help a laugh. "I guess I've nothing better to do. And I have to admit, it does feel good to finally talk about it."

"You've never told anyone any of this?"

"Sophie and I never talked about it much. She begged me to stop provoking him, but I couldn't. If I did, he'd turn on her, and I knew I was the stronger of us."

"You've an amazing strength, Alexandra," Evan said. "We've been here without food for longer than a day, and you've hardly complained. You're not the usual lady of the peerage."

She shook her head. "That is for sure. Though I'm still looking forward to finally eating."

"As am I."

"I wonder how much my mother has told your father about all this."

Evan cleared his throat. "I know she's told him some because my father said she'd been through a lot during her time with your father. I can't tell you how much I wish he were still alive, Alexandra, because if he were, I'd go and kill him with my bare hands."

Her heart leaped. "He's not worth the effort, Evan. Believe me, I'm glad he's gone, though I wouldn't mind seeing him taking a pummeling from you."

"Yes, of course. You've been free of him for two years, and for that I'm thankful. And I'm beginning to see what my father sees in your mother."

"Oh? You didn't before?"

"No, I don't mean it that way. She's a lovely woman. Very pretty and smart and she clearly cares deeply for him. I'm talking about her strength—the strength she passed on to you."

"If I'd been stronger, I'd have gotten all three of us out of there."

"For God's sake, you were only a child. And your mother was bound to him by law. There truly was nothing you could do."

"Still..." Her hands itched, the same feeling she used to get when her mind was nearly exploding with all the thinking she did about how to get them out of his house. Again the invisible worms climbed upon her arms and legs. She'd learned long ago that brushing them away was futile.

She'd learned long ago that a lot of things were futile.

Evan held her against his strong body, and she found comfort there.

"Nothing like that will ever happen to you again. I promise you."

"You're right about that," she said. "I made myself that same promise the day the bastard died." And she had. No one would ever beat her down again. And never again would she worry about not having enough money. She'd see to that. "Goodness, enough about me. Tell me a bit about yourself."

"I've had a very good life," he said. "Even as a second son. My father wasn't like Lybrook's. He included me in the affairs of the estate. But I knew it all would go to Jacob someday, and I'd be left with nothing."

All the more reason to continue her pursuit of Mr. Landon, Ally thought, despite the fact that Evan had turned out to be quite something after all—not the stuffy peer she'd thought he was. They'd shared a beautiful intimacy, but he didn't have anything to his name. Once his father died, his lot in life would be up to his older brother, and why would Jacob want to share his fortune with Evan?

"Do you resent your brother?" she asked.

"Not really. Not anymore, at least. It's not his fault he was born first. Neither of us had any say in the matter. And at least my father educated me. That's more than Lybrook can say."

Ally nodded. Lily's new husband, Daniel Farnsworth, the Duke of Lybrook, had had his title thrust upon him when his father and older brother unexpectedly passed on. His father hadn't taught him anything about estate affairs. He was learning as he went, and doing a fine job, thank goodness.

"What will you do when your father passes on?" Ally asked.

"I've got plans in the works. Business deals." He cleared his throat. "I'll be fine, I can assure you."

She nodded.

He sighed against her. "We need to figure something out."

"What?" she asked.

"Where we go next."

Next? There was no "next" for them. They would go home, and she would continue with her plans to marry Mr. Landon. "What do you mean?"

"I mean," he said, "we must marry."

CONFESSIONS OF LADY PRUDENCE

by Madame O

Dearest Amelia,

I confess, the reward I'd promised Christophe and Joshua plagued me for days on end, until one evening when my cherished maid, Hattie, came to attend me.

She has blossomed into a beautiful maiden of eighteen years. Lovely blond tresses and firm pink lips—my goodness, my heart patters as I write this.

"Hattie," I said as she unlaced my corset, "have any young men about the estate asked for your favors yet?"

"Oh, no, my lady. I'm a good girl. Mr. Savage once cornered me in the alcove on the third story, but I screamed until he let me go."

"Mr. Savage?" One of the stablemen. What had he been doing on the third story? I made a mental note to have him dismissed. "No others? No stolen kisses...?"

"Only a few clumsy kisses with a lad when I was younger."

Oh, Amelia, she was ripe for the picking! I decided then and there to take her under my wing and teach her all that you taught me. And once I did, she could join Christophe and Joshua and be part of the reward I'd promised.

My cunny pulsated as she helped me out of the restricting garment. I removed my chemise and turned to her, clad only in my drawers, which were already damp from my juices.

She blushed an adorable raspberry shade when I gazed

up and down her body. "You are lovely, sweet Hattie," I said. "I have missed you."

She cast her blue eyes downward. "I've missed you too, my lady."

I trailed my fingers over her porcelain cheek and brought her gaze back to mine. "Dear Hattie," I said, and pressed my lips gently to hers.

She backed away, her lovely mouth dropping into an O. "My lady! Goodness!"

"Do you not wish to kiss me, Hattie?" I asked. "Do I not please you?"

Her blush deepened. "You are beautiful, my lady. But I..."

"I learned much in the Americas," I told her. "And the most important thing was that one should never turn away from pleasure."

"But we're both...women."

"Yes. And no one knows a woman's body like another woman." I smiled, my nipples hardening. How I wanted those firm lips around one of them, tugging, pulling.

Such an ache between my legs, Amelia!

"I'd like to kiss you again, Hattie. Your lips are so soft..." I edged closer, my diddeys tingling. Slowly I untied the strings to my drawers and let them drop around my ankles, baring my whole body.

She gasped.

"Don't be afraid." I moved closer and slid my hands up her arms. "Please. Kiss me." I leaned in and touched my tongue to the seam of her lips. "Open for me, my dear. Let me show you how lovely kissing a woman can be."

Hattie pressed her lips together at first, and I tantalized her with tiny pecks against her firm crimson flesh, the sweet smacking sounds sending lightning to my moist pussy. I drew her plump lower lip between my own and sucked on its soft sweetness. A moan escaped her throat.

Oh, as I write this, I find I must reach into my drawers and slide my fingers through my wet folds. Hattie is so beautiful. If only you were here, Amelia. The three of us could have such fun.

With a little prompting, she opened her lovely lips and I swept in to taste her sweet mouth. Vanilla and spice infused my taste buds. Such a delicious mouth Hattie had! I coaxed her with my tongue, and soon we were kissing frantically, our tongues entwining, circling. My nipples grew harder, and I grabbed her hands and brought them to my breasts.

CHAPTER SEVEN

Alexandra lurched upward into a sitting position. "Marry? Have you gone completely mad?"

"I've ruined you, sweet. As a man of honor, it's my duty to marry you."

"Don't be absurd. It was never my intention to trap you into marriage."

"I never thought you were trying to trap me, Alexandra. But what's done is done. We can't fix it. We must marry."

Ally rolled her eyes. "That's ridiculous."

"Oh? I might have gotten you with child. Have you thought of that?"

Truthfully, she hadn't. "Why didn't you pull out then?"

"I...should have. You're absolutely right. But my God..."

"I'm sure I'm not with child. I finished my courses only days ago."

"That means nothing."

Embarrassment flooded her. Had she truly just mentioned her courses to a gentleman? A gentleman who had just thoroughly fucked her, but still...

"That method is completely unreliable. And how do you even know about that?"

"I've told you before. I *read*."

"We should marry at once."

"You've gone dotty. I'm not going to marry you."

"I can take care of you fine."

"I don't want to be taken care of fine, damn it! I want to be rich. I'll not go through those worries again. Ever. I'm going to marry Mr. Landon."

"Oh, I see." Evan cast his gaze downward. "And Landon, as we all know, is worth millions."

"Exactly."

"Well, he hasn't proposed to you yet, has he?"

"He will." And she had no doubt he would, after Evan caught them together. Of course that plan was spoiled now. They'd go back to the Brighton estate, and she'd need to plan another trip to London—one that didn't coincide with the worst rainstorm in decades.

"This is ridiculous, Alexandra. You and I must marry, posthaste. I'll not hear another word about it."

"Pardon?" Who did he think he was? "I'll not be ordered around by anyone, certainly not by my stepbrother and a second son."

Even in the darkness, his eyes blazed. She'd gone too far. He was angry.

"You will marry me, damn it." He rolled on top of her and clamped his mouth onto hers.

The kiss was angry, punishing. And arousing. She squirmed beneath him, trying to free herself, to no avail.

She didn't really want to be freed. She returned his passionate kiss, opening to him and taking his punishment. No kiss had ever been like this. He was sucking her soul from her, and she was happy to let him. He continued kissing her while he trailed one hand down her arm and toyed with her folds, which were already slick with moisture. When he entered her with a finger, she gasped.

Still he punished her with his mouth, taking, demanding,

and she responded, giving herself to him willingly.

She sucked in a breath as, within seconds, he replaced his finger in her pussy with his hard, thick cock.

He pummeled into her, still punishing, and Lord, how good it felt to be taken so roughly, with such feral exuberance. She arched upward, trying to get him to go deeper. And still he pounded into her.

Though still sore from before, his cock inside her completed her, eased the emptiness that so often plagued her. And she shattered, her climax ripping through her like a thunderbolt.

"Evan, oh Evan!" she cried out.

"That's right, Alexandra. Come for me." He continued to plunge into her depths, taking her to new heights, until he finally groaned, and with one final thrust, pushed hard into her.

"Damn it!" he said when his breathing had returned to normal.

"What?"

"I should have pulled out. What is the matter with me?"

She couldn't answer. For the idea that he filled her with his essence aroused her unnaturally. No, she did not want to be with child, but for some unknown reason, she wanted him to come inside of her.

"Don't worry about it. As I said, the timing is not right."

"And as I said, that method is completely unreliable."

She truly wasn't worried. She planned to seduce Mr. Landon anyway, so what did it matter if she *were* with child? She'd just tell him it was his.

Her heart seized. None of that felt right. Something niggled at the back of her neck, bothering her about her plans. Still, no reason she could see existed to change them.

"Please, Evan, let's not worry about that for now. Let's go to sleep so we can rise with the sun and get the bloody hell out of here."

"Very well," he said, turning away from her. "Good night."

★ ★ ★ ★

Ally jerked upward. "Evan, what is that?"

Someone pounded on the door.

Evan's eyes shot open. "Someone's here. Stay here. I'll take care of it." He moved to rise, but—

"Hello?"

The door opened. Two men stood in the doorway. And Ally and Evan were both naked as babies.

"Oh, my lord. I'm sorry," one of the men said, looking away.

Evan threw the comforter over Ally and rose, taking a bed linen with him and wrapping it around his waist.

"Do you recognize them?" Ally asked.

"Yes. They're servants from the estate."

"My lord...er... We got word from the caretaker that you hadn't arrived in London, and Lady Sophie was concerned... So we..." The servant's face turned bright crimson.

Evan cleared his throat. "We're thrilled to see you, of course. But if you could give us a couple of moments?"

"Yes, yes, of course." They moved backward and shut the door behind them.

Evan's cheeks were rosy, and Ally was sure her own visage was as scarlet as the servant's had been. "What will we do now? He saw us nude!"

Evan shook his head. "I'll see they're compensated for their discretion. And if they breathe a word of this, they'll be dismissed. I feel certain I can trust our servants."

His voice didn't sound as sure as his words did, but Ally had no choice but to trust him.

"Come," he said, "we need to get our garments on. Yours should finally be dry by now."

Ally's chemise and drawers had been dry for a day, but her traveling outfit was still slightly damp. Nothing to be done. Either wear it, or go back to the Brighton estate wearing bed linens... No, not on today's agenda. By the time Evan was dressed, Ally needed help with her corset.

He came to her without her asking and tightened it for her. "These things always seemed barbaric to me," he said.

"Trust me, they are." She sucked in her breath. "But what choice do we ladies have?"

"You don't need one," he said. "You have a lovely shape without it."

Thankfully her back was to him. Her cheeks and chest warmed.

"I hope your friend in London hasn't been too worried about you," Evan said, still tightening her laces.

"My friend?"

"The one you were supposed to visit?"

"Oh. Yes, of course." Ally cleared her throat. "Miss... Spofford. I'll send her a wire when we get back. I'm sure I'll be able to visit her soon."

"There are still a few balls in London as the season finishes up," Evan said. "Perhaps you and Sophie would like to attend one? We can plan another trip in a week or two, after we've rested up and fully healed from the accident."

How perfect that he suggested it! "Yes, I think that would be acceptable," she said, trying to sound casual.

"Perhaps your friend Miss Spofford will be in attendance."

"Yes...perhaps." Ally bit her lip.

"There you are. That's as tight as you go."

"Thank goodness. Anything more and I might swoon." She did so hate her corset. She pulled up her dress and stepped into it. "I'll need you to fasten me."

He quickly did so.

Ally bit her lip again. "What are you going to tell those men?"

"That this is none of their concern. They'll be fine, and if they aren't, they will no longer be employed. Most of our servants are notoriously loyal. We treat them well, so there's no reason for them not to be."

She nodded, hoping he was right. "Do you think they brought any food with them?"

"Lord, I hope so," he said. "I am certainly famished."

"We should have woken up earlier and left before they got here."

"Yes, we should have," he agreed, "but I assure you there will be no trouble from this. And honestly, it's better this way. We haven't eaten in two days. We're weak, and the trek to the road would have been arduous for both of us."

True. But it would have been a lot less embarrassing.

Evan opened the door. "After you."

Ally walked outside. The sun was shining, finally, and the two men stood next to two saddled horses. Evan walked to them and had some words with them out of her hearing. Just as well—she was embarrassed enough, and if she heard the words, no doubt she'd turn seven shades of red. She looked around. Where was the carriage? Not even a buckboard?

Evan returned to her. "I'll take one of the horses. You will ride with me."

Lord in heaven. Ally was not much of a rider.

"I'm sorry there's no sidesaddle. You'll have to ride astride."

"Why didn't they bring adequate provisions?" she asked. "How far must we ride?"

"They couldn't. They knew they might have to go off road. Which they did. I'm sorry for the discomfort, but it will only be a few hours."

"Did they bring any food with them?"

"Yes, some sandwiches in the saddlebags. They're getting them now."

"Thank God."

One of the men strode toward them and handed them each a sandwich. Ally rammed half of it in her mouth.

"Slowly, Alexandra. If you eat it too quickly, you'll get sick."

"I don't rightly care at the moment." She finished the sandwich in a total of four bites. "That's not nearly enough."

"I know," Evan said, munching on his own sandwich, "but we'll be fed well once we return to the estate. Sophie will have Chef prepare us a veritable feast."

They went back into the shack and each drank a dipper of water. Then they mounted the horses and were off.

Sitting astride behind Evan was certainly no hardship for Ally, even though the terrain was rough until they made it to the road about forty-five minutes later.

The breeze blew through Ally's long hair, tangling it into a worse mess than it was already. But nothing to be done at this point.

Several derriere-pained hours later, they arrived back at

the Brighton estate. Evan dismounted and helped Ally down, and the servants took the horses to the stables.

"Oh, a meal and a bath...or a bath and a meal," Ally said. "I'm afraid I don't know in which order I want them. Perhaps one of the maids can serve me in the tub."

"A meal for me first," Evan said. "I'm famished."

She was as well. But after their ordeal, Evan looked merely disheveled. And terribly sexy. She, on the other hand, had strings of hair filled with snarls tangling around her shoulders, and her dress was still damp and felt sticky next to her skin. The curse of being a woman. It was the same with growing old. Men looked handsome and distinguished. Women looked wrinkled and crone-ish.

The unfairness of it all.

He walked her to the main door of the mansion and opened it.

"Sir!" Graves strode toward them quickly. "Thank goodness. Did Marley and Silverton find you?"

"Yes, yes, and we are so grateful. We are a mess from the storm, as you can see, and in need of a hefty warm meal."

"At once. Let me inform Lady Sophie that you've returned."

A few minutes later, Sophie ran toward them and embraced Ally. "Thank goodness! Oh, what a mess! I can only imagine what you've been through."

"Sophie, it was horrid, but we're alive and in one piece. Unfortunately, poor John didn't fare as well, nor the horses."

"You must tell me everything."

"We will, but we really do need a meal first."

"Yes, of course, but Ally..."

"Hmm?"

"You have a caller."

"A caller?" She looked down at her mussed dress and the hair sticking in tangles to her shoulders.

"Yes. But don't worry, I'll tell him—"

"My lady?"

Ally jerked at the gentleman's voice.

Out of the parlor walked Mr. Nathan Landon.

CONFESSIONS OF LADY PRUDENCE

by Madame O

Though it pained me, I stopped the kiss for a moment. "Do you like my diddeys?" I asked.

"I... They're lovely, my lady."

They swelled even as she said it, Amelia, I swear to you.

I smiled into her cerulean eyes. "Pinch my nipples, Hattie. Please."

"But the kissing, my lady? I..." Her blush heightened again, and a tiny smile curved her lips upward.

My cunny throbbed! She was enjoying the kissing as much as I.

"Never fear," said I. "We shall continue the kissing. But my nipples long for your fingertips, my dear. It will feel good to me, I promise you. My titties are aching for your touch."

With a tentative hand, she touched my turgid nipple.

"Oh, yes, sweet Hattie." I closed my eyes. "Twist that firm little bud. Harder. Harder!"

She closed her fingertips around my aching nipple. A jolt thundered through me.

Dearest Amelia, I nearly climaxed then and there! Oh, her fingertips were heaven.

"The other, Hattie. The other," I begged.

And her free hand cupped my second breast, her thumb easing over the tight nipple.

"Do you like it, my lady?"

"Yes, yes, I love it. Twist them, Hattie. Pinch them." I held my breasts out to her in offering as her fingers continued to work their magic.

I slid my own fingers into my drawers and glided them over my wet cunt. My clitoris—such a funny new word that you taught me, Amelia dear—was rock hard and swollen, and with only a slight brushing of my hand, I launched into climax.

My whole body trembled, Amelia, much like it did when you sent me to climax oh so many times. I grabbed Hattie and pushed my tongue back between those luscious lips. I drank from her essence as I came down from the highest peak. And Amelia, she kissed me back with such a frenzy! Her vanilla tongue twirled with mine for endless moments, until she gasped and broke away.

"My lady! We should be ashamed."

"Of what, my dear? Of enjoying ourselves? 'Tis folly to be ashamed of such a thing." I hesitated a bit. "You did enjoy yourself, didn't you?"

Again that lovely blush veiled her face and neck as she fidgeted. "Y-Yes, my lady."

I walked forward, pushing her backward until her legs hit my bed. "I should like to see you unclothed, Hattie. Here"— I turned her around—"let me undress you."

"I... I can't."

I turned her back around and looked straight into those blue orbs. "You can't? Why on earth not? I am your mistress. You can and should do whatever I ask of you."

"But my lady, it's not... I just can't."

I smiled and took her lovely face in my hands. "You can't because you shouldn't? Or you can't because you don't want to?"

"I... I shouldn't, of course."

"So you do want to, then?"

"My lady—"

"You may think of this kind of play as forbidden fruit, yet that makes it so much sweeter, doesn't it?" I turned her back around and fiddled with the knot on the back of her head until her blond locks tumbled free. "Such lovely hair you have, sweet Hattie."

CHAPTER EIGHT

Evan couldn't help smiling. Alexandra, though a mess, still looked gorgeous to him. But to her paramour, Mr. Landon? What would he think?

Her cheeks turned crimson, and he imagined the rest of her luscious body bore the same blushing color. How would she react to this?

Sophie clasped both hands to her mouth. And Alexandra just stood, immobile, as if petrified.

"My lady," Mr. Landon said, "your sister was just telling me that you'd been lost on your way to London. Thank goodness you are all right." He turned to Evan. "And you as well, my lord."

"Yes, Landon, thank you," Evan said. "We're fine, but in need of some sustenance at the moment."

Ally stood, still paralyzed. She said nothing.

"Mr. Landon," Sophie said, "I'm sure you understand that my sister and stepbrother need to see to a few things."

"Yes, yes, of course." He took Alexandra's hand and kissed it.

A jolt of possessive jealousy surged through Evan.

"I shall call on you again soon," he said, as Graves showed him the door.

"Oh, of all the..." Ally shook her head.

"I'm so sorry, Ally," Sophie said. "He just arrived a few moments ago, and I was explaining that you were being looked for. I'm thrilled you're here and all right, of course. I never dreamed he'd come out of the parlor."

"He'll probably want nothing more to do with me," Alexandra said. "I look an absolute fright."

"If he doesn't want you because of how you look, he's not worth your time anyway," Sophie said.

"Rubbish, Sophie." Alexandra shook her head. "Please excuse me. I must see to a bath and then have a nap.

"You don't wish to take a meal?" Evan said.

"Not at the moment. I've suddenly lost my appetite." Alexandra ambled up the stairway.

"Sophie," Evan said, "would you care to join me in a meal?"

Sophie nodded. "I haven't been able to eat due to worry. Suddenly, I have quite a hunger. Plus, I'm anxious to hear all about your ordeal."

Sophie joined him in the informal dining room while he ate and told her of the carriage accident and how they'd found shelter. Of course he left out the part where he'd slept with her sister.

"How very terrible for the coachman," Sophie said. "But how very fortunate for the two of you. I don't know what I would do if anything happened to Ally."

"She is fine, though a bit frazzled," Evan said. "She'll be all right. Have you heard any word from my father?"

Sophie shook her head. "I doubt we will. Why would they send word while on a wedding trip?"

"Just some business dealings I was hoping to get his input on," Evan said. "Jacob and his solicitor are due here within a few weeks, and I need to have up-to-date information. I guess it will fall to me to get things in order."

"Yes, please don't bother your father," Sophie said. "He and my mother have waited so long for happiness. They do so deserve it."

Evan swallowed the bite of chicken sandwich he'd been chewing. Sophie was right. He'd learned a lot about what her mother had endured during her first marriage, and he did want her to have happiness now. He was still a bit irked that his father hadn't found that kind of happiness with his own mother, but at least his mother had been taken care of and had lived a good life. If only she could have had love...

But what of love? Evan himself had been ready to marry Lady Rose Jameson, and though he cared for her, he hadn't been in love with her nor she with him. Was love simply an illusion? Love was not the act itself. He'd engaged in the act many times, but had never loved the one he was with.

Though with Alexandra... He'd felt something different—something almost primal and protective. But no, it wasn't love.

Not that he'd know the difference.

Evan finished his meal. "If you'll excuse me, Sophie, I must get cleaned up after our...difficulty."

"Yes, of course." Sophie rose as well. "I'll see to my sister. In fact, I'll have Chef prepare her a tray. She must eat something."

Evan nodded and climbed the two flights of stairs to his suite on the third floor. He bid Redmond to prepare him a bath. When the tub was ready, he peeled off his soiled clothing and lowered himself into the steaming water.

Ah, heaven.

"Do you require anything else, my lord?" his valet asked.

"No, Redmond. You may go. I may just sit here until the water becomes tepid."

"I couldn't help but notice your bruising. Do you wish me to call your physician?"

"No, there's no need. We were thrown a bit in the carriage. I assure you a hot bath is the best medicine for me right now." That, and perhaps another tumble with Alexandra. But that wouldn't happen.

"Very well, then." Redmond bowed and left the room, only to come back a moment later. "I beg pardon, sir, but Mr. Graves requests an audience with you."

"Can't it wait? I'm exhausted."

"I'm sorry, sir, but he says it's of the utmost importance."

Evan sighed. "Fine, send him in."

Graves entered, the expression on his face unreadable. "Forgive the intrusion, my lord, but I received an urgent message from your printing office in Bath."

"Well, what is it?"

"I'm sorry, my lord, but I was told that only you could read the missive."

Evan let out a breath. Why now? All he wanted was a warm bath and his own bed. And then, of course, perhaps another meal later.

"Redmond," he said, "fetch my robe, please."

Evan dried quickly and stepped into the robe that Redmond held for him. He turned back to Graves and took the letter the butler was still holding. Sighing, he broke the seal and took out the folded piece of parchment.

He widened his eyes. "Thank you, Graves. You may go. Redmond, please ready my grey suit. I'm going to have to go into Bath."

★ ★ ★ ★

Having finished her bath, Ally sat in front of the looking glass, combing out the snarls from her finally clean hair.

A knock at the door startled her.

"Yes, who is it?"

"It's just me," came Sophie's voice from the other side of the door.

"Of course, do come in," Ally said.

The door opened, and Sophie ambled in, carrying a tray. "I figured you would be hungry," she said. "I know you must have been fraught with embarrassment when Mr. Landon saw you so disheveled, but still, Ally, you must eat. You haven't eaten in nearly two days."

Her sister was right, of course. Ally *was* hungry. But so many images were swirling in her mind. The intimate moments she had shared with Evan, and then the man she intended to marry, Mr. Landon, seeing her looking no better than a common peasant. She sighed. How would he ever feel the same way about her? He thought of her as glamorous and socially intelligent. Not that she felt that way herself. Her past wouldn't allow that. But damn it, no one would know of her past if she could help it. No one but Sophie and her mother knew now. Well, except for Evan, and he had assured her his confidence. Up until now, she had put on a good show for Mr. Landon. Perhaps he would understand that she had been in a carriage accident and had been without amenities for two days. If only he hadn't been there to see her when she returned.

"Thank you, Sophie."

Sophie set the tray on the table and uncovered it. "Chef outdid himself today. Roast chicken sandwiches with tomato and fresh mozzarella salad and creamed vegetable marrow. Lemon spice cake for dessert."

Ally feared it would all taste like sawdust to her right now. But her stomach wasn't going to allow her to wait any longer for sustenance. "Do join me, won't you, Sophie?"

"Of course. Evan told me about your ordeal over lunch, but I need to hear your version. It must have been horrid, Ally. I don't know how you got through it."

Ally shook her head. "Really, Sophie, we've been through so much worse. This was merely an inconvenience."

"I'm so very glad Evan was with you. I know you are angry that he wouldn't let you travel alone, but thank goodness he was there. What would you have done if he hadn't been?"

Probably not made a huge mistake. But of course she couldn't bring voice to those words. Even though her intimate moments with Evan were the most precious moments she'd ever experienced, they had been a mistake. Still, Sophie was right. If Evan hadn't been there, Ally might not have survived. But she was not going to appear weak. "I would have been just fine, Sophie. Goodness, if there was one thing life with Mother and Father taught us, it was how to take care of ourselves."

"During life with Mother and Father, we were never without shelter."

"Yes, that is true. However, there were certainly times when I went to bed hungry."

"Well perhaps our bellies weren't always filled to the brim as they are now," Sophie said, "but you went nearly two days with no food at all."

"We had water. Fresh water at that, from the rain."

"I'm just so thankful that neither of you were seriously injured. And also that you were able to find the small shack for shelter. What did you do while you were there?"

Ally couldn't help a small smile. If her sister only knew! She'd lost her virginity to the man least likely to have taken it. But Sophie could never know that. Mother and the earl could never know that. She needn't fear anything from Evan. He would want to keep this as quiet as she did.

"We talked a bit. He wanted to know about our childhood, but I was quite vague." Ally hated lying to her sister, but she didn't want Sophie to be embarrassed around Evan. "He told me a little bit about his mother, and about how he wished she had been loved by his father, the way he loves Mama."

"I'm glad you kept it vague about our childhood," Sophie said. "It's not that I'm ashamed of it, but it was just so horrible I would rather pretend it never happened. The more people who know, the more I can't erase it."

"It's a part of who we are, Sophie. Believe me, I wish it had never happened either. But it did, and like it or not, it has shaped who we are. We just can't let it color our futures."

Sophie sighed. "You are correct, of course. What else did you do in the shack? If you were vague about our childhood, I can't imagine that you spent forty-eight hours talking about Evan's mother."

No, they certainly hadn't. Her cheeks warmed as visions of making love with Evan twirled in her mind. "We were lucky enough to find a deck of cards in one of the cupboards. We played a little whist."

"With only two of you?"

Oh, she had put her foot in it now. Why hadn't she said some other game? Of course, she was ignorant as to card games. "We had to change the rules a bit. But at least it was something to do." *Now please, Sophie, don't ask me any more questions.*

"I'm just happy you're all right." Sophie smiled. "Do you feel you should see a physician?"

"Oh, heavens, no. I'm absolutely fine. A little banged and bruised is all. Millicent brought me a headache powder, and it's already starting to help. The warm bath did wonders also."

Ally filled her plate from the tray. The food did look good. She took a bite of chicken sandwich. Her mouth was dry, but she chewed and swallowed with a loud gulp. It didn't taste like sawdust after all.

★ ★ ★ ★

"My lord, we were just getting ready to close." Mr. Jenkins, the clerk at the printing office walked toward Evan.

"I'm afraid I'm going to need some information."

"Of course, my lord. What may I help you with?"

"You can tell me, Jenkins, why I was summoned near the end of the workday, when I have just returned from being stranded from a carriage accident, to be informed that my company has been printing obscene material."

CONFESSIONS OF LADY PRUDENCE

by Madame O

"Oh, my lady." She sighed. "Your breath on my neck, it's so...so..."

I pressed my nearly nude body against her still fully clothed back, my nipples poking into the soft cotton of her garment. I blew against her neck, the wisps of hairs drifting slowly.

"My dear Hattie," I said, "I still wish to see you unclothed."

Slowly and deliberately I untied the laces on the back of her gown. Most servants in our household don't wear foundation garments, and I quivered with excitement. Only a gown and a chemise stood between me and Hattie's ripe flesh.

She did not stop me as I eased her gown and then her chemise over her shoulders. They landed in a brown-and-ivory puddle at her feet. I turned her to face me, and we were so close our pert breasts touched, sending a tingle to my core.

"May I touch your lovely bubbies?" I asked.

She nodded shakily.

Her brown nipples beckoned. They were already tight under my appraisal. Oh, Amelia, they were nearly as lovely as yours! I cupped the ripe mounds and thumbed the buds lightly.

Hattie swayed backward against the bed. "Oh...my lady..."

"It feels nice, doesn't it?" I said. "Let me pinch your lovely nipples, Hattie." I took both between thumb and forefinger and squeezed hard.

"Oh my!" Hattie gasped.

I pinched her harder. "Do you feel something between your legs, dear heart?"

"My lady, oh my! Yes, it's a tickle, it's a..."

I plunged one hand into her drawers to find her pussy. Slick, dear Amelia. Slick as dew. I wanted to rip off those offending drawers and suck her cunny dry then and there! But I settled for finding her nub and touching it ever so lightly.

She gasped and trembled against me. "My lady, that feels...oh!"

I continued to slide my fingers over her clitoris whilst I twisted one nipple with my other hand. "Might I kiss this nipple, my dear?" I asked.

"Please," she begged.

I lowered my lips to the lovely bud and flicked my tongue over it, still working her hard button with my other hand. I itched to slide a finger into her quim, but I held off. Slowly, Amelia, the way you taught me. I closed my lips around the nipple and sucked. Such softness beneath my tongue, Amelia. How I've missed frolicking with you! I kissed the flesh around the nipple, and then clamped back on, nibbling gently.

Her quim gushed over my hand. Oh, that I had a hard cock to shove into her at that moment! But alas, I'd have to settle for eating that delicious cunt. And that would wait until later.

And then...oh, Amelia, it was thrilling! She climaxed against my hand, my lips still around her nipple. She quivered against me, moaning, groaning, and I bit down hard on that tight little nipple. By now, I was so wet I was ready to climax again myself without much coaxing.

CHAPTER NINE

Jenkins reddened. "I have no idea what you're talking about, my lord."

"Someone found an underground newspaper circulating in Bath. Apparently it's been traced back to this printing house."

"Where did you get this information?"

"From a loyal source, I assure you. Now do you care to tell me what is going on?"

Jenkins cleared his throat. "You'd have to ask the night crew, my lord. I can assure you that nothing of that sort has come through on my watch."

Evan looked into the back—the whirring of the presses, the typographers making prints... He loved the printing and publishing business. He loved printed matter, especially books, and now that the industrial revolution had dawned, the demand for mass-produced printed media was high.

He had bought the business—which also included branches in London and in Edinburgh—a few years ago. His business was now thriving and was responsible for the majority of the printing in the area. He prided himself on having the newest presses and was delving into lithography as well. Evan had attended the great exhibition organized by the Queen's husband, Prince Albert, in 1851. It had attracted 13,000 exhibitors from all industrial nations. Evan had taken advantage of the new technology he witnessed during the exhibition and had brought as much of it as he could to his business. While he printed newspapers and flyers and material for the theaters and other businesses in town, he prided himself on his printed novels, and most recently on his new color printing. There was no careless work at his company—no upside-down lowercase B was ever used for a lowercase G. Nor did his company use the excessive ornamentation that was so prevalent in current society. This was a high class operation.

Evan knew that his brother, Jacob, would never insist that he leave the Brighton estate once he inherited the earldom, but Evan did not want to be a burden on his family. He had decided long ago that he would make his own way in the world, and he had done quite well for himself. Perhaps he was not worth as much as Alexandra's Mr. Landon, but he was well on his way.

Drat. Why had he thought of Alexandra and Mr. Landon? The man was nowhere near good enough for her. She was smart and beautiful and had been through so much in her short life. She deserved better than a common philanderer.

"Very well, then," Evan said. "I shall return early in the morning before the night clerks leave. And we shall get to the bottom of this."

Evan left the building and got into his carriage. Then he thought better and spoke to the coachman. "We won't be going home after all. I'd like to take a room in town for the evening."

"Of course, my lord. Which inn would you prefer?"

"Wherever I can get the best meal. I need a few hours of sleep before I sneak in on the night crew."

★ ★ ★ ★

After gorging herself on the meal Sophie had brought her, Ally changed into her night rail and readied for bed. Exhaustion weighed heavily upon her. She ached all over, though the headache powder had helped a bit. The biggest problem was that she couldn't get her new stepbrother out of her mind. Though still sore between her legs, she longed for more of him.

She would definitely keep to herself her pact to sleep with Mr. Landon. That is, if he would look twice in her direction after seeing her at her worst. She would have to look spectacularly dazzling the next time they came in contact, and she had every intention of doing just that. Her cousin Lily owned an amazing red velvet dress that she had worn the night her betrothal to the duke was announced. It was audacious, yet Lily had stolen the entire evening by wearing such an outrageous costume. Ally was built quite a bit like Lily—tall, full bosom, narrow hips. She was quite sure the dress would show off her best assets as it had for Lily. Surely Lily would allow her to borrow the dress. The only problem was the fabric was a velvet and really too warm for the summer.

No, the red dress would not work after all. She would have to summon Lily's modiste to come and make her a new dress, one that would make Mr. Landon's eyes pop out of his head and make sure he totally forgot the image he had seen of her earlier today.

Of course, Evan would never allow her to leave the house wearing a dress anything like Lily's red dress. She would have to find a way to get back to London without him. He had mentioned attending a few balls in London. The season would be over in a couple of weeks, when Parliament closed in early August.

Mr. Landon often commented about the events he attended during the season, so she was sure he would be at one or more of the balls signifying its end. In fact, she was counting on it.

If only his kisses stirred her the way Evan's had. After the debacle with Wentworth in April, she had been certain she didn't ever want to kiss another man. Mr. Landon had changed her mind. He was lovely to look at, his hair shorter than Evan's and darker than her own. He had lovely amber eyes. Evan was, of course, taller. Evan was taller than most men. Broader too, and most definitely more defined. The man could have been sculpted by one of the Renaissance artists. He cut quite an athletic figure.

But he was the second son. He would never have an estate of his own, nor a title. Ally didn't care about the title, but she did care about the estate. She wanted money. As mercenary as she knew it sounded, she had made up her mind long ago that she would never live in near poverty again. Sophie thought her shallow in some ways, mostly because of her determination to marry for money. In truth, Ally was not shallow at all. She loved her family and would move heaven and earth to help them if they needed her. With money, she could make sure she would have the means to help them if they needed it. Mama's recent marriage had negated the need on her part, but she still had Sophie to consider.

If Mr. Landon would not have her, she would simply find someone else who would. She hoped against hope that he wasn't shallow and that he didn't care how horrid she'd looked earlier today.

Ally let out a heavy sigh. *Marriage*. It was a fate she'd resigned herself to long ago—a fate that didn't necessarily include love. After all, the only example of marriage she'd had in her short life was her mother's loveless one. Since her father's death two years previously, she'd been privileged to see firsthand the marriage between her aunt and uncle. Theirs was a love match, and both her cousins, Lily and Rose, had found love matches for themselves. And now even Mama had found her love match. Ally had never considered the possibility of a love match, and she wasn't about to start considering it now.

She patted her full tummy. She was fraught with exhaustion and could not wait to sleep in her own bed tonight. But she wanted to do some writing first. She sat at a small table, took a quill and parchment, and began.

★ ★ ★ ★

After a hearty dinner and a couple of good brandies, Evan readied himself to return to the printing house. He would damn well find out who was behind the obscene literature.

Evan was very well acquainted with the night staff. They were responsible mainly for daily news journals that had to be delivered at first light. The day staff, under Jenkins, dealt more with books and other such literature, which were Evan's main interests and why he got into the printing and publishing business in the first place. He had nothing against erotic literature, but he didn't want his business associated with it because it was illegal under the Vagrancy Act of 1824, more specifically its amendment in 1838.

The carriage pulled to a stop in front of the business. The front door would be locked, of course, since normal business hours were during the day. Though Evan had a key, he chose to go around to the back entrance.

He strode in nonchalantly. "I need to speak with Mr. Charles Gunderson, please." In actuality, he had never met

Gunderson before. All the night staff had been hired by Jenkins and his superior.

"He's in the back, sir," a workman said. "May I ask who wishes to speak with him?"

"Lord Evan Xavier. I own this business."

The young man, who couldn't have been more than sixteen years old, arched his eyebrows, his lips trembling—only a touch, but Evan noticed.

"Yes, of course, my lord," he said, his voice shaking. He went into the back room where the presses were rumbling.

A few moments later, the boy returned with an older man greying at the temples.

"Good evening, my lord. What brings you in at this hour?"

Evan cleared his throat. "I did not realize I needed to have a reason to check on one of my own enterprises."

"Of course not, my lord."

"I have had word from a reliable source that a piece of underground erotic literature is being printed here on my presses."

"I don't know what material you're speaking of," Gunderson said, "but I can assure you that any business we do here is completely legitimate. If any erotic literature is being printed here, you have my assurances that it has been properly paid for, and profit is being made."

"Let me make something clear, Gunderson. I believe in freedom of expression and all that, but I run a clean operation here, not one that prints what some people consider to be obscene. There are laws against that, you know."

"Let me check the records, my lord. If we have any clients who are printing material of that nature, what would you like me to do?"

"Cancel the contracts, of course."

Evan said the words, but in no way did he believe that there was a contract with his business to print such literature. This was going on under the table, and he had a feeling Gunderson knew all about it. Jenkins seemed to be in the clear because he had clearly not warned the night staff that Evan had made inquiries. Whatever was going on, Evan would find out about it and put a stop to it.

"I think I'll take a look around and see what's going to print tonight," Evan said.

"Absolutely, my lord. The morning journal is about to go to print in a few hours. They haven't sent over the final copy yet. Right now we're finishing up a pamphlet printing for the ladies' garment store on Orchard."

"Excellent," Evan said. "I'd like to take a look for quality control. If you could please show me around, I would appreciate it."

During his tour through the presses, Evan found nothing to indicate that anything untoward was going on. However, something did not sit right with him. Either Gunderson or someone who worked under him was lying. He could feel it in his gut. He had become the businessman he was not only because of his business sense, but also because of his gut instinct. He had learned to trust it.

"Thank you, Gunderson. You seem to be running a tight ship here, and I appreciate it."

"You're very welcome, my lord. I take my work here quite seriously."

"I'll be in touch." Evan nodded and left via the back entrance.

His mind was whirling. Though he knew he needed

rest, he was agitated and needed to work off some energy. He dismissed his coach, deciding to walk back to his rooming house.

Alexandra invaded his thoughts. Though he'd always thought her beautiful, he'd never known what internal strength she possessed. Unconventional, yes, but who wouldn't be after the life she had lived?

His cock pulsed. Damn it all. Just what he didn't need tonight. What the hell? He knew damned well where he could sate his appetite. There was a high-class gaming hall and brothel nearby, and he hadn't frequented the place in a while. He turned off the road to his hotel and ambled toward the seedier section of the city.

"Evening, sir," a long-haired boy said. "Care for a bit of reading material?"

"Thank you, no," Evan replied.

"Sure you do, old bloke. This is a free sample. If you like it, you can find it in several places in Bath and in London." The boy pushed a paper into Evan's hand and walked swiftly away.

Evan shoved it in his pocket and continued to the gaming hall. He entered, ordered a brandy, and looked around. No shortage of beautiful women here, but for some strange reason none of them appealed to him. He was looking for a tall woman with chestnut hair, sparkling brown eyes, and the most luscious breasts he'd ever been privileged to see. And she certainly wasn't here.

He sighed and gulped down the rest of his brandy. As he got up to leave, the paper the young boy had handed him crunched in his pocket. He pulled it out and held it up to the lamp on his table. He squinted to read the calligraphic title.

The Ruby.

CONFESSIONS OF LADY PRUDENCE

by Madame O

My skin was so tight, my nerves so tingly. I eased Hattie's drawers over her hips and then disposed of mine as well. She had a triangle of honey-blond curls over her mound, and I ached to run my fingers through their softness.

Instead, I pressed against her in a soft hug and whispered, "Would you lie with me on my bed? Kiss me some more?"

She nodded hesitantly.

I took her hands, and together we lay down atop my quilt. I took her into my arms and pressed my mouth to hers. She opened for me quickly, thrust her tongue into my mouth. Pure heaven, Amelia, kissing her. She might not have had much experience, but kissing came very naturally to her.

We ate at each other's mouths, sighing, moaning, swirling our tongues around each other's, sucking and licking. My quim grew wetter and wetter, and my nipples hardened again, aching for her twisting fingertips. She hadn't yet tasted my nipples, but I could no longer stay away from the sweet heaven that beckoned me.

I broke our kiss with a loud smack. "Hattie?"

"Yes, my lady?"

"I should like very much to kiss you...*other* places."

"Like what? My cheek?"

I gave her cheek a playful peck, laughing. "Silly. No. Your cunny. That beautiful heaven between your legs. I should very much like to kiss it the way I was kissing your mouth."

"My lady, that cannot possibly be..."

"Be what? Any fun?" I let out a giggle. "I assure you it is wonderful."

"But why would you want to do that? There are much better places to kiss me."

"Why don't you let me be the judge of that?" I slid downward on the bed and spread her lovely long legs. Her cunt glistened with nectar, and my own pussy throbbed.

I fingered her delicate folds. I tentatively licked her slit from bottom to top.

"Oh!" She gasped and squeezed her thighs against my face.

"Relax, love." I pushed her thighs apart again. "You taste like springtime. May I please kiss your beautiful cunny?"

CHAPTER TEN

Evan widened his eyes as he read through the page. Such outrageous titles!

Life Among the She-Devils.
The Libidinous Adventures of Miss Constance Cooke.
Confessions of Lady Prudence.
A House Party at the Estate of Lord and Lady Peacock.

Under each title were a few sentences leaning toward the erotic, though not quite obscene. This was a sample, after all.

And down at the bottom, where it always appeared on work printed at his business, was the seal.

Evan shook his head. Whoever was behind this didn't get any points for intelligence. Any worker worth his salt who wanted to print something in secret would have removed the seal. This "free sample" had definitely come from his printing house. He shoved the paper back in his pocket and raked his fingers through his hair, which was thankfully clean now. He left the hall and started back toward his hotel.

He would deal with this on the morrow.

★ ★ ★ ★

Ally felt tons better the next day. After a hearty breakfast and a walk about the grounds, she retired to her chamber for a long hot soak in the tub. Afterward, she dressed in a pink afternoon gown, descended for a light luncheon with Sophie, and then retired to the front parlor with a thick novel. Just as she was engrossed in a spicy scene, the parlor door opened.

"Lady Alexandra, you have a visitor," Graves said.

Well, at least it wouldn't be Mr. Landon. "Who is it, Graves?"

"Mr. Nathan Landon, my lady."

Her stomach lurched. Had he come to tell her good-bye? That had to be it. Why would he come back here wanting more of her after he had seen her at her absolute worst? Perhaps she should refuse to receive him. That would make it easier. At least she wouldn't have to listen to his rejection.

"I'm afraid I'm not receiving today, Graves. Tell him to send me a written message, and I shall respond in kind."

"As you wish, my lady." Graves left, closing the door behind him.

Ally's nerves skittered. Goodness, just when she was enjoying a restful afternoon. Sophie had gone to her chamber for an afternoon nap, so Ally was basically alone in the large house but for the servants. She hadn't seen Evan all day. Perhaps he was in Bath on business.

She looked up as the parlor door opened once again.

"My lady, beg pardon," Graves said, "but Mr. Landon insists upon seeing you. He is being quite persistent. I thought it best to ask again before I had him thrown out."

What on earth could this be about? She didn't want him thrown out, so she had no choice. "Fine. Send him in, Graves. But he won't be staying long."

Mr. Landon strutted into the parlor, proud as a peacock and dressed in dark green velvet. "My lady, I was fraught with disappointment when you chose not to receive me today."

"Well, it appears I have received you nonetheless, so no need for disappointment," she said.

"I wish to see how you are recovering from your carriage accident. I've been in a constant state of worry over it."

She warmed a bit. Perhaps he did still care for her, despite her frazzled appearance the previous day. On the other hand, he was probably just being gentlemanly. Whatever the reason, she must be a good hostess.

"Mr. Landon, it's a pleasure to see you as always. Thank you for your concern, but I assure you I am completely fine. Just a few bumps and bruises. Our poor coachman did not fare nearly as well. He was thrown and killed on impact. I'm thankful Lord Evan and I were inside the coach. It clearly saved our lives."

"I am so sorry this horrible incident has befallen you. May I sit?"

"Of course." Ally nodded to the settee across from where she was sitting.

Mr. Landon instead crossed the room and took a seat next to Ally on the divan. She shuddered for a moment at his closeness. But the quiver was different than what she was used to around Mr. Landon. She trembled not from arousal, but from... Was it fear? Of course not. She had been with Mr. Landon many times before. And she certainly wasn't feeling the rapid heartbeat of fear or the instinct to run screaming. Since she couldn't quite put her finger on what she was feeling, she chose to ignore it.

"I'm so pleased to see that you have recovered." Mr. Landon took her hand and lightly brushed his lips over it.

"As you can see, I'm no worse for the wear." Ally smiled

shakily.

Mr. Landon continued to kiss the top of her hand, moving to her wrist and then to her forearm as he rained the gentle kisses over her skin. She gasped, waiting for the goose bumps that usually accompanied his kisses.

They failed to erupt.

Mr. Landon looked up when she drew her hand away.

"My lady, I will be leaving for London tomorrow. I'm planning to attend the remaining balls of the season. I hope very much that I shall see you at one or more of them."

"Sir, I do believe my stepbrother, sister, and I will be making the trip. I do so look forward to a dance with you."

"As do I, my beautiful lady." He took her hand once more and drew it to his lips. Instead of pressing gentle kisses onto her palm, this time he pulled her toward him, caught her in an embrace, and kissed her lips, sliding his tongue along the seam.

She and Mr. Landon had kissed on many occasions, and Ally had never hesitated to open to him. His kisses were smooth and succulent like a fine wine. But what she craved now were Evan's kisses. His kisses were rough and passionate, raw with power and desire, not so much like a fine wine but more like a hearty Scotch whiskey, that although smooth, burned one's throat. They were hard and drugging and took all one's energy, but they were the best experience in the world. Ally would never stop craving Evan's kisses.

Yet Mr. Landon was the man she intended to marry. So she opened her mouth and accepted his tongue. The kiss was acceptable. More than acceptable, really, considering her experience. In fact, only three days hence, she had considered his kisses perfect.

Mr. Landon broke away from her lips and kissed her

neck, sucking on her pulse point and gliding his tongue over the contours of her neck and shoulder. He grazed over the top of her sleeve, baring more skin and pressing his lips upon it. The experience was pleasant, and yes, it even felt good. And since this was the man she intended to spend her life with, she wanted to experience more. He moved his mouth from her shoulder, down her décolletage, and to the top of her bosom.

"Oh, Lady Alexandra, how beautiful you are," he said against her skin. "I hunger for you, my darling. Might you grant me one small favor?"

Ally sucked in a breath, and her nipples hardened as she thought of Evan tugging and kissing them. She longed to feel that intensity again. No reason existed to believe that it could only be felt with Evan.

"Mr. Landon..."

"Please, my darling, Nathan."

Odd, that she still thought of him as Mr. Landon after all this time. He had told her on many occasions to call him by his Christian name, but it had never felt right to Ally. She nearly laughed aloud at the thought. Here, sitting beside her, kissing the tops of her breasts, was the man she intended to marry, and she had never called him by his Christian name. She let out a soft chuckle.

"Is something funny, my lady?"

"No, of course not...Nathan." She gently cleared her throat. "What favor do you ask of me?"

"Just a glance at your lovely breasts, my lady. I've dreamed so long of seeing the beauty you hide beneath your garments."

Oh, she was tempted. But for Sophie, she was alone in the house. Graves and the others wouldn't dare barge in. But Evan... If he were home, he would not hesitate. He felt responsible for her. She hadn't seen him all day, but that didn't mean he wasn't here.

"I don't dare, sir. My stepbrother might—"

"Lord Evan is in the city today," Mr. Landon said. "I saw him taking breakfast at the Grand House several hours ago."

Breakfast at a hotel? He had spent the night out? A dull thud landed in Ally's belly. She swiftly pushed it away. What did she care? He could break his fast anywhere. He was certainly no concern of hers.

"He may still be there, for all I know," Ally said. "But I can't take the chance. He might have come home after you saw him and could walk in on us at any moment."

"Darling Alexandra, your decision pains me. But alas, I am a patient man, and I can wait to sample your lovely jewels. However, I cannot wait forever." He rose.

Was that some sort of ultimatum? It did not sit well with Ally. She had to work with haste to get him to marry her before he grew tired of waiting.

"Sir, I will be at one of the balls, at least. If you will wait for me, I promise you will not be disappointed."

"I do look forward to that with bated breath, my lady." Mr. Landon bowed and saw himself out of the parlor.

Ally let out a sigh. She'd made up her mind months ago that she would marry Mr. Landon. And if she had to give him a taste of her nipples, she would do so, but not in this house. She would do so at a ball, out on the terrace in a dark corner. In fact, she would let him do whatever he wanted. She just had to make sure someone was watching.

She adjusted the sleeves of her dress and picked up her novel. A few moments later, Sophie entered.

Ally looked up. "Did you enjoy your nap, Sophie?"

Sophie's eyes looked sunken and sad. "Not especially."

"Is something the matter, Sophie?"

"Oh goodness, nothing to get me so upset. After all you and Evan have been through over the past couple of days, I feel like a shallow ninny for being bothered by anything."

"You could never be shallow, Sophie dear." Ally patted the seat next to her. "Come and tell me what is bothering you."

Sophie sat down, wringing her hands. "Lord Van Arden stopped by to call on me while you and Evan were gone."

"Yes? Were you not happy to see him?"

Sophie shook her head and sniffled. "Of course I was happy to see him. The problem is he was not exactly thrilled to see me."

"Then why on earth did he come here?"

"It's all so silly really. He came to tell me that he would no longer be coming by. He has fallen in love with a common woman."

Ire pulsed through Alexandra. "How dare he? That little snake."

Sophie sniffed. "Oh, Ally, it's not his fault he fell in love with someone else. I do wish I had kissed him though. I know I said I would never allow any liberties, but a girl gets curious. And who knows when I will get another opportunity? Gentlemen aren't exactly lining up for my favors. I fear I will end up like Mother, twenty-five and no prospects due to my timid nature. I don't want to be forced into marriage the way she was."

Ally embraced her sister in a tight hug. "You are only twenty-three. Not twenty-five. And you know very well Mother and the earl would never force you into anything. She wants better for us."

Sophie pulled out of Ally's embrace. She grabbed a

handkerchief out of her pocket and wiped her eyes and nose. "I know Van Arden wasn't the catch of the season, but he was a nice man, a gentle man, and I know he would never have hurt me."

"It seems to me he *has* hurt you," Ally said.

"I meant physically. The way our father hurt Mama."

Ally nodded. "Unfortunately, there are all kinds of hurt, Sophie. I wish I could shield you from all of it."

Sophie gulped. "You shield me from enough of it, dear sister. I always hated how he picked on you and hurt you. May God forgive me for not being able to stand up for you."

"There's nothing to forgive. The man was a tyrant. Believe me, he didn't even hurt me after a while. You get numb to it. I almost felt powerful, to be honest. It was like I had this control over him. I could make him want to hurt me, and I had the power not to be hurt."

"You're so strong, Ally. I envy you."

"You have no reason to envy me. You are beautiful and smart, and any man who doesn't want you is an idiot."

Sophie let out a shaky laugh. "You always could make me smile."

"What were your feelings for Van Arden? Did you fancy yourself in love with him?"

Sophie shook her head. "If what Lily and Rose said is true, and you know without a doubt when you're in love, no, I was not in love with Van Arden. But I was very fond of him, and I think I could have been happy as his wife."

Despite the experiences of Lily and Rose, Alexandra still wasn't sure she believed in love. Love had never been a requirement for her own marriage. She didn't love Mr. Landon, and she didn't labor under any delusion that he loved her. Sophie, though, would hold out for love. And her sister needn't worry. Ally would have plenty of money to take care of Sophie if need be. Never would her sister be forced into a loveless and abusive marriage like their mother had been. Ally would see to that.

"He is not the last man on earth, Sophie. There are others, and the right one will find you."

"I do hope you're right. I couldn't bear the thought of being forced into an unhappy marriage."

"Sophie, I'll say it again. Mother and the earl would never force you into anything. She knows better than anyone that spinsterhood is preferable to an abusive situation."

"Spinsterhood? I can't bear the thought of that either." Sophie wiped her eyes again with her lace handkerchief. "Perhaps I should have allowed a few kisses. Van Arden was never insistent, but he did ask a couple of times."

Ally wasn't certain how to respond. She had done her share of kissing, but it was out of her own curiosity rather than to give the gentleman in question anything. Today she had the chance to allow Mr. Landon a few more liberties, and she had wanted to try, but her heart hadn't really been in it. Her curiosity had been sated. She had done what she wanted and more with Evan.

"If you are not comfortable with allowing him a kiss, you did the right thing," Ally said. "When you are ready to give a kiss, you will know, and you will be doing it for yourself, not for someone else."

"Is that how you truly feel, Ally? Did you truly only allow Mr. Landon liberties because you wanted them?"

"Absolutely. I have the intention to marry Mr. Landon, but I myself was curious. And if my curiosity can help me show a gentleman that my treasures are worth sampling for the rest of his life, all the better. But believe me, Sophie, I wanted the liberties as much as he did."

"But it's not ladylike to want such things. As ladies, we are supposed to be the sensible gender and rebel against our baser instincts."

"Yes, that is what convention dictates, is it not? However, we are all human beings, and women have needs just as gentlemen do."

"Ally! How can you speak of such things? Ladies aren't supposed to have such thoughts."

"How can you even say that anymore? You and I have both watched Lily and Rose succumb to their baser desires, and neither of them regretted it one bit. I've done a lot of reading, Sophie, and there are parts of the female anatomy that are meant solely for pleasure."

"My goodness, those cheap novels—if one can even call them such—cannot be relied upon for accurate information."

"I'm not talking about the novels, though they are terribly amusing and you would do well to read a couple of them. I am talking about basic anatomy. Have you perused the library here at the estate? The earl has myriad reference books, and the library over at Lily and the duke's estate has even more. You know what a voracious reader I am. I've devoured nearly all of them."

"My goodness, Ally, what on earth could you be speaking about?"

"I'm speaking about sexual desire, Sophie."

Ally smiled as her sister's cheeks turned red as a beet.

"No need to be embarrassed, sister dear. Did you know that women have an organ in the body whose sole function is sexual pleasure?"

"Ally, really. Must we discuss this? And of course men have an organ for sexual pleasure as well. Even a lady as naïve as I knows that."

"Well, of course. But that organ has several functions other than sexual pleasure. Excretion for one, procreation for another. The organ I'm talking about has only one function, and that organ is found only on the female body."

"You can't possibly be serious."

"Oh, I am more than serious. In fact I—"

Ally and her sister both looked up as the parlor door opened swiftly. Evan stood in the doorway, his large frame nearly taking up the entire space.

"Sophie, Alexandra, I must speak with you."

Sophie, her cheeks still bright red, said, "Of course, Evan, what is it?"

"I'm afraid some business has come up that I cannot ignore. I will not be able to take you to London for the last balls of the season as I promised."

"Well of course, we understand—"

"The hell we do." Ally stood, clenching her fists. "I will return to London, with or without you."

CONFESSIONS OF LADY PRUDENCE

by Madame O

Hattie squirmed beneath me. "My lady, 'tis not proper. You shouldn't—"

And then my mouth was upon her. Oh, Amelia, you can't imagine how sweet the taste of her pussy. If only Christophe had been there and I were sitting on his face grinding into him as I ate my fill of Hattie. She writhed against my probing tongue as I continued to plunder her sweetness. When she finally erupted, convulsing against me, I slowed my attack.

I knew she wasn't ready to return my favor, and I was willing to wait. But now, she having experienced such sweet diversion for the first time, I hoped it would be easy to convince her to join Christophe and me at our next lesson.

"Hattie, dearest," I said, "would you like to experience even more pleasure?"

"My lady, I'm not sure there is any pleasure that could be more fulfilling than what I just felt."

I couldn't help chuckling a bit, dear Amelia. Such naïvety! And to think, if not for you, I would still be as naïve as innocent Hattie. "My dear, I can assure you that we have only scratched the surface of pleasure. My art instructor, Christophe, has given me amazing gratification, and I wish for you to experience it as well."

"I don't know..." She reddened from head to toe and wrapped her arms over her succulent breasts. "What we just did was scandalous enough. I don't know if I should partake in any more such activities."

"Didn't I just tell you only moments ago never to deny yourself pleasure?" I smiled.

"You did, indeed, and I certainly would like to experience more..."

"If you felt being with a woman was scandalous, perhaps you will find being with a man slightly less so." I raised my eyebrows and smiled again.

"Perhaps..."

And then, Amelia, I knew I had her. I so look forward to my next lesson with Christophe. I hope very much he will bring Mr. Peck with him.

I shall write again when I have more exciting adventures to tell you. Until then, I remain yours, affectionately,

Prudence

CHAPTER ELEVEN

And here we go again. Evan sighed. The woman was bound and determined to get to London. Evan doubted very much it had anything to do with her friend, Miss Hortense Stafford or whomever it was. Knowing Alexandra, she had something completely different up her sleeve. Still, he had made a promise to her, and he hated having to break it. Plus, Sophie certainly deserved to get off this estate and have some amusement, as well. Shy and timid she may be, but she had seemed to enjoy the balls they'd attended at the duke's estate.

"My apologies to both of you," he said calmly. "I know you were looking forward to seeing the end of the season. However, there is a problem at one of my businesses in the city of Bath, and I must get it resolved."

"Well, that is not an issue as I see it," Alexandra said. "Sophie and I can simply travel to London alone and attend the balls."

"You know damned well"—Evan jerked when Sophie gasped at his language—"that I cannot allow the two of you to travel to London alone. Look at what happened last time we tried to go. You and I ended up stranded."

"Oh, for God's sake, Evan, we just won't travel during the worst rainstorm of the century. Surely that won't happen again." Alexandra stomped her foot on the Oriental rug.

"Ally," Sophie said, "if we can't go to the balls, it's not the end of the world. We shall both have our seasons next year."

"It's not the damned season—"

Sophie gasped again at Alexandra's words.

"—I'm concerned about. I just want to have a little bit of fun. Ever since Mother and the earl left on their wedding trip a month ago, we've been stuck here. I've nearly exhausted all the literature in the library, and I've knitted and crocheted so many baby booties that I want to hurl my crumpets."

"I am very sorry," Evan said again. "If there were any other way—"

"Of course there is another way," Alexandra said. "If it's a chaperone you are concerned about, send us with one of the servants—one you trust completely. I'm sure he would be happy to escort the two of us to the balls in London."

Oh, Alexandra was beautiful, and when she got that dander up, sexuality just oozed from her pores. Evan felt feral. He wanted to run to her and crush his mouth to hers in a carnal and passionate kiss. But he couldn't—not in front of Sophie. And not at all, for that matter. She had refused his suit, and she no doubt would not appreciate any more of his attentions. He'd have to hope like hell he hadn't impregnated her.

The thought of his child growing in her belly filled him with a raw and possessive need. To see her body change, to see a baby born with her chestnut hair... But no. It would be much better if she was not with child.

"Don't be absurd. I can hardly have the two of you attending London society balls on the arms of a servant."

"Why not?"

"Because it's just not done, that is why." He turned and then looked back over his shoulder. "And I'll not hear one more word about this."

"Oh, you will hear more than one word about this," came

Alexandra's voice from behind him. "You can be certain of that."

Evan closed the door to the parlor a bit more loudly than he meant to. He walked quickly to his office on the first floor. His father, being aware of his business investments, had allowed him to use a room on the estate for his work. He sank down into his leather chair. The musky scent of cowhide wafted to his nose. What was he going to do about Alexandra? She never left his mind. Even when he was focused on work, still her visage tormented him behind his eyes, her berry scent always in his nose, and the touch of her skin a memory beneath his fingertips.

He shuffled some papers on his desk, looking for a particular file, when a knock sounded on the door.

"Yes?" he said.

"It's Graves, my lord."

"Yes, Graves, do come in."

Graves entered with an envelope. "This was just delivered for you." He laid the message on the desk.

"Thank you," Evan said. "Tell me, what has been going on about the estate while I've been gone?"

"It has been quiet, my lord. We did have one caller."

"And who was that?"

"Mr. Nathan Landon. He came to call upon Lady Alexandra."

Jealousy stirred in Evan's gut. Why was Nathan Landon hanging around Alexandra? Landon was a notorious skirt chaser. The peers put up with him because he was a cousin to the Duke of Lybrook. He wasn't sure why Lybrook himself had allowed his wife's cousin to associate with Landon, knowing the type of man he was. An astute businessman, yes, and nice enough—but Evan had seen Landon in many situations that even gentlemen of ill repute would not be seen in. Somehow, he had to steer Alexandra away from Landon. Keeping her out of London would be a good start, but what could he do about Landon coming to call?

In truth, he needed to resolve this problem at his printing business, but he could easily have one of his associates look into it. It was not a big enough issue to require his presence. God knew he wasn't the first business owner to deal with the dregs of the city trying to use his business for their own gain. Still, it gave him an excuse to stay in Bath rather than travel to London for the remaining few weeks of the season. And that would keep Alexandra right here where she belonged.

"My lord?"

Evan jerked in his chair. He had quite forgotten that Graves still stood in front of him. "And anyone other than Mr. Landon?"

"No. As I said, it has been quiet."

"Very well, then. You may go, Graves."

The door had no sooner closed than Alexandra stormed in, her face red, her fists clenched, her beautiful lips trembling.

"We need to talk," she said.

"I can't imagine what about. Other than the fact that I'd appreciate a knock before you barge into my office."

"You know damned well what we need to talk about. I am going to London. My friend is expecting me. And you promised to escort me to the end of the season balls."

"Yes, I know that," he said calmly. "However, as I said before, there is some unforeseen business that requires my attention."

"Summon your brother. He should be spending his time

here anyway. It will be his estate someday. Instead, he's living it up in London, he and his intended. He should be here taking care of business while your father is out of the country. That is his responsibility, not yours. Why would any business keep you here? You're nothing but a second son."

The derision in her words sent an arrow through his heart. She truly did look down upon his station. "My brother is seeing to the estate while he's in London, and he and his solicitor are due here in a little more than a week." Evan's hands shook. Though his legs ached to stand and thunder toward Alexandra, he glued his behind to the chair. "The business to which I'm referring is my own, not the estate's."

"What kind of business could you possibly have?"

"That is none of your concern."

"It certainly is my concern if it's keeping you from escorting us to London. However, it doesn't need to be my concern. All you need to do is find someone suitable to take Sophie and me to London. And if you don't, we will be going alone."

Unable to hold himself in check any longer, Evan stood, walked around his desk, and grabbed Alexandra's upper arm, gripping her tightly. "You will respect my authority, and you will not travel to London."

"I *will* go to London," she said.

Evan's body tensed. His cock swelled and pulsed against his trousers. What she did to him! He had to have her.

"You will not!" He slammed his mouth down on hers.

He glided his tongue over the seam of her lips, probing for entrance. They remained tightly sealed. No problem there. He could wait. He nipped at her full lips slowly, suggestively, and then he sucked her lower lip between his own. Her lips had to have been forged by God himself, so perfect they were. And then, with a sigh, she parted them, and he drove his tongue into her mouth. She responded immediately, twirling her tongue around his, soft groans coming from her throat.

Yes, yes, he had her now. He continued kissing her while he cupped one of her peachy breasts. It swelled beneath his hand. Her dratted corset kept him from feeling the nipple that he knew would be hard under his touch.

She sighed against him, kissing him with passion. And then he jolted. She had gripped his erection through his trousers. He nearly spent right then and there. He was nothing more than a youthful lad with her, so eager was he. He was not inexperienced by any means, but in Alexandra's presence, all of that drifted away with the wind.

He tore his mouth from hers, regretting the loss almost instantly. "Turn around," he commanded.

She complied, and he began unfastening her gown.

"What is it about you?" he whispered against her neck. "Why do I ache for you so much? What have you done to me?"

"Faster, Evan. Undress me. I need you."

She hadn't answered his question. He worked her buttons as fast as his thick fingers would allow, his breathing more rapid with each new bit of skin he exposed. When her dress sat in a puddle on the floor, he loosened her corset and removed it. He turned her around and brushed her soft chemise off of her shoulders. She stood before him naked but for her drawers, her engorged breasts held out like an offering. Her nipples were puckered and pink. He bent to taste one.

"Oh, yes," she sighed. "That feels so heavenly."

He nibbled on the nipple, biting, tugging, sucking. The texture was like silk and the taste like the sweetest pear. He feared he could never get enough of her. He moved to the other nipple while continuing to work the first with his fingers. She moaned, such sweet sounds from her throat. He nipped and tugged until he brushed his hands down her sides and over the swells of her hips, pushing her drawers to the floor. Her dark bush of curls beckoned him. He left her nipples, kissing down her abdomen and then inhaling the earthy scent of her sex. Lord, she intoxicated him. The lips of her pussy were just visible at the apex of the triangle. They were already red and wet. On his knees, he tongued her clitoris.

"Oh," she sighed. "I was just telling Sophie earlier that there was an organ on the female body that was meant solely for pleasure." Her breaths came rapidly. "She didn't...believe me..."

Evan chuckled. He continued licking her for a few moments but then ceased. "Turn around, sweet, and sit on the edge of my desk. And then spread your legs for me."

She obeyed, and there she was, glistening and pink, engorged and beautiful, just waiting for him to plunder her. He slid his tongue from the bottom of her opening to her clitoris, stopping to suck on the tight nub. She gasped. Yes, it was an interesting little part of the female body, one he'd learned to love. Nothing was better than bringing a woman pleasure, and that little nub of nerve endings was the key to the process. Not to mention it was close to that part of her that held him so beautifully, hugged him so tightly, and gave him the utmost pleasure.

He continued to lick her sweet pussy, circling her opening, rubbing his cheeks against her wetness. Pure heaven. Here she was, bared for his pleasure, while he was still fully clothed. His cock pulsated against his britches, longing for release—release that only she could grant him. Would she take him between those ruby lips? Suddenly, he wanted that more than his next moment on this earth, to have those luscious full lips pleasuring him. But he didn't want to scare her. He would settle for being embedded in her lovely cunt.

She writhed on the desk, squirming, gasping, groaning. "I'm going to climax, Evan, please, please!"

He thrust two fingers into her, and she shattered around him, her walls clamping down around his fingers as the orgasm took her. God, she was beautiful. All women looked beautiful in ecstasy, but Alexandra—she was something special, something unique. Her flushed cheeks, her swollen lips, her rosy engorged breasts, her silky hair tumbling free from its confined style— she was simply stunning.

He stood hastily, unbuckling and unbuttoning his trousers. His cock was thick and swollen, and it ached to be inside her sweet suction. With one smooth thrust, he plunged inside of her. She hugged him so completely he nearly spent as soon as he was all the way in. His body still ached from the carriage accident, but in his lust he hardly felt it. He held himself in check for several seconds, breathing, focusing, until he could withdraw and thrust in again.

"God, what you do to me." He clenched his teeth. "You embrace me so completely, hold me so securely." He thrust again. "Kiss me, Alexandra."

Their lips met and their tongues tangled. He took her, branded her, plunged in and out of her body. He broke away from the kiss and sucked in a much-needed breath.

"Oh, Evan," she said. "I-I... I am going to come again!"

She let out a scream, and he clamped his mouth onto hers again to muffle it. Her slick walls contracted against his hard cock, milking him, and soon he was joining her in orgasm. This time, he remembered to pull out, and his seed spewed upon the milky-white skin of her belly. As good as the release felt, it paled in comparison to the two times he had come inside of her. He panted, pulling her close.

"Why did you do that?" she asked.

"Do what?" He continued to breathe rapidly.

"Pull out?"

Reality struck, and he pulled slightly away from her. "You know damned well why I did that. I don't want to get you with child."

"Isn't that a moot point now?"

"Absolutely not," he said. "Why tempt fate?"

"I suppose you're right." She slipped off the desk, picked up her drawers from the floor, and stepped into them. "It's just that..."

"It's just that, what?"

"It's just that... I liked it when you...you know...inside me."

He shuddered. He had liked it as well. In fact, at this very moment, he could think of nothing he would like more than to release inside her every night. But this needed to stop. Just moments before, she'd been putting him down as being only a second son. Clearly, she was not the woman for him. If only they could fight this attraction that boiled between them. They would have to put a stop to it once their parents returned from their wedding trip. What would his father and her mother say? They had left her in his care, trusted him to see to her and Sophie's best interests. Taking her to bed had not been on that agenda. He wanted to tell her he liked it too, that coming outside her body had not satisfied him nearly as much. But he held those words back and quickly pulled up his trousers and fastened them.

"Here," he said, wiping off her belly with his handkerchief and then holding up her chemise, "let me help you."

She stepped into the garment, and then he helped her with her corset, tightening it. Finally, he buttoned her dress.

"I shall go straight to my chamber." Alexandra fidgeted with her hair. "I'm sure I must look a fright."

A fright was hardly how she looked. She looked beautiful and satisfied, which made him smile. "You will pass," he said. He wanted to say more, but his lips didn't move. He turned away and absently looked over the papers on his desk.

"Evan?"

He turned toward her again. She was biting her lower lip. His cock, completely spent, jerked inside his trousers. What was it about this woman? "Yes?"

"Could you possibly reconsider? Sophie and I would so much like to attend the last balls of the season."

Back to this again? Had she come in here planning to seduce him if he refused to accompany them to London? And he'd fallen right into her trap. Anger roared to life within him. "Absolutely not."

"In that case, you force me to take drastic measures."

He cocked his head, his curiosity piqued. "And what type of measures might those be?"

"I will be forced to send a message to my mother and your father, telling them in no uncertain terms that you have taken advantage of your position as my guardian."

Evan widened his eyes. What on earth was she going on about? "I beg your pardon?"

She stared straight at him, her eyes blazing. "I shall tell them that you raped me."

CONFESSIONS OF LADY PRUDENCE

by Madame O

Dearest Amelia,

After much anticipation, the day finally arrived for my next art lesson with Christophe. Rather than convince Hattie to attend along with me, I chose to arrange for her to interrupt us in the act. That way I could bid her join us, and Christophe would have the reward I had promised him.

I had hoped he would bring his friend Mr. Peck with him as he had last time, but he did not. However, that was probably a blessing. If Hattie had walked in on the three of us engaged in improper behavior, it might have scared her away. With just Christophe and me, the chance was much better that she would agree to join in our merry escapades.

Christophe arrived, and we did spend the first half hour actually studying art. I had arranged for Hattie to barge in forty-five minutes after our lesson began, so I was eager to get started. When Christophe came behind me and took my hand, showing me the proper strokes, I had my chance. I backed into him and circled my hips so that I created friction against him.

"I see you have missed me, my lady," he said, his voice smooth as whiskey.

"I have indeed, good sir." I laid the brush down on the easel and turned toward him, my breasts skimming against his chest.

He gripped my shoulders tightly and lowered his lips

to mine. We enjoyed a frantic kiss, our tongues dueling and tangling, our passion growing. I turned quickly back around.

"Undress me, Monsieur. I fear I can wait no longer to have your lips upon my nipples."

He did not disappoint me. He unfastened my dress and loosened my corset, and soon the two offending garments lay on the floor. He got rid of my chemise and drawers with quick aptitude. And I stood before him, naked as the day I was born, my nipples hard, my pussy wet.

"Suck my sweet cream, good sir." I spread my legs, gripped his shoulders, and pushed him down onto his knees.

He darted out his tongue and grazed my sweet bud. Tremors shot through me, and I sighed. Oh, yes, how I had longed to have my pussy sucked while I was initiating Hattie. And now, finally, my desire was fulfilled.

"Your quim is so sweet, my lady," Christophe said against my nether curls. "I have thought of nothing but you since our last meeting." And he continued to plunder me.

"Yes, yes." I cupped my breasts and scraped my fingernails over my hard nipples. "Fuck me with your finger, good sir."

He did as I bid, and soon I was creaming all over his hand, flying in ecstasy as my climax whisked me to the moon. As I floated downward, a knock on the door startled me.

I looked down at Christophe, his cheeks red.

"Whatever shall we do, my lady?"

"Nothing whatsoever," I said, knowing Hattie was behind the door. "Come in," I called.

The door opened, but Hattie did not enter. Instead, Lars, one of the estate's new footmen, stood in the doorway, his eyes as big as saucers.

I had promised Christophe a reward, but that would have

to wait until the next lesson apparently. Lars was a handsome, tall man, barely out of his teens, with a shock of long auburn hair pulled back in a queue.

And suddenly I was no longer concerned with Hattie's absence.

I recalled the deliciousness of both Christophe and Joshua focused on me. Lars was young—long and lean—and I quivered with anticipation.

Oh, yes, he would do quite nicely.

CHAPTER TWELVE

Evan's fist came down on the mahogany desk so hard the room rattled. Ally trembled, her body chilling. Oh, she had gone too far. His eyes were glazed over with fire, his nostrils flaring. Tiny beads of sweat emerged on his forehead. His dusky full lips parted slightly, his jawline tight, the muscles in his neck tense.

Ally bit her bottom lip. *Say something. Tell him you didn't mean it. Do something, Ally, anything at all!*

"You will *what?*" He glared at her.

She wanted to tell him she was sorry, that she would never do such a horrible thing, but no words emerged.

"I'm afraid I have no other choice than to put you under house arrest," he said, his voice low and stern. "Clearly, you cannot be trusted."

"Evan, I—"

"I do not want to hear it," he said through gritted teeth. "To think for one minute I actually thought..."

"Thought what?"

"Never you mind. This conversation is over. And whatever this...*thing* is between us is also over. I shall begin searching for a suitable husband for you first thing in the morning."

"What?" Ally clenched her fists. "You cannot be serious. I will not be forced into any marriage!"

"You will do as I say. I am responsible for you. And quite frankly, you are more than I can handle. I will foist you off on someone else so you're no longer my problem."

Raw anger pulsed within her. Ally's skin tightened, and her heart surged. *No. No. No. Absolutely not.* She opened her mouth to speak, but again she was rendered mute. His harsh presence frightened her, and also aroused her. Oh, he was a formidable man, a man whose very existence could light fires.

"I wash my hands of this." Evan walked from behind his desk and left his office.

Ally sank into a chair, her eyes misting with tears. *Dear Lord, what have I done?*

★ ★ ★ ★

Later that night, Ally sat in her hotel room in Bath. She had waited until both Evan and Sophie had retired for the evening, and then she had sneaked to the stables and paid one of the servants handsomely to take her into the city. She would leave on the rail at first light and be in London by the afternoon. She had packed her best gowns, and if her plan went accordingly, within a few days she would be Mrs. Nathan Landon.

She munched on the roast beef and potatoes for which she'd paid dearly to get the cook out of bed after hours. She shouldn't have bothered. The meat was dry and the potatoes were lumpy and soggy.

She hated how she had left things with Evan. He was high and mighty and controlling, but he didn't deserve to be accused of rape. She would never have gone through with it. But now, because of her hasty words, she was facing a forced marriage. She was of age and could legally marry whomever she wished. Still, it would behoove her to find a husband before Evan's plans fell into place. There was a ball tomorrow eve. Mr.

Landon would no doubt be in attendance, and so would Ally.

She sighed. Once lunch rolled around tomorrow and she hadn't surfaced, Sophie would begin making inquiries. Ally had thought of that, however. She'd left a note on her pillow stating that she was spending the day out walking the estate and had taken a picnic lunch with her. It wouldn't keep Sophie at bay for long, but no one would notice she was truly gone until she didn't come home for the evening meal, and by then it would be too late to get to London until the next day. Not a great plan, but she had been pressed for time.

She pushed the tray away. She really had no hunger.

Would Evan be able to forgive her hasty words? She bit her lip. Within a few days, she would be someone else's problem, as he wished. And whatever had been between them would truly be over.

Her body still aching a bit from the bumps and bruises caused by the accident, Ally fell into bed.

★ ★ ★ ★

Evan lay in bed, thoughts of Alexandra plaguing him. Every time he thought that perhaps he had been wrong about her, that he had misjudged her, she proved him wrong. Would she really accuse him of rape? She knew damned well that it hadn't been rape. His father would likely disown him. Not that it mattered. He wouldn't be inheriting anything of his father's anyway, being a second son. Still, he loved his father, and the relationship meant a lot to him. He could not allow Alexandra to sour his father against him. He would find a suitable mate for her and have her out of all of their hair by the time his father and new wife returned.

But what would Iris think? She would hardly be pleased that he had married off one of her daughters while she was abroad. What to do? Alexandra would be the death of him. Mr. Nathan Landon seemed to be interested. Of course he was interested in any beautiful woman in a skirt. No way would he agree to marry Alexandra. Women had been trying to drag him to the altar for years, ever since he'd made his fortune, and not one had succeeded yet. Of course, Alexandra was in a league of her own. How could any man resist her? She had beauty, she had intelligence, she had cunning, she had passion, and she had fire... The woman had everything—everything that Evan wanted but had never thought he wanted, if that made any sense at all. Never in one million years had he imagined he would have any interest in a woman like Alexandra.

He had courted Lady Rose Jameson for a couple of months. She had been the epitome of what he thought he wanted—socially adept, from a good family of peers, beautiful, intelligent, soft, and gentle. Alexandra might be beautiful and intelligent, but she certainly didn't fit in any of the other categories he'd thought were so important to him.

None of it mattered now anyway. She had proven what kind of person she was.

He was done.

Done or not, though, he did need to speak to her. He had to make sure she didn't go running to Mummy and new Daddy crying rape. He slipped on his robe and poured himself a brandy. Rather than sipping, he swallowed the amber liquid quickly, burning his throat.

He walked out of his suite and down the staircase to the second floor. The hallways were dark, and he hadn't brought a candle with him, but he knew this place like the back of his hand. Alexandra was probably sleeping, but he didn't care. They needed to talk. When he got to her room, he knocked gently.

No response.

He knocked harder. Still no response. "Alexandra?" He knocked again.

Still nothing.

He inched open her door a bit. "Alexandra?" he said again.

He walked through the sitting area and stood at the doorway into her bedchamber. He knocked again. Still nothing.

This had gone far enough. He opened the door and walked in. "Alexandra," he said, "I need to speak with you."

He lit a lamp on her bed table.

No!

She was not there. His heart beat rapidly and his breathing accelerated. He looked around the chamber. A small piece of parchment lay on her pillow. He unfolded it.

Sophie,
I rose early and decided to spend the day out of doors. I packed a small luncheon and plan to be gone with a good book most of the day. Please do not worry.
Ally

That little minx! Evan knew very well where she had gone—London.

No chance of sleeping for him this night. He'd have to go after her.

A half hour later, after interrogating the servants, he found out that one of them had been paid off to get Alexandra to Bath. His business would have to wait. Evan promptly dismissed the man in question and rode his stallion, Leopold, into Bath. After checking the inns and rooming houses, he located Alexandra, ironically, at the same hotel where he'd spent the previous night. Rather than abducting her and taking her back to the estate, he booked a room himself. He would deal with this in the morning.

And he would deal with it in London. Forcing her to go back to the estate would be futile. She would only run again. The woman was determined to go, so rather than trying to stop her, he would simply follow her.

★ ★ ★ ★

Alexandra woke early the next morning, her backache increased from sleeping in a bed she was not used to. She rang for a hot tub, bathed quickly, dressed in her traveling clothes, ate a light breakfast, and walked to the railway station.

Freedom! Within days she would be a married woman, and her freedom would be limited. However, her purse would not be limited. Still, she would relish these last few days of liberty. She inhaled the summer breeze on this sunny July day.

Big mistake. She was no longer in the country. In the city, the aroma was vile. Clearly not everyone had indoor plumbing in Bath. She wrinkled her nose. London would likely be no better.

But London was where her future lay. She reached the railway station, purchased her ticket to London, and sat down to await her train. She gazed around at all the people. Other women her age appeared to be riding the train alone, so she didn't feel too out of place. Despite what her stepbrother might think, young women of an age frequently traveled alone. People from all walks of life gathered at the station—young women like herself, many young businessmen, families with small children, and older couples as well. She looked back toward the ticket booth. A man stood, his back to her, purchasing a ticket. With broad shoulders and a shock of wheat-blond hair, he could have been Evan. But of course Evan had no idea where she was. She turned her head and gazed in the other direction. She had bigger fish to catch.

The train ride was rickety, and she'd purchased an inexpensive ticket, so her seat was lumpy and uncomfortable. She hadn't packed a lunch, so by the time they reached London she was quite famished. She disembarked and found a small café near the station where she took a repast. Then she hired a coach and asked him to take her to the Brighton townhome.

When she knocked on the door, an older gentleman opened it.

"Yes, madam, may I help you?"

"Yes, you may. I am Lady Alexandra MacIntyre, the earl's new stepdaughter. I will be staying here for a few days while I visit a good friend in town."

"Of course, my lady. I am Forrest Clay, the caretaker. I will summon the butler at once. We have been expecting you. We were so sorry to hear about the accident that you and Lord Evan were involved in. Is he with you?"

"No, I'm afraid he could not make it this time. He had some business that could not be avoided."

A throat cleared behind her. "Lady Alexandra is mistaken. I am here, and I will be acting as her chaperone."

Alexandra's neck heated. She turned to face Evan's angry glare. "What are you doing here?" How had he found her? Drat, he would ruin everything.

"I live here, Alexandra." His lips were pursed into a thin line.

"Very well, then." Alexandra entered.

Another man appeared, dressed formally. "Lord Evan, it is wonderful to see you." The man took Evan's valise.

"May I present my stepsister, Lady Alexandra MacIntyre. Alexandra, this is our butler, Woods."

"A pleasure, my lady." He took her satchel as well. "Lord Evan knows where his chamber is, but let me escort you to yours."

Alexandra followed Woods up a winding staircase and down a hallway of doors. He stopped in front of one and opened it. "Here you are, my lady. I will send Mary to attend to you."

"Thank you, sir. I appreciate it."

The butler took his leave, and Alexandra looked around her chamber. It was a good size, though nothing like her chamber at the estate, which included a sitting room and a bath chamber. This would do nicely, however, and she was thrilled to be here. All except for that thorn in her side—Evan. Most likely he would insist upon accompanying her to the balls.

She chuckled to herself. Just days ago, when he had insisted upon accompanying her to London, she had thought it a splendid idea. Who better to catch her in the act with Mr. Landon? Now, given their past couple of days together, she wasn't sure he was the right person at all. Nothing to be done about that. He was here, and he would be going to the balls.

Her maid, Mary, arrived shortly and helped her out of her traveling clothes.

"Is there anything else I can do for you, my lady?"

"Not at the moment, thank you. I believe I will take a short nap. I will be attending the ball this evening, so if you could be here later to help me prepare, I would appreciate it."

"Of course, my lady." Mary curtsied politely and left.

No sooner had Ally fallen asleep than another knock came on the door. "Drat!" she said. *Who on earth could that be now?* "Come in," she called.

Mary entered again. "I'm so sorry to disturb you, my lady, but Lord Evan has requested that you ready yourself for dinner."

Requested, had he? "You may tell Lord Evan that I will be skipping dinner this evening and napping until it is time to get ready for the evening's festivities."

"I'm sorry, my lady. Lord Evan is master of the manor when neither his father nor brother is present. I cannot tell him anything of the sort."

Ally sat up and let out a heavy sigh. "That's absolutely fine. I shall tell him myself. If you would, please select a gown for me and help me dress."

"Yes, my lady."

A while later, Ally walked down the hallway to Evan's suite and knocked loudly. He came to the door, looking as dashing as ever in his dinner clothes.

"Good evening, Alexandra."

"I have come to tell you that I shall not be attending dinner this evening," Alexandra said calmly.

"To the contrary"—Evan adjusted his cravat—"you *will* be attending dinner, and you *will* be ready to go within an hour and a half."

Ally's dander rose. "I have been traveling all day, as have you. I am still full from my repast after the trip. There is no reason for me to go to dinner with you."

"There is every reason for you to go."

"And what may I ask might that be?"

"Because I have said that it will be so." He gave her a smirk.

Oh, he had a lot of nerve, this one. So determined to be controlling.

"You have no authority over me." Her cheeks warmed. How she wished that were so. But her mother and stepfather had left Evan to look after her and Sophie. And Evan, being an honorable man, took his post seriously.

"Very well, then. You do not have to go to dinner. However, if you do not accompany me, I will place you under house arrest for the remainder of the evening, including the ball later. And don't think you can pay any of these servants off. They have been in the Brighton employ for decades, and they are not so easily swayed. Besides, I have instructed Woods that you are not to be trusted."

The nerve! She clenched her hands, grabbing fistfuls of her satin gown. "Does it make you feel like more than a second son to exercise such control over another human being?"

"Alexandra, none of this gives me any pleasure. If I had it my way, I would still be in Wiltshire at the estate, passing a pleasant and relaxing evening reading a good book in my bedchamber after having dealt with my business issues, which I've had to neglect due to your insolence. I have no use for the season or its balls. And I have no use for dining with the Earl of St. Clair and his wife this evening. However, his daughter is betrothed to my brother, and it would be bad form not to accept their invitation. As you are now the daughter of my father's new countess, it would also be bad form for you not to attend when you are in town."

"Well goodness, we would never want to have bad form, would we?"

"May I remind you that none of this is of my doing? It is because you ran off to London that I was forced to follow."

"No one forced you to follow me. I would be perfectly happy being here alone."

"Yes, yes, of course. Visiting with your friend Lady Hortense, if she indeed exists."

"Who in the hell is Lady Hortense?" The man was obviously losing his mind.

"Whatever the name is you gave to your fictitious friend. I am not such a complete dolt that I didn't see through that."

"Oh." Ally laughed nervously. "You are speaking of Miss Prudence Spofford. Of course, I plan to see her tomorrow."

"Prudence, Hortense, whomever. I don't for a moment believe that this person exists. However, if you insist upon keeping up the charade, fine. I would love to make Miss Spofford's acquaintance tomorrow."

"Absolutely. Perhaps you will find her to your liking. She's rather stiff and conventional." Now she had done it. She'd have to find someone to masquerade as Miss Spofford. Or she would just say that Miss Spofford had taken ill and couldn't receive anyone. Yes, that would work.

"I look forward to it. Now, if you'll excuse me, I must continue to prepare for dinner." He looked her over. "Is that what you're planning to wear?"

Ally looked down at her pale yellow satin gown. Not exactly appropriate for dinner. It was more of an afternoon dress. Pale yellow was not the best for any type of eating. She would have to change again for the ball later. Why should she change now? Just because Evan didn't find her dress appropriate was no reason in her mind. "Yes, what of it?"

Evan nodded. "It is lovely and quite becoming. Please

be waiting for me in the parlor in half an hour. We will take a coach to the St. Clair London residence."

Ally's cheeks heated, and the top of her breasts were rosy pink when she looked down. How his words affected her. She tingled all over and suppressed a shudder. Before she could respond, Evan dismissed her by closing his door.

★ ★ ★ ★

Evan slacked against his door and loosened his cravat, which suddenly seemed to be cutting off the air in his throat. This woman would surely send him to an early grave. He was certain there was no such person as Miss Spofford, and tomorrow he would set out to prove that. Tonight he had to go to the St. Clair residence and make nice with his brother's future in-laws. They were perfectly fine people, and he didn't mind their company, but he was not in the mood to socialize. Perhaps it was best that he was not the heir to the Brighton estate. His brother, Jacob, was good at this sort of thing and even enjoyed it. But not Evan. He was happy tending to his businesses, or riding Leopold, or writing poetry in his journal, or reading a good book.

If Alexandra hadn't run away to London, none of this would be happening. And he still needed to talk to her about her behavior yesterday. He did not truly think she would accuse him of rape. He believed she had spoken in haste and on impulse. However, her words had been cruel, and he needed to resolve the issue with her.

He let out a sigh, and then jerked away from the door when a knock vibrated through him. He turned and opened the door. Woods stood before him.

"Yes?" Evan said.

"I'm sorry to disturb you, my lord, but we have a bit of an... issue."

CONFESSIONS OF LADY PRUDENCE

by Madame O

Poor Lars's face was red as a ripe tomato. He covered his eyes with his hand. "I beg your pardon, my lady. Please forgive my intrusion."

I ambled toward Lars and shut the door to the parlor, locking it. I gently removed his hand from his eyes and squeezed it. "No need to apologize. And no need to cover your eyes. Please, look upon me."

If possible, he reddened even further.

"Does the sight of me naked please you?"

"I... Er..." Lars's voice cracked.

"Oh, how rude of me. May I present my art instructor, Monsieur Christophe Bertrand."

Lars shifted his gaze to Christophe, who was still fully clothed. "Sir, please let me apologize..."

"If Lady Prudence is not upset by your presence, far be it for me to take offense," Christophe said.

"I am far from offended," said I. "In fact, I would take it as a great compliment if you would see fit to join us."

"Oh... I..."

I thrust my hand outward and grasped the bulge in his trousers. "I see the sight of me does please you. Come, please suck on my nipples while Christophe fucks me."

"My lady, I am new in your aunt's employ. I cannot take the chance of losing my post."

"Whatever makes you think you will lose your post? Would it not be more likely that you would lose your post if you did not please me, her niece?" I held up my breasts. "Tell me, Lars, do you like my pretty titties? Do you not want to nibble on them?"

"My lady, they are quite...beautiful, and I would be lying if I said you were not enticing."

I grasped the back of his head, weaving my fingers through his silky copper hair, and pulled him downward to my breast. "Then kiss my nipple, Lars. Please."

He bent to obey. His firm lips clamped around the tight bud, and shudders ripped through me.

"Christophe, please come and suck the other one. Never before have I experienced two sets of lips pleasuring my diddeys."

Oh, Amelia, I can hardly describe the sensation! Christophe's lips were firm and demanding while Lars's were soft and timid. It was wonderful, and I nearly thought I might reach climax from the stimulation alone. Before I could, though, Christophe reached to my pussy and started stroking my tight button. Oh, I must have been dripping wet with cream! What euphoria! His fingers circled my opening, and as they both tugged on my nipples, my climax built within me. Just when I thought I would burst, Christophe removed his hand.

"Christophe! Please! I was ready to come."

"Yes, my lady, I know. But I thought it only polite to give our newcomer a chance to taste the glory that is you first."

CHAPTER THIRTEEN

An issue? Evan rubbed his jawline. Was it Alexandra? Had something befallen her? His heart stampeded at the thought of her being in any type of peril. But of course not. She had left him only a moment ago. "What type of issue, Woods?"

Woods cleared his throat. "Somewhat of a delicate nature, I'm afraid."

"Is anyone hurt?"

"No. Everyone is fine. It's just that..."

"Out with it, Woods. What is going on?"

"We found some...er...*literature*...outside the front door. I am wondering if it belongs to you. Perhaps it fell out of your valise?"

"I don't recall bringing any literature with me," Evan said.

"I can't imagine that it belongs to Lady Alexandra."

"What exactly is this literature of which you are speaking?"

Woods cleared his throat again. "It is of an...*erotic* nature." He pulled some crumpled papers out of his pocket and handed them to Evan. "I found these right outside the front door."

Evan held back his gasp. *The Ruby*. And there, of course, was the seal of his business. Well, these couldn't possibly belong to Alexandra. "Has anyone else been by today?"

"Not that I'm aware of. The house has been closed as you know."

"I doubt this is anything to worry about. They probably

fell out of someone's pocket, and the wind blew them onto our property. Just dispose of them."

Evan readied to hand the papers back to Woods when something caught his eye.

"Lady Prudence, this is my good friend, Mr. Joshua Peck. Josh, Lady Prudence Spofford."

Lady Prudence Spofford. Wasn't that the name of Alexandra's friend? This was too similar to be a coincidence. Yes, he'd known that her "friend" never existed. However, he'd never imagined that the name had come from an underground erotic paper printed at his own printing house, no less.

The papers must belong to Alexandra. Where on earth could she have found them? And why would she bring them to London? And why would she have them in the first place? Questions flooded his mind—questions that both confounded and excited him.

Clearly, much existed that he did not know about her. Damn it all. Tonight they had to dine with the St. Clairs. And then later, the ball.

Alexandra was too much for him to handle. He would marry her off, and soon.

He folded the papers and laid them on a table next to the door. "On second thought," he said to Woods, "I will deal with this myself."

"I understand completely, my lord," Woods said with a glint in his eye.

"Oh, I didn't mean—"

Woods chuckled as he closed the door.

★ ★ ★ ★

The St. Clair townhome was a bit bigger than the Brighton townhome, but not by much. Vladimir Brooks, the Earl of St. Clair, was a jovial gentleman short of stature but long on humor. His wife, Paula, the countess, was nearly a foot taller than he. She was reserved and quiet, but perfectly friendly. And quite pretty. The St. Clairs' height difference was even vaster than the difference between Ally's own parents. Ally had inherited her mother's height, while Sophie was a bit shorter, clearly inheriting her height from their father's side.

Marvella Brooks, the daughter of the Earl and Countess of St. Clair, was betrothed to Evan's older brother, Jacob. She was pretty but also reserved and quiet like her mother. No doubt she would make a good Countess of Brighton, a title currently held by Ally's own mother.

Jacob looked like an older and slightly smaller version of Evan himself. Though he was fair of face, he did not have Evan's incredible physique. Ally had only met Jacob and Marvella once, at the wedding, and hadn't spoken to either of them for any length of time. They were both quiet and reserved, possessing genteel natures.

Also joining them was John Brooks, the earl's son and heir. Thankfully, he too had inherited his mother's height. He was dark of hair and eyes, and had the jovial personality of his father.

They were all very friendly and made Ally feel welcome in their home. Oddly, at dinner, Ally was seated next to John Brooks rather than next to Evan. He was very attentive, keeping her wine glass filled and engaging her in conversation.

"I do hope you'll save me a dance at the ball this evening,

Lady Alexandra."

"Indeed, I would be delighted."

It wasn't totally an untruth. Viscount Brooks was handsome—not Evan handsome, but who was?—and she might enjoy a dance with him. But she couldn't take her eyes off of her goal. Dances with too many others, and she would lose her focus on Mr. Landon. She had to find a way to get him alone so he could compromise her. On top of that, she had to arrange for someone to see them.

"Tell me," Brooks said, "why have you not been around this whole season?"

"My sister, Sophie, and I decided to skip the season this year. When our mother became betrothed to the Earl of Brighton, we stayed at the estate in Wiltshire to help her plan the small wedding."

"And your sister? Why did she not accompany you to London this trip?"

"Oh, London is of not much interest to her."

"Is she as lovely as you are?"

Alexandra caught her breath. Brooks was flirting with her. She had not expected such. But why not? He was unmarried, and so was she. And he did have a title. But Alexandra knew little about the monetary values of titles. Many of England's aristocrats were actually penniless, as her own father had been. They looked to find wives with healthy dowries for that very reason. Thanks to her new stepfather, Ally now had a dowry.

She looked around the informal dining room. It was elegantly decorated in cherry with gilt-edged wallpaper and dark cherry crown molding. The china from which they took the repast was bone white with silver trim. Their tablecloth was fine tatted lace.

No, the St. Clairs did not appear to be in any type of financial straits. Still, Ally had her sights set on Mr. Landon. Very few peers were as wealthy as he, and she had already put a lot of time into her conquest. Starting over now would be a waste of her valuable time.

Evan, who sat across the table from her, hardly looked her way. He talked estate business with his brother and the earl. Ally found it odd that Brooks did not join in, but he seemed content to engage in small talk with her. However, she was finding it tiring. By the time the cheese tray arrived, she was uncomfortable and really wanted to leave.

When the dreaded meal finally ended, she looked forward to a few moments to chat with the ladies while the men retired for cigars and port. However, Brooks came up behind her and touched her on the elbow.

She turned. "Yes?"

"Lady Alexandra, I would be most pleased if you would accompany me to the back terrace."

"Don't you intend to join the gentlemen for a cigar?"

"Honestly, I never did develop the taste for tobacco. And I find port far too sweet. I do enjoy a good cognac, but frankly, I would relish the chance to talk to you a bit more and get to know you better."

Ally fidgeted. Really, she should not accompany him. They would be unchaperoned, although this was his residence. Of course, when had she let the lack of a chaperone stop her?

"I'm afraid it would not be proper, my lord. Lord Evan would never allow it." At least that was the truth.

"My lady, it was Lord Evan's idea."

"What?" Ally clenched her fists at her side, her breathing coming faster. Evan? Stiff and conventional Evan? And then it hit her like an anvil punching her in the stomach.

He had been serious. He meant to marry her off. So that was why Brooks had been so attentive at dinner.

"Why, yes. He suggested that I show you the terrace. In fact, he insisted upon it."

"Oh, he did, did he?" Ally smiled sweetly. "Then we mustn't disappoint him." She tucked her arm in his. "Please, my lord, I would love to accompany you to the terrace. I'm sure it will be most enchanting."

★ ★ ★ ★

Evan's insides twisted as, out of the corner of his eye, he saw John Brooks leading Alexandra to the back terrace. Why had he thought for a moment that she would refuse him? Of course she wouldn't. He was a first son, heir to a title and to the money and estate the title commanded.

Evan hadn't had a chance to peruse *The Ruby* yet, and he couldn't be sure the papers did belong to Alexandra. But where else would she have gotten the name Prudence Spofford? It was hardly a common name. Damn it all to hell. She did seem to know a lot about the pleasures of the flesh. Yet she had been a virgin when they coupled. She had bled, and she had gasped upon his entrance. Although he had never deflowered a virgin before, he was very experienced in the act itself, and he had felt the difference, a slight hesitation, when he entered her for the first time.

So how could a virgin learn about such acts? Her two cousins, both of whom she was very close to, had recently married. They could have told her everything.

Or she could have learned it from this type of literature. Underground papers were more common than the average person might realize. Being in the printing and publishing business, Evan had come across his share of them. None, of course, that had been printed at his own house but for this one.

His guts twisted again. And he had sent her outside to be mauled by John Brooks.

He willed his stomach to settle. Brooks was an honorable man. Evan had no reason to believe he would act improperly. He truly wanted to be free of the albatross around his neck that was Alexandra. Marrying her off was the easiest and best way to accomplish this. So why did the idea make him want to punch every suitor that came near her into oblivion?

He should have resisted her. He shouldn't have made love to her when they were stranded. He'd fooled himself into thinking that he was only doing it because they were alone, facing starvation, trapped in a foggy storm.

But that had been a lie. He had wanted to make love to her, plain and simple. She touched a part of him that no woman had. Several months ago, when he was courting Lady Rose Jameson, Rose had attempted to seduce him. He had been tempted, yes. He was human, after all, and Rose was a beautiful woman. But he had resisted.

He hadn't been able to resist Alexandra.

He must find her a husband and quickly. If he did not, he had no idea what might happen between them.

And there was still the chance that he might have gotten her with child. If that were the case, they would have to marry.

Part of him hoped he had gotten her with child. Part of him wanted to marry Alexandra.

And that part scared the hell out of him.

"Are you coming, Xavier?" St. Clair slapped him on the back.

Evan looked down at the shorter man. "In a moment, perhaps. I'd like to get a little fresh air first."

"Of course, of course. Just join us when you're ready." St. Clair retired to the cigar room.

Evan made haste toward the doors leading to the back terrace. Whatever was starting between Alexandra and Brooks, he was going to stop it. If Brooks was going to marry his stepsister, he would do so as a gentleman. Evan would not allow any liberties.

He walked out onto the terrace, inhaling the London night air. He wrinkled his nose. How he'd much rather be back in Wiltshire on the estate where the air was fresh and clean. He looked around. Where were Alexandra and Brooks? Had they descended onto the lawn? His heart thrummed wildly. Had he dragged her into a dark corner? Was he compromising her at this very moment?

His skin tightened around him and his muscles tensed. This would not happen. He marched across the terrace and down the stairs. "Alexandra!" he called.

Nothing.

He walked around the yard, his pulse racing, looking for any clue. Where in God's name was she? What had he done with her? His gut tightened. If that rake had done anything to her, by God, Evan would see him in hell.

When he had searched every crevice of the lawn, he doubled around to the front of the house, searching there. He finally gave up and went back inside. The butler showed him to the smoking room.

"St. Clair, where in hell is that son of yours?"

"Xavier, I'm glad you decided to join us. John is right here."

Evan looked farther into the room, and there sat John Brooks, puffing on a cigar.

"I thought you were with Lady Alexandra." Evan calmed his rapid breathing.

"Only for a moment," Brooks said. "She decided to join the ladies. But I must tell you, Xavier, she is an absolute delight. Thank you for introducing me to her."

Evan breathed a huge sigh of relief. "You're quite welcome. Now, it would be my pleasure to take you up on that glass of port."

★ ★ ★ ★

Ally smiled to herself. John Brooks was a gentleman—too much of a gentleman for her taste, really. Their short walk had been pleasant, but then she had decided to join the ladies. After a grueling hour of trying to make small talk with Marvella and the countess—nice women but not gifted in the art of conversation—she was exhausted. Now, back at the Brighton townhome, Ally lay on her bed relaxing for a few blissful moments before getting ready for the ball.

Brooks was handsome, but his presence did not stir her. In fact, Mr. Landon's presence had failed to stir her the last time they had met. It seemed she was only stirred by one man these days—Evan.

Still, her sights were set on Mr. Landon. His fortune was greater than most peers in England, and he had businesses all over the world. With him, she could travel, see everything the world had to offer, experience life to its fullest. The title meant nothing to her. Her mother had possessed a title—the Countess of Longarry—and what had that title gotten her? A life of abuse and near poverty. No, Ally cared not about title.

For a moment, she considered the fate of her cousin Rose. Rose had fallen in love with a commoner, Cameron Price, and had been ready to live with him as his peasant wife. However, fate had intervened when Cameron found out that he was the grandson of the Marquess of Denbigh. Now the Earl of Thornton and heir to the Denbigh Marquessate, Cameron, while by far not the richest peer in England, was well enough to do, and Rose would never have to live as a peasant.

Mr. Landon, though related to the Duke of Lybrook on his mother's side, was indeed a commoner—a commoner with immense wealth, and Ally meant to have it all.

A knock on the door startled Ally. She rose to answer it. Mary stood before her.

"I have a message for you, my lady." Mary held out the parchment.

Ally swiftly took the paper. "Thank you, Mary. Please return in ten minutes' time to help me prepare for the ball."

Mary curtsied politely and left.

Ally opened the parchment and widened her eyes.

No, it couldn't be.

CONFESSIONS OF LADY PRUDENCE

by Madame O

Lars's cheeks reddened and a spray of light freckles became apparent across his nose, making him look younger than his years. Oh, Amelia, such timidity! It aroused me all the more. I had to have his tongue upon me, and soon.

"Yes, please, Lars," I said. "Do lick me, I beg of you."

Lars stood, seemingly paralyzed, yet his erection was still apparent beneath his britches. It took all my strength not to push down his trousers and stroke him to climax.

"Lady Prudence has asked a favor of you," Christophe said slyly. "It would be bad form not to comply. After all, her aunt is responsible for your employment."

"Do you not find me attractive, Lars?" I asked.

"I... I...find you beautiful, my lady. What man wouldn't find you to his liking? You are indeed lovely."

"I assure you I am loveliest in the secret place between my legs." I winked seductively. "Please, Lars, I have already begged you. Must I get down on my knees?"

Lars's lips trembled as he again reddened even further. "Yes... If you would get on your knees, it would please me."

"But then how would you—"

Christophe placed his hand over my mouth. "He wants you to submit, my lady. Some men find that arousing."

And suddenly I wanted nothing more than to please this newcomer. I fell to my knees. I had no idea what he had in mind, but my curiosity was piqued and my body ablaze.

"Does this please you?" I asked.

Lars smiled, the red on his cheeks now as fiery as the pulses between my legs.

"You do look lovely on your knees, my lady."

"What is it that you wish of me?"

"Turn around," he said. "Unbuckle Monsieur Bertrand's trousers and suck his cock while I watch. I will lick you from behind."

I complied, and Christophe stood in front of me, smiling wickedly. I unbuckled him. When his cock sprang free, I licked its tip and nearly bit down when I felt the soft slide of a tongue in the crease of my arse. Within seconds, Lars had positioned himself between my thighs as I knelt, and he began to work on my quivering quim.

I ground into Lars's face as I worked Christophe's member with my mouth.

"Yes, yes," Christophe said, his breathing rapid. "Does that feel good when he licks your little pussy? Do you like my hard cock in your mouth?"

I grunted and groaned, wanting to shout, "Yes, yes!" But of course my mouth was full. I continued to writhe on top of Lars's face, my orgasm imminent. And when I burst, Christophe spurted into my mouth, his fluid coating my throat.

Amelia, I cannot tell you how aroused I was at that very moment! And I had yet to have a cock inside my pussy. But these two men were not going to leave before that happened.

CHAPTER FOURTEEN

Ally quickly folded the parchment, slid it between the pages of a book on the shelf, and vowed not to think about its contents. Nothing could be done now anyway. She had to prepare for the ball.

How she wished she had a gown that would turn all eyes toward her, like her cousin Lily's red velvet gown the night of her betrothal announcement. Because she'd left the estate so quickly, she hadn't had time to summon the modiste. Alas, she would have to make do with her lavender silk, which her new stepfather had gifted her with after his engagement to her mother. He had given Sophie a ball gown as well, in colors accenting her own.

Mary arrived shortly and laced and tightened Ally's corset.

"Mary, tighten it more around my bosom. I want to push it up so my cleavage is more apparent."

Mary shook her head. "I do not advise that, my lady."

"I understand. My sister would not advise it either. However, I have an agenda this evening, and showing a little more bosom than usual will help it along. So please do as I ask."

"Of course, my lady."

Mary tightened the corset until Ally had achieved her desired effect. Together they got Ally into the ball gown, and then Mary arranged her hair in a lovely upswept style with a few curly ringlets hanging about her neck.

"Oh, my lady." Mary breathed in. "I can't say I agree with showing so much bosom, but my goodness, you do look breathtaking."

"Thank you very much for your assistance." Ally smiled. "I am very pleased with the result."

Mary curtsied and left, and Ally sat down on a settee, wringing her white gloves between her fingers. Had she made a mistake this evening with Viscount Brooks? He was pleasing to the eye, polite and intelligent, and heir to a title. Probably not as wealthy as Mr. Landon, but by virtue of the London townhome, the St. Clair estate appeared to be in good condition. Any other time, Ally would have been thrilled by the attentions of such a worthy suitor.

But she hadn't been able to shake the thought that Evan had put Brooks up to the courtship. Of course, it wasn't a courtship. It was simply a walk on the terrace. Would he have tried to take a liberty? The question was moot now, because Ally had ended the encounter before she could find out.

How could Evan throw her into the arms of another man? Did he have no feelings for her at all? Had he forgotten their lovemaking so quickly?

She frowned. Why should he care at all? She had behaved horribly by threatening to accuse him of rape. Her heart thundered as she recalled the dark anger on his features after she had said the words. They hadn't spoken of it, but how could he ever forgive her? She wasn't sure she could forgive herself.

Nothing to be done about it now. The ball was imminent, and Mr. Landon would be there. Ally would find a way to lure him into a dark spot and make sure that someone of prominence caught them in the act.

The grandfather clock chimed, and Ally rose to descend

to the entryway. Her breath caught as Evan appeared in his dark burgundy evening attire. Another man so splendid could not possibly exist in the universe. If Sophie were there, she would have complimented their stepbrother on how fine he looked. However, Ally stood speechless, her tongue immobile.

"I see you are ready to go." Evan held out his hand to her. "The coach is ready."

Nothing about how she looked? He hadn't given her ample bosom a glance. Perhaps he truly meant to be rid of her.

The ride was short and not exactly unpleasant, though she hardly spoke. He escorted her into the manor where the ball was being held, and a servant announced them. Evan found a place for them at a table with his brother and Lady Marvella. Ally tried not to look too bored. She glanced around pointedly. Viscount Brooks was there, along with Sophie's former suitor, Marshall Van Arden. On his arm was his new betrothed, who couldn't hold a candle to Sophie. His loss.

Yes, there he was, speaking to two young ladies who giggled flirtatiously. Mr. Landon clearly enjoyed the attention. Ally had never been in his presence at a seasonal ball. He'd attended a few balls at the Lybrook estate in Wiltshire, but this was a London ball. All of England's most eligible debutantes were in attendance, many of whom would be vying for favors from one as wealthy as Mr. Landon.

An odd sensation crept up Ally's spine. She'd never had to compete for his attention before. The two ladies speaking to him were both lovely. How would she make herself more irresistible than they were? A quick glance around—she wasn't the only woman here who thought to show off her charms. Though a fair amount of women wore more conservative attire, there was no shortage of cleavage in the ballroom.

Should she approach Mr. Landon, or wait for him to come to her? What was the proper etiquette?

She was lost in this conundrum of thoughts when warmth touched her forearm.

"Lady Alexandra?"

She looked up into the blue eyes of a handsome man she'd never met. "Yes?"

"I am Lord Michael Owen. Lord Evan suggested I come over and make your acquaintance."

"Oh he did, did he?" Ally wrung her hands, sweltering in the gloves. But then she smiled. Two could play this game. "I'm ever so pleased to meet you," she said.

"I'm afraid Xavier did not tell me how beautiful you were."

"Goodness, my lord, you flatter me." If only she had a fan to flutter over her face, the image would be complete.

"Would you care to share a dance, my lady?"

Ally smiled, coquettishly she hoped. "I would be absolutely delighted."

Lord Michael was a good dancer. Ally hadn't danced a lot, but he led her expertly, and she did not miss a step. Her heart fluttered when Mr. Landon approached Lord Michael from behind and tapped him on the shoulder.

"Mind if I cut in, my lord?"

Lord Michael cleared his throat. "Not at all, Landon."

From Lord Michael's expression, Ally was certain he did mind, but what could he do? It would be bad form not to allow it. And although she had enjoyed dancing with Lord Michael, Mr. Landon was her ultimate quarry this evening.

Mr. Landon took her in his arms, squeezing her a bit tightly. "My lady, you look absolutely stunning."

"I thank you, kind sir."

"I can't recall ever seeing you look lovelier." He winked. "With your charms so elegantly on display, I'm surprised that every eligible man here hasn't danced with you yet."

Ally's cheeks warmed, but she was determined to play her part. "I haven't been here long, Mr. Landon. There is all the time in the world for me to dance with many men."

"I hope you will save several dances for me, my lady." He led her in a complex twirl, but she followed along with no problem.

She let boldness overtake her. "It would be my pleasure to dance every dance with you, sir."

"In that case, perhaps you would consider accompanying me to the terrace later? This is a beautiful manor, and it would be my pleasure to show you all it has to offer." His eyes gleamed with mischief.

Ally's nerves skittered. Her breathing became rapid, but she willed herself to calm. This was perfect, exactly what she'd wanted. Her nerves would not stop her. "Indeed, I would be delighted. Shall I meet you there later?"

"Yes, that would be more discreet, wouldn't it?" Mr. Landon smiled down at her. "Five minutes before the clock strikes twelve, slip out the back doors to the terrace, I will meet you there. And"—he lowered his voice—"I mean to have a taste of those beautiful breasts tonight."

Ally trembled. Yes, she would go through with this. After all, had this not been her plan all along? So why was she having second thoughts? All was working perfectly. She had an hour to find someone who could catch her in the act. But whom could she ask? She knew no one here, only Evan and her new acquaintance, Viscount Brooks. Surely he wouldn't agree to catch her. But what if she asked him to meet her five minutes later on the terrace? She would be with Mr. Landon, being compromised, and Brooks would find them.

Yes, that would work. She mentally applauded her genius.

The dance ended, and Mr. Landon brushed his lips lightly over her gloved hand. "Until later, my beautiful lady." He smiled.

Ally swallowed. She hoped she hadn't bitten off more than she could chew. She looked around for Viscount Brooks, but before she could find him, another young gentleman asked for a dance, and then another. Goodness, had Evan instructed every man here to dance with her? This was becoming ridiculous. Where was Evan, anyway? She had barely seen him all evening. After he'd led her to a table, Lord Michael had swiftly escorted her away.

Did Evan have his eye on someone? After all, he had been ready to marry her cousin Rose only months ago, despite not being in love with her. And he had insisted that she, Ally, marry him after their escapades while they were stranded.

Perhaps he was ready to get married, and he didn't really care who he married. The thought struck Ally hard. Kind of like a punch in her gut. Though she was absolutely sure she would marry Mr. Landon, she didn't want Evan marrying anyone.

Be rational, Ally. You're not being fair.

Her loving stepbrother hadn't even asked her for a dance. It wasn't polite to ignore one's own family members at a ball. Lily and Rose's brother, Thomas, always danced with each of them whenever the three were out and about.

She glanced at the large grandfather clock across the room. A half hour remained before her date to meet Mr. Landon. She had to find Viscount Brooks and arrange to meet him slightly thereafter. But first, she would find out why Evan was being so impolite.

She scanned the room. Yes, there he was, standing by the refreshment table, speaking to two other gentlemen. She hesitated to approach him. He'd most likely force the two other men to dance with her. But this had gone far enough. She marched swiftly toward the group.

She infiltrated the group quickly and without pretense. "Excuse me, my lord." She tugged on Evan's sleeve. "Might I have a word with you?"

"I'm in the middle of something," Evan said tersely.

"Xavier," one of the men said, "is this the lovely Alexandra you've been telling us about?"

Evan cleared his throat. "Yes, this is my stepsister, Lady Alexandra MacIntyre. Alexandra, Mr. Jonathan Talkington and Viscount Clinton Canterwood."

The gentlemen were tall and nice-looking, but Ally had no interest in meeting either of them. To be polite, she held out her hand. "Charmed."

Before either man could say another word, she tugged on Evan's sleeve again. "I'm sorry, Evan, but it is a matter of some importance."

Evan looked at her sternly. He wasn't happy with her, but she couldn't care less. She would find out what was going on in that head of his.

"I beg pardon. If you could excuse me, gentlemen."

Ally led him to an unoccupied corner of the ballroom. "What is going on with you?" she demanded.

"I'm sure I don't have the slightest idea what you could be talking about."

"Oh, don't give me that. You know exactly what I'm talking about. You haven't paid me a speck of attention all evening, despite the fact that you escorted me here and we are now family. It is bad form for you not to dance with me at least once. Instead, you've sent every drooling bachelor my way."

"Alexandra, I told you I was going to find you a husband, and I intend to do so."

She balled her hands into fists. "I told you that I have no intention of being forced to wed anyone. I shall choose whom I marry, and when I'm ready, I shall do just that. In the meantime, I will invite you and everyone else to stay out of the matter. Now"—she smiled sweetly—"I should like to dance with you, brother."

The word brother felt all wrong on her tongue. Despite the marriage of their parents, Ally would never think of Evan as a brother, hardly even a stepbrother. They had known each other for only months, and the attraction between them could never be denied.

Evan let out a sigh. "Very well, then." He took Alexandra's hand and led her to the dance floor.

He held her a polite distance away. No time like the present to make her feelings known.

"Evan, I've told you before I will not be forced into marriage. I've seen arranged marriage at its worst. I will not go through what my mother went through."

Evan looked down at her, his expression grave. "How could you think that of me? I would never arrange a marriage for you with a tyrant like your father. But of course, why would you believe me?"

"And what exactly is that supposed to mean?"

"Just yesterday you accused me of rape, my lady." Evan pursed his lips into a tense line.

Ally's stomach fell. How could she apologize for her hasty

words? She would never have gone through with it, but how could she get him to believe that? "Evan, I—"

"You've made it quite clear what you think of me, Alexandra. Well, here's what I think of you. You are impulsive and self-centered, and I won't have you being a hardship on me or on my father."

"I would never be a hardship on anyone. Trust me, I have plans in motion that—"

"I am not interested in your plans. We have seen how your plans work out. You do not know what is good for yourself, so I will have to take care of you. Believe me, once I explain the circumstances, my father will be very happy that I took care of things in his absence."

"And what of my mother? Do you really think she will be happy that you married off her daughter?"

"Your mother is a sensible woman. If I find a match for you, a good match, where you are treated well, why would she have any issues with that?"

"Because she has finally found love, Evan. I should think she would want that for me as well." Alexandra choked out the words. The truth of them stung her. Here she was, ready to marry Mr. Landon solely for his money, when what her mother wished for her was a love match.

Well, she'd say it again—love was overrated. And she certainly wasn't going to wait until she was fifty-two years old, like her mother, to find love. She was going to think of now, and she was going to make sure that she, Sophie, and their mother were taken care of. Once the earl died, her mother would be the dowager countess, and her financial stability would be in Evan's brother's hands. Ally couldn't take the chance that they would be left destitute again.

"What makes you think any of these suitors are going to have the least bit of interest in me?"

"Oh, they are definitely interested. Can't you tell?"

Tell? Sure, they looked at her bosom. All the men did. That didn't prove they had any interest. All that proved is they wouldn't mind getting into her drawers. And speaking of...

"And what will we do, dear stepbrother, if I end up with child? With your child?"

Evan's whole body tensed, his arms strengthening their hold. His cheeks reddened. "I have not forgotten about that. We will know soon enough if you are with child, and if you are, I will ask for your hand."

"I've already told you that I'm not marrying you."

"If you're carrying my child, you will damned well marry me."

"If that is your decision, why on earth are you sending every eligible gentlemen and peer this side of Britain after me? If they're as interested as you think they all are, surely one of them will decide to ask for my hand in the next week. Then what will happen if I do end up expecting your child?"

"We will call off the betrothal, and you and I will be married."

Ally shook her head. What a convoluted scheme! And ridiculous, as well. Was he punishing her for accusing him of rape? She certainly did deserve reprisal for that slip of the tongue, but for goodness' sake, he wouldn't even let her apologize. Every time she brought it up, he cut her off. And as far as a child was concerned, Ally truly was not worried about it. As she had told him, she had just finished her courses a few days before they were intimate, and she knew her body well enough to know that pregnancy was unlikely.

The dance ended, and Ally curtsied politely. "Thank you, my lord." She turned to look at the grandfather clock in the corner. Only a few minutes left. She had to find Brooks and arrange to meet him so he would find her with Mr. Landon. "Now, if you will excuse me please, I'm sure I have myriad more gentlemen to dance with." She rolled her eyes, turned, and strode away.

★ ★ ★ ★

Evan strode out of the ballroom and toward the gentlemen's smoking area. He poured himself a brandy and took a sip, letting the amber liquid settle over his tongue and down his throat. No matter how many men he sent Alexandra's way, his guts twisted every time another one took her out onto the dance floor.

He sucked in a deep breath and let it out slowly. He hated the warmth and desire that floated over him every time Alexandra and he talked about the possibility of her being with child. Did he want her to be carrying his child? A primal and animalistic part of him did. Was he ready to be a father? More to the point, was she ready to be a mother? She truly did seem to be impulsive and self-centered, but that did not stop the incredible desire and passion he had for her. It was unlike anything he had ever known. He hadn't felt it for Rose or anyone. And though he'd enjoyed his exploits in the past, the act itself with Alexandra was something else altogether.

He had to get her away from him. She was most likely right about the timing of her courses. She seemed to know a lot about her own body and about the world of pleasure. Odd, since she had clearly been a virgin when they made love for the first time.

He would marry her off quickly. How else could he curb this desire for her?

He poured himself another brandy and sipped it, saying hello to a few men who walked in, making a bit of small talk. Finally, he decided to get some fresh air on the terrace.

He raked his hands through his long hair, inhaling the night air. Lord, London was not Wiltshire. How he longed for a true breath of fresh air. He walked along the terrace, ignoring the whispering couples coveting their privacy. Nervous energy rippled through him. He knew what he needed, and from whom he needed it. But that would not happen tonight or ever again.

The moon was a round white globe in the sky, casting its silver curtain over the lawn and the couples who thought they were being discreet. Evan turned a blind eye until a cherry-red nipple caught his gaze—a beautiful nipple he knew well. His ire throbbed within him as a mouth—a mouth that was not his own—descended toward it.

CONFESSIONS OF LADY PRUDENCE

by Madame O

But Lars had something else in mind. My quim still pulsating from my climax, my mouth still coated with the essence of Christophe, Lars lunged forward and grabbed me, taking a chair and arranging me on his lap. My arse was bared to him, and he slowly brushed his hands over my buttocks. I shuddered all over, the aftershock of my climax still surging through my veins, my blood still boiling, my pussy still wet.

"Such a lovely arse, my lady," Lars said.

I turned and looked up at him, my cheeks warm and my pulse racing. "I am so very glad you find it to your liking, sir."

"Yes, yes," he said, still rubbing my arse. "And because you have been so good today, I shall not spank your lovely arse."

Spank? Amelia, my heart nearly stopped! I'd heard of such things, but never had I expected any gentleman to speak of such prurient behavior. Of course, Lars was a servant from a peasant's background, not a gentleman. Suddenly I could not contain my excitement! I wanted a spanking more than I wanted anything at that moment.

I turned my head the other way and espied Christophe sitting across from us on a settee, his eyes glazed over, his expression unreadable.

I turned back toward Lars and looked into his flushed face. "Do you wish to spank me, Lars?"

"Such a beautiful arse is made for such pleasures." He

smiled lasciviously, so different from the shy and awkward footman who had entered the room only moments ago.

"Then by all means, please spank me."

His hand came down on my arse with a loud swat. I jolted, a rush of pain surging through me, out to my limbs and then back inward, until the pain metamorphosed into pleasure, landing between my legs. Amelia, I cannot even describe the bliss. Before I could process the feeling cascading through me, he slapped my arse again, and the sharp pain traveled through me once more, changing into pleasure and culminating in my most secret spot.

Christophe stood and came toward us. He squatted down next to us and began working the folds of my pussy, which were slick and wet. Another slap came down upon me, and Christophe's fingers surged into my pussy. Oh, Amelia, never have I felt such all-consuming passion and need! The next slap became more important to me than my next breath, and Christophe's fingers fucking me whilst Lars spanked me was the most delicious sensation ever. Soon I was climaxing again, and then again.

"Your arse is such a lovely shade of pink, my lady," Lars said, now massaging my buttocks.

"Yes, indeed, my lady," Christophe agreed. "I do believe spanking becomes you."

"Please, please. I must have a cock inside me. I beg of you, both of you. Please, one of you must fuck me."

"As I have already done that many times," Christophe said, smiling, "I will give that honor to Lars today."

Quick as a flash of lightning, Lars bent me over the divan, unfastened his pants, and shoved his cock into my waiting cunt. He fucked me hard and fast, grunting and groaning, his ballocks slapping my clitoris as he thrust and he thrust.

Amelia, my orgasm, when it came, was the most amazing burst of stars I have ever experienced. And then, when he spurted over my bare back, his own climax taking him, I felt a pleasure I'd never yet known.

I cannot wait until our next encounter. I hope Lars will interrupt us again, and I hope Hattie will not lose her nerve. What fun the four of us will have!

Until then, I am yours, affectionately,

Prudence

CHAPTER FIFTEEN

Ally scanned the terrace. The night was more illuminated than usual. She hadn't counted on a full moon this evening. Well, all the better for Brooks to see them when he arrived a few moments later for their rendezvous.

Mr. Landon freed her breasts, kissing the tops of them. "Lady Alexandra, I always knew they would be the most beautiful I've ever seen."

Ally's heart thumped. Having him see her like this felt all wrong. But it was a means to an end, and she would go through with her plan. She had to, not only for herself, but also for Sophie and her mother.

A shadow approached. Good, Brooks was right on time.

Mr. Landon descended to her nipple.

"Get your goddamned hands off of her." The voice was low and primal.

And it did not belong to Viscount John Brooks.

She turned and met Evan's gaze. Excellent. Her conventional stepbrother would see that Mr. Landon did right by her. Everything had worked out perfectly. So why did she feel so violated and ashamed? And why was she wishing Evan's lips were the ones descending toward her hard nipple?

Mr. Landon looked up. "I beg your pardon?"

Evan grasped Mr. Landon by the shoulders and pulled him off of Ally. "I said get your fucking filthy hands off of her," he said through clenched teeth.

A dull thud echoed as Evan's fist slammed into Mr. Landon's nose. Mr. Landon fell onto the terrace, blood gushing from his nostrils.

A scream lodged in Ally's throat, but before she could let it out, Evan grabbed her arm, forcing her across the terrace and back into the ballroom. She ran, pushing her breasts back into her loosened corset, trying to keep up with his big heavy strides. Through the ballroom they raced, Evan seemingly on a mission. Ally nudged several people and murmured her apologies, though she was sure those affected hadn't heard her since Evan was pulling her through so quickly. They reached the front door and he hauled her outside. He dragged her to their carriage, nearly threw her inside, and told the coachman to take them to the Brighton townhome.

He didn't speak to her during the ride. He didn't even look at her. She cringed, both fear and arousal bubbling through her. What would he do to her?

When they arrived, he pulled her out of the carriage and forced her up to the door and inside the townhome.

"My lord?" Woods began.

Evan ignored Woods, dragging Ally along to the staircase. He lifted her in his strong arms.

Her heart hammered, her cheeks warmed, and her body throbbed. "Where are you taking me?" Terror—or was it lust?—paralyzed her.

Evan gazed down at her, his eyes afire. "To my bed. Where you belong."

Ally gulped, still unable to move, unable to resist. She saw no point in trying to stop him. He was an animal, and she was his prey. She *wanted* to be his prey.

He raced to his chamber, set her down, turned her around,

and unfastened her gown.

"My God, you're so beautiful," he whispered, turning her to face him. "I want you so much. To see him, his hands on you..." His eyes were dark and smoking as he descended and bit into the side of her neck.

Ally sucked in a breath. The pain of his teeth sinking into her skin twitched through her, followed by a wave of clenching nirvana. Pleasure-pain. She had heard of such things. She had read of such things. But to actually experience the exquisite torture of it... And she ached to feel it again.

"You're mine, Alexandra." He brushed her gown off her shoulders and sank his teeth into the soft flesh there.

She gasped again at the pleasure and pain coursing through her, gritting her teeth while she tried to inch forward. Had to get nearer...nearer to his body heat, to his raw masculine presence.

"I won't ever let anyone else touch you. Only I will possess you, Alexandra."

He turned her and removed her corset, and soon she stood before him wearing only her chemise and drawers, her legs trembling.

He tore her chemise down the middle and yanked it off of her onto the floor. She gasped again as he made the same work of her drawers. She stood before him naked, while he was still fully clothed, her pulse drumming, her nipples puckered and hard, her sex throbbing between her legs.

He pulled her close and whispered against her mouth, "Tell me you're mine, Alexandra."

She opened her mouth, but no words emerged. Inside she was shouting, *Yes, yes! I am yours, yours and only yours, forever!*

He gripped her more tightly, his short fingernails clawing

into her flesh. "Say you're mine. Say it, Alexandra."

She quivered, and her blood turned to hot lava. "I'm yours, Evan."

"And who is taking you this night?"

"You are. Only you."

He crushed their lips together, and she melted against him, her whole body lost in a molten heat of passion and desire.

He kissed her hard, grinding against her, punishing her. It was a kiss of passion, yes, but it was also a kiss of punishment. Punishment she was only too happy to take. His groans were a vibration into her mouth rather than a sound. He growled like an animal, marking her, making her his mate. His brown eyes were feral and glazed over.

When he finally broke the kiss, they both sucked in deep breaths, as if coming up from water. Alexandra shook, her heart racing, her body on fire.

Evan cupped her breasts, thumbed her nipples gently at first, and then gave them each a hard pinch. "Did he put his mouth on them? Did he touch what is mine?"

Ally shook her head, her lips trembling, her body sizzling from his touch. "No. No, he didn't. You stopped us before—"

She fought for breath as his lips clamped down on one nipple. No gentle love this time. He sucked hard, he bit, all the while tugging on the other one with his fingers. And in that moment, she had never been happier that Mr. Landon had not put his mouth on her breasts. Only Evan had, and that thought filled her with elation.

She squirmed, her sex quivering, her juices dampening her thighs. She was melting, melting into this amazing man who affected her like no other. She was his, limp in his arms. He could do with her what he would, and she was powerless to stop him.

He continued to torture her breasts, sucking, licking, nibbling.

"Evan, please..."

His stubble scratched at the sensitive skin of her bosom. Oh, such exquisite torture! As amazing as his attention to her nipples was, she needed him lower, touching her, inside her.

"Please..." she said again.

"Please...what?"

Ally gasped, her breath coming in rapid pants. Why was she having trouble putting her needs into words? It wasn't as though they'd never done this before. But something was different about this time. Evan was controlling, punishing, needing her in a way he hadn't previously.

"Please... I need you..."

He let her nipple drop from his mouth with a soft pop. He looked up at her, his eyes blazing, his skin ruddy and shiny with perspiration. "You need me to do...what?"

He was going to make her spell it out. No matter, she could do that. "Inside me, Evan. I need you inside me."

He smiled, his dusky pink lips full and swollen. "All in good time, Alexandra. I will reclaim all of your body this night. I will take what is mine."

He stood, removed his cravat, and then slowly, enticingly, he undressed. With each inch of golden skin he bared, Alexandra's heart fluttered more wildly. How glorious he looked, a god come to life. When he finally stood before her, completely stripped of all garments, she sucked in a breath at his male beauty. Mr. Landon, nor anyone else, could possibly look as good. Those sleek broad shoulders, that defined chest and rippling abdomen. The soft blond hairs, the copper nipples peeking through. The patch of light brown curls from which his erection sprang. The thunderous thighs, the well-formed buttocks, the strong calves, and even his feet were beautiful.

"Lie on the bed, Alexandra, and spread your legs. Offer yourself to me."

She did as he bid, her skin tingling and her nipples tightening even further. Her clitoris craved his touch. She lay, completely exposed, naked and vulnerable.

His.

He knelt at the bedside, gripped her buttocks, and pulled her to his mouth. He flicked his tongue over her clitoris, and she burst, the orgasm rocketing through her. So fast, and she was unprepared for the exquisite torture.

"Yes, yes," he said against her vulva. "Come for me, my sweet Alexandra."

He devoured her then, sucking at her, licking her, forcing his tongue inside her slit. She writhed under his ministrations, her mind whirling. Her nipples hardened into tight buds, and she brought her fingers to them, teasing them, pinching them, pretending her fingers were Evan's lips and teeth.

When Evan thrust two fingers inside her pussy, she shattered once again, wailing as he took her to the precipice. She pinched her nipples hard, taking the pleasure to pain and then back again. And he continued to stroke her with his fingers and lick her hard button. Just when she thought she would die an untimely death if he did not fuck her, he moved from between her legs and flipped her onto her stomach.

So he wanted it this way. Fine, she didn't care, as long as he fucked her. But instead of his cock, it was his tongue that touched her...in a most forbidden place.

She had read of this, of course. Many men enjoyed this

aspect of the act, not only with other men but also with women. But she wasn't sure...

But oh, how wonderful the feel of his silken tongue against that secret part of her. He stroked her smoothly, lusciously, starting at her clitoris and ending at her anus. Had he done this before? She could never know, and in this moment she didn't much care. She wanted to experience everything with him. If he demanded entrance, she would grant it.

He slipped one finger into her cunt, slowly finger fucking her as he continued to lick her other opening. She moved her hips in tandem with his thrusts, finding his rhythm, becoming one with him. She wanted more, his cock—in her mouth, in her pussy, even there.

And as if reading her mind, he breached that forbidden hole with his finger. She squealed.

"Easy, love. Relax, let this happen."

"Evan, I..."

"I will stop if you ask me to."

"No, Lord, don't stop." She breathed in deeply and let it out slowly, willing her muscles to relax.

"Good, good," he said. "You are mine, Alexandra, even this part of you. I will claim all of you."

Ally relaxed, and slowly, purposely, he slid his finger in and out. He continued to probe her pussy as well, and as she got used to the double penetration, her nipples tightened once again, her skin tingled, and she found herself reaching, soaring for that now known ecstasy.

"Yes, you're responding." Evan pressed a kiss to her buttocks. "I will make this good for you. I promise."

Alexandra moaned, squirming, her deep-seated lust taking over. How wonderful it felt, how perfect. And just when she thought she could take no more, Evan removed his finger from her pussy and replaced it with his cock.

Still he fingered her hole as he fucked her deeply, passionately. Thrust, thrust, thrust.

"Sweet God," Evan groaned. "So good, Alexandra. So tight. You were made for me."

"So good," Ally said, her teeth gritted. "It feels so good, Evan."

He plunged into her again, and then again. He kept going while she shattered once, twice, and then once more. Her orgasms kept coming, coming, taking her to new heights. She danced in the stars against the backdrop of the sun, rainbows, kaleidoscopes, everything in the world vibrating into her. Yet he kept fucking her, fucking her, and fucking her, hard.

"Evan, I can't take it any longer. My God." And she came again.

Finally, he groaned and plunged into her so deeply she was sure he touched her womb, and perhaps...her heart.

"Lord." He pulled out and flopped onto the bed.

Her muscles limp, she crawled next to him. An odd little sack lay next to his now flaccid penis. She reached to touch it.

"A French letter," he said.

Of course, she knew about French letters. They protected against pregnancy and against some nasty diseases one could catch from sexual contact.

She should be glad he had taken such a precaution. But for some reason, the sight of the item unnerved her. He'd said he was taking her, claiming her. Why did he not want to join with her free of barriers? After all, they had done it before.

But before she could ask, Evan let out a soft snore next to her. She chuckled lightly, snuggled into his arms, and closed her eyes.

★ ★ ★ ★

Evan awoke, stood, and walked to the window. The moon still shone brightly, a full silvery-white sphere lighting up London. He turned and gazed at Alexandra, so beautiful and innocent in sleep.

He had acted irrationally. But seeing Landon about to put his mouth on her had awakened a beast within him. Landon would not have Alexandra. She would be Evan's. After all, he had planned to find a suitable husband for her. Who would be more suitable than he himself? This time he wouldn't give her an option. He turned and stared out the window once more.

"Evan?"

He spun around. Alexandra sat up in bed, her full breasts hanging gently, beautifully.

Evan walked back to the bed and sat down. "I'm sorry. I didn't mean to wake you."

"It's no matter." She patted the space next to her. "Come, lie down."

She was so beautiful, so welcoming. Sometimes Evan thought there were two Alexandras—the one he knew by day, who spoke quickly and without thinking, whose actions were often irrational and illogical, and then this Alexandra, the one he knew at night, the one who made love to him like a vixen, with everything she was, who accepted him, who gave in to his needs and met them with her own.

Which Alexandra was he in love with? For this *was* love. This was the feeling he had grasped for but that had never materialized with Rose. And now it had hit him like a steam engine, taking him over.

He smiled. There were not two Alexandras. He was in love with every part of her, even her impulsiveness and self-centeredness. It wasn't even self-centeredness, really. Her childhood had been hell, and she was determined never to relive it. What he had mistaken for self-centeredness was impulsiveness, strength, and the willingness to go after what she wanted at all costs.

Oh, she was beautiful, outside and in. Her strength alone was enough to make him love her.

He turned to her, brushing his hand across her cheek. It was time to say the words.

"Alexandra..."

She arched her eyebrows. "Yes?"

"I love you."

She opened her mouth, but he placed two fingers upon her lips, quieting her.

"I love you and only you. I have fallen so hopelessly in love with you that I can't imagine life without you."

She smiled, her perfect beauty radiant in the moonlight streaming in from the window. "I love you too, Evan."

His heart soared. They would be together. They would be married. He pressed his lips lightly over hers.

"Come back to bed now," she said. "Being with you is so wonderful. I adore it, and I adore you. There is absolutely no reason why we can't continue our liaison once I marry Mr. Landon."

CONFESSIONS OF LADY PRUDENCE

by Madame O

Dearest Amelia,

Unfortunately, Lars was occupied during my next art lesson, and Christophe did not bring Mr. Peck with him either. Fortunately, I was able to persuade Hattie to join us.

I told her that my "guest" and I would be requiring tea half an hour into our lesson, and to just enter without knocking. I was tempted to dispense with the lesson altogether, but I couldn't get Christophe too excited too quickly. I had to get him just right to the edge before Hattie interrupted us. We discussed color and light for a bit, and finally, when Hattie was due to enter within about five minutes, I turned to my handsome instructor, grabbed his cock through his britches, and melded my mouth to his.

His member rose instantaneously, and I fondled him through the fabric as our tongues dueled together. A few moments later, he turned me around and fumbled with the fasteners on my dress. When he brushed it over my shoulders and began loosening my corset, Hattie entered.

Her cheeks turned crimson at the sight of us. "My lady, I do beg pardon."

I smiled. "Please bring the tea in, Hattie. Monsieur Bertrand and I would love to partake of it later."

Hattie walked toward the table, her gaze cast downward, and set down the tea tray. She turned.

"Hattie dear, do not leave yet."

She stopped but did not turn around.

"Please, dear Hattie, come here to me. I have told Monsieur Bertrand all about you, and he is very excited to make your acquaintance."

Hattie turned, her cheeks still crimson, her bottom lip red and pouty.

"Do not be fearful," said I. "Please, do come to me."

As Christophe continued to loosen my corset, Hattie moved forward. When I could reach her, I pulled her to me and kissed her sweet red lips.

She sighed into me and opened, giving me her tongue. I still wonder at the differences between men and women, dear Amelia. While the kisses I have shared with men are succulent and amazing, those I have shared with you and now with Hattie are sweeter and gentler, so very innocent. Once she warmed up, we passionately kissed together. She wasn't wearing a corset, and when Christophe divested me of my own, her nipples hardened against my bosom.

Oh, Amelia, how much I wanted to taste that sweet little quim! But I was determined to let Christophe have his reward that I had promised him a few lessons ago.

I broke the kiss. "Dearest Hattie, would you please help me undress Monsieur Bertrand?"

"My lady..."

"Have I ever made you do anything you didn't want to do?"

"No, of course not, my lady." She cast her gaze downward once again.

I tipped her chin upward. "And you need not do anything you don't want to do now," said I. "You are free to leave. If you want to."

She trembled beneath my touch. "I do enjoy it when you kiss me, my lady. And...I do not think...I want to leave."

"Do you find Monsieur Bertrand pleasing to the eye?"

She smiled shyly. "Oh, yes, my lady. He is quite handsome, indeed."

"I can assure you he looks even better without his garments. Now, would you please help me undress him?"

Hattie ran her tongue over her lower lip. "Yes, my lady."

CHAPTER SIXTEEN

Ally trembled as Evan rose from the bed, fire in his eyes.

"I confess my undying love for you, and you tell me you're going to marry another man?"

Ally gulped. "Well, I must marry Mr. Landon. He has compromised me. You witnessed it, and so did several others once you punched him." Her voice shook.

"I compromised you long before that rogue Landon ever laid a hand on you."

"And what if you didn't?" Ally said hotly. "What if you were not my first? Perhaps Mr. Landon was."

His face reddened and his nostrils flared. "How dare you? I know you were a virgin when I took you. I've been around the block enough times to know when I'm deflowering a woman. And you told me last night that he hadn't touched your breasts. Were you lying to me?"

Ally bit her lower lip. "No," she said shakily.

"You told me you love me."

She nodded. She could not lie to him about that. "I... I do love you, Evan." And she did. It had come to her last night, as Mr. Landon's lips hovered over her breast. She didn't want him to touch her. She didn't want anyone touching her but Evan. He invaded her thoughts night and day. She loved him. She could no longer deny it. She no longer wanted to.

She longed to be with him, but she'd made a promise to herself long ago. She would marry for money and nothing else.

She had to make sure she, her sister, and her mother were taken care of. Mr. Landon could make that happen.

As much as she loved Evan, he was still a second son—a son with no inheritance. Sophie would say that didn't matter. No, it shouldn't, but Ally had gone without for long enough. She wouldn't risk ending up with nothing. And she would never be a burden on another person, especially not Evan. When Father had died, she, Mother, and Sophie had been supported by Lily and Rose's parents, the Earl and Countess of Ashford. The Countess was Mama's younger sister.

Ally had hated being a burden. She would not do it again, and certainly not to someone she loved.

Evan's eyes still glared, but something new and hollow had invaded them. Sadness?

"You love me, yet you'd marry someone else?"

"You don't understand—"

He grabbed her wrist. "I understand perfectly. You're lying to me. You don't love me."

"No." She vehemently shook her head. "I'm not. I would never lie about something like that."

"But you'd lie about something else? About what then?"

"No, no, no." That had come out all wrong. "I... I have a plan. I've had it in the works for months, and I—" Fear slammed into her when she recalled the ominous note she'd received earlier. It could have two distinct meanings, and she knew not to which it referred. "You don't want to marry me anyway. I'm not...good enough for you."

She was right about that. All she'd been through... She was damaged. Part of her head might never be right due to the abuse she'd suffered. She still had nightmares, the horrid dreams she'd probably never shake.

"Not good enough! What the fuck do you mean by that?"

She shook her head, willing the threatening tears away. How many years of her life had she spent berating herself? Her father had blamed both Sophie and her for not being boys, the heir that he wanted. But once her father had died, she had become goal-oriented. She was smart, attractive, strong. She'd make a good partner for the person she chose. And that person would have so much wealth that Ally would never have to worry about anything again.

She'd never thought she would actually fall in love. It had sneaked up on her, invaded her senses, personified in the man with whom she'd felt most likely never to fall in love. She'd always appreciated Evan's male beauty, his strength, his quiet demeanor. But his seriousness and adherence to convention had racked her nerves.

Here she was, completely in love with this beautiful man, and miracle of all miracles, he seemed to love her as well. She did not doubt his sincerity, and their physical attraction and chemistry was beyond obvious. But what she felt for him went so much further. She felt at one with him—at peace with herself.

And that was a new feeling. She wasn't sure she was ready for it.

Part of her was broken. Her father had seen to that. Evan deserved better.

She'd never felt guilty about her desire to marry only for money. She would use her husband, and he would use her as well, for the physical necessities of marriage as well as to bear him children. She had plans to be a good wife. She would be by his side at all social gatherings, looking her absolute best and attending to all social graces. She was prepared to be a whore in the bedroom if that was what he required. She would earn her keep, and she would earn it well. The fact that she was broken in some ways wouldn't matter because she didn't need her husband's love, and he would not have hers.

No, she could never be with Evan.

Evan's eyes, though still clouded with anger, misted. "Are you going to answer me sometime this century?"

Ally hedged. "I'm not sure how to answer you, Evan. I've known for some time that I would never marry for love. There are certain things I may never be able to give you, and you deserve everything."

"I love you, damn it. You are all I want and all I need."

Ally shook her head. "You only think I'm what you want. We have a good time between the sheets. Don't mistake that for love."

Evan scowled. "You honestly think I could mistake sex for love? You ought to know by now that I am by no means inexperienced in the act. I have had many women, and never have I fallen in love with any of them. I courted your cousin, a beauty by anyone's standards, yet I could not fall in love with her. I've never said those words to anyone, Alexandra, and I do not say them lightly. However, it appears that you do."

Alexandra swallowed. She did not say the words lightly either. But she had made a mistake in saying them, even though they were true—most probably the truest words she'd ever spoken. She could not say them again.

"I intend to marry Mr. Landon," she said, willing her voice not to shake.

"Then leave my chamber," Evan said, the words like ice.

She stood. In a white haze, she gathered a linen around her, retrieved her garments, and did as he bid.

★ ★ ★ ★

Sophie rose, took a light breakfast, and decided to take a morning walk about the grounds of the estate. Graves had informed her that Evan and Alexandra had gone to London, and the mansion was quiet. But Sophie didn't mind. She was an introvert by nature, quite content in her own company. Though she missed Ally, she found it nice not to have to make constant chatter with her sister.

Sophie adored her alone time. She could go to the conservatory, play the pianoforte, and sing to her heart's content, not worrying that anyone other than servants might hear. She could sit on the divan for hours at a time with her nose in Mr. Dickens's latest book and worry not about being interrupted. Or, like this morning, she could enjoy the crisp morning air, the summer blooms, the light breeze as she walked about the grounds, admiring the greenery and the lushness of the scene.

No one followed her. No one was around to follow her. She smiled and opened her mouth to croon one of her favorite ballads.

She jumped when a hand clamped over her mouth.

"Do not scream, my lady. Do as I say, and you will not be harmed."

Sophie tensed, terror coursing through her. What was going on? She was alone on the estate, and now, with a stranger's hand over her mouth, she couldn't scream. Would anyone have heard her anyway? She was far away from the mansion and the stables. Most of the servants were at either of those two places. She had no choice but to do as her captor bid. She was held so fast that she couldn't turn to see who he was. Her heart beat quickly, wildly, and her knees threatened to give way. The captor forced her forward, and she took jagged steps for another mile or two before they came to a horse tied to a tree.

Before she could get a look at him, her captor blindfolded her, gagged her, and set her upon the horse. He mounted behind her.

Surely someone would see them. Someone would wonder why this man was riding along with a blindfolded and gagged woman. But after riding for a bit, the horse stopped, and Sophie was forced into a waiting carriage.

Now no one would see her or hear her.

Where was he taking her, and why? She shivered, and nausea threatened to overtake her. She couldn't take a deep enough breath through the gag.

Within a few moments, blackness descended upon her.

★ ★ ★ ★

Evan seized with anger. Had he truly thought Alexandra could return his feelings? After what they had shared, how could she be so intent on marrying someone else, especially a rake like Nathan Landon?

Love.

He was near twenty-seven years old, still a young man, but a few months ago he felt it was time to get married, so he had begun courting Lady Rose Jameson. They ended their relationship when they both decided to hold out for real love. Rose had said he would know when he was in love, and she'd been right. It had hit him like one hundred stones. Alexandra. She was a pain in his arse, yes. Headstrong and impulsive, socially inept, disrespectful of authority and convention. But strong, so strong. And intelligent and beautiful. No flower, that one. Evan had been surprised to find that he didn't want a wilting flower. He wanted an equal, a woman who would always challenge him, a woman who wasn't afraid to speak her mind. And a woman who wasn't afraid to ask for what she wanted behind closed doors either.

He had fallen hard. Why had she lied to him? Why couldn't she have just admitted that she did not love him?

Was it possible that she did?

But if she did indeed love him, how could she even think of marrying someone else?

Alexandra had not had an easy life, he knew, and what he did know probably only scraped the surface. His heart ached for what she had gone through as a child and teenager.

Now, she expected him to go to Nathan Landon and force him to marry her.

It would be easier to cut his heart out with a jagged blade.

But he loved her despite himself, and if Landon was what she wanted—truly wanted—he would get him for her. The rake would marry Alexandra. Evan would make sure of it. And in so doing, he would resign himself to a life of bachelorhood. A life of bachelorhood on the continent, for he couldn't stay in England and watch his beloved bear another man's children.

He threw himself on his bed, his heart aching, his body numb. The wild berry scent of her still permeated his bedding. He inhaled, closed his eyes...

A few hours of sleep would do him good. But he only tossed and turned.

★ ★ ★ ★

Sophie awoke in a dark room. Her blindfold had been removed, but her gag was still in place. She was lying on a hard cot. Though she tried to scream for help, the gag muffled her words.

She jerked upward when the door of the small room opened. In walked a woman dressed modestly in grey. Her garments resembled mourning clothes. Her mousy brown hair was pulled back severely into a tight bun. She held a tray containing a sandwich and a cup.

"I see you're up. Good." The woman set the tray on the table next to the cot. "I have to take your gag off so you can eat. But you're to say nothing, do you understand?"

Sophie nodded, shaking.

The woman removed the gag. "Here you are. It ain't much, not what a genteel lady like you is used to, I'm sure. But you reap what you sow, don't you?"

Reap what she sowed? Sophie arched her eyebrows and opened her mouth.

"I told you, don't say a word. I'm not interested in what the likes of you has to say. Now eat your luncheon. I'll be back to clear it later." She swiftly left the room, locking the door behind her.

Sophie worked her jaw and massaged her cheeks. She ached where the gag had been. In fact, she ached all over, although they had not hurt her, thank goodness. She had taken her share of beatings in her short lifetime, and she wasn't anxious to begin again. What could they possibly want with her? She truly was nobody.

She was too frightened to be hungry, but who knew when she would be allowed to eat again? The bread was slightly stale and the roast beef flavorless. Still, she forced it down, hydrating herself with the glass of watered-down wine.

How would anyone know she was missing? Ally and Evan were gone in London. No one would notice she was gone until evening, and then it would be too late to do anything about it until the next day. Her eyes misted, and a tear fell. What would become of her?

★ ★ ★ ★

Evan banged on the door to Mr. Nathan Landon's townhome.

The door opened, and a butler appeared. "Yes, sir, may I help you?"

Evan barged past the man. "I need to see Landon. Now."

"I beg pardon, sir, but the master is still abed."

"I don't give a bloody damn if he's in bed. I will see him now. If you do not get him for me, I will find him myself. I'm sure this huge mansion is full of bedchambers, but if I keep looking, I will eventually find the correct one." And he'd no doubt find a woman there as well.

"I'm afraid I cannot disturb the master. He left explicit instructions—"

"Did you not hear me, man?" Evan grabbed the butler's collar. "I will see him now. And if you think I won't pummel right through you to get to him, you can think again. He has compromised my stepsister, and I am here to see that he does right by her."

The man cleared his throat. "Sir—"

"It's 'my lord.' I am Lord Evan Xavier, son of the Earl of Brighton."

"I beg pardon, my lord. But I assure you, the master

cannot be disturbed."

"I assure you that I will physically remove you to get to him. Do you think me incapable of such?"

The mousy man eyed Evan up and down. "I suppose you are more than capable, my lord."

"I assure you that I am. Now are you going to get Mr. Landon, or should I?"

The butler nodded. "Yes, my lord. Please wait here." He left the foyer, his heels clicking on the marble flooring.

Evan looked around. So this was what one million pounds could buy. It was huge—marble flooring, sculptures gracing every corner, Oriental rugs, and silk brocade covering the chairs and settee. And this was only the foyer.

It was the money. How had Evan been so blind to the fact? Alexandra had come from near poverty, and the stars she saw when she looked at Landon were not stars at all but pound signs.

Evan paced the large foyer, glancing at the grandfather clock at the end of the hallway every couple of moments. Ten minutes passed, and then fifteen. His anger intensified. What on God's green earth was taking so damned long?

After a half hour had passed and the butler had not returned, Evan left the foyer and walked toward the large staircase. He walked swiftly upward, passing several shocked maids on the way. He tried all the bedchambers on the second floor, to no avail.

Up to the third floor he strode, walking toward the end of the hallway where ornate double doors stood. Yes, he had found Landon's lair. He grasped the ornate crystal doorknob, but it didn't turn. Locked, of course. He clenched his teeth and banged on the door.

"Landon, goddamn it, open the door this fucking minute."
Nothing.

"I'm not kidding, Landon. I will kick the door down myself if you do not open it."

Evan clenched his teeth and tensed his muscles, ready to give the door a swift kick, when it opened. Nathan Landon stood there, wearing nothing but a red silk robe.

"Xavier," he said. "I told my butler very succinctly that he was to dismiss you. How in the hell did you get up here?"

"I'm not so easily dismissed." Evan stalked toward the other man. "You and I need to talk, Landon."

Landon cowered. "If this is about what happened between me and Lady Alexandra, I have—"

Evan gathered all of his strength, willing himself not to pummel the man. Instead, he pushed him back into the sitting room and followed him in, closing the door. "You have compromised Lady Alexandra, and now you are going to do right by her."

"Xavier, if I had to 'do right' by every woman I've compromised, I'd have several dozen wives by now."

Evan saw red. He grabbed the silk of Landon's robe in a clenched fist. Just as he was about to land a punch on the man's nose, a woman, also clad in red silk, walked through a door that must have led to Landon's bedchamber.

"Nathan, what is going on?"

Evan shook his head. "I should've known. You try to get beneath my stepsister's corset, but when you fail, you find the next common whore to warm your bed."

The woman walked forward, her eyes glaring. "Nathan, aren't you going to defend me? Are you going to let him speak about me that way?"

"Of course not. Go back to bed, Christine. This won't take long."

The woman huffed and slipped back through the bedchamber door.

Evan shook his head. "Alexandra is way too good for the likes of you."

"Just as well. I'm not going to marry her."

"Oh, yes, you are, if you value that pretty face of yours."

Evan readied himself to pummel the shit out of the rake, when two servants entered and grabbed him by the shoulders.

"What in bloody hell took you lads so long?" Landon said. "This fool barged into my chamber."

Evan easily outmaneuvered the two servants, freeing himself. "Really, Landon, did you think these two weaklings could stop me?"

"Perhaps not, but this will." Landon opened a drawer and pulled out a pistol, pointing it at Evan.

CONFESSIONS OF LADY PRUDENCE

by Madame O

Together Hattie and I divested Christophe of his clothing. His erection sprang at attention, and Hattie's eyes became wide as saucers.

"Oh, my lady..."

"Yes, he is spectacular, isn't he?" I took in Christophe's golden broad shoulders, his muscular chest and abdomen, the smattering of dark curls surrounding his copper nipples. Oh, Amelia, I was so ready to be fucked!

Hattie's mouth trembled. "But he's so..."

"Large, yes, I know. But you need not concern yourself with that part of his anatomy just yet, my dear. I have other things in mind for you today."

"What, my lady?"

I smiled deviously. "You shall see, but first we must undress you. I cannot wait for Monsieur Bertrand to see the lovely jewels you are hiding under your clothing."

Once undressed, Hattie covered her breasts with one arm and her lovely triangle of light curls with the other hand.

I strode forward, also naked. "Hattie, do not be shy. Monsieur Bertrand likes what he sees, do you not?" I nodded to Christophe.

"I do, indeed." Christophe smiled and strode toward Hattie. "May I look more closely?"

Hattie nodded shyly. Christophe gazed at her, not

touching her.

"May Christophe give you a kiss?"

Hattie nodded again, and Christophe pressed his lips lightly against hers. As Hattie's lips parted and Christophe delved between them, my nipples tightened. Amelia, watching the two of them mesmerized me. To see such a beautiful man and a beautiful woman coming together—what could one want more? Except to be a part of it, of course.

I knelt between them and took Christophe's cock into my mouth. I sucked on him for a bit and then finagled myself between Hattie's legs and swiped my tongue in between her folds. I worked between the two of them for several moments until they were both gasping.

"Monsieur," I said, "if you would lie down, I bet I could persuade Hattie to sit on your face."

Christophe did as I asked, and I showed Hattie how to squat over his face and move with him as he licked her sweet quim. Christophe's cock begged for attention, and my pussy was soaked and ready. I straddled him, taking him between my cunt lips, descending until I filled my pussy with his massive arousal. I moved slowly, upward and downward, taking him in and then rising. He groaned as he continued to plunder Hattie. Hattie writhed, facing me, her lips pouty.

"Let me kiss you, Hattie dear."

I leaned forward and captured her lips with my own. We kissed fervently, our tongues whirling and twirling, gasping and moaning into each other's mouths. I continued to fuck Christophe wildly, and soon I was close to climax. I wanted the three of us to climax together, Amelia. I wanted it so much! But was simultaneous climax for three people even possible?

Hattie and I continued to kiss. I brushed my hands over

her shoulders and down to cup her beautiful breasts. I found her nipples, and they formed tight little knobs.

She followed my lead, as I was hoping she would, and began toying with my nipples. Oh, how good it felt, Amelia! All the while I rode Christophe, his cock filling me and completing me.

When Hattie gasped and broke her kiss, I knew she was right on the edge. I rode Christophe harder, faster, willing him to climax, and as Hattie started screaming, I dropped my hand from her beautiful breast and fingered my clitoris, bringing forth my own explosion.

Christophe grunted and forced my hips upward, releasing his cock and squirting onto my belly. We had done it! We had all climaxed together.

We collapsed in a heap, all breathing rapidly. And I dreamed of my next encounter. Until that time, I am yours, affectionately,

Prudence

CHAPTER SEVENTEEN

Evan rolled his eyes. Truly, did this man really think he could scare him? Evan had fought off better men than Nathan Landon, two and three at a time.

"You're not the first person to pull a gun on me," Evan said.

"You may be strong and full of muscle, but I assure you, you're not immune to a bullet," Landon said.

"I can have that gun out of your hand before you even pull the trigger." In a flash, Evan executed a circular kick to Landon's hand, knocking away the gun. It slid across the wood flooring.

Landon's face turned scarlet. His mouth formed an O. No words emerged.

"Now, are you going to come along and do right by my stepsister? Or do I need to beat you into submission?"

Landon let out a sigh. "Fine. She's a lovely little thing. It will be no hardship bedding her."

Orange rage rose within Evan. His blood boiled. Images swirled in his head of Landon's mouth about to come down on Alexandra's nipple, the two of them in bed, Landon fucking her pussy, her arse...

He drew in a breath. It was what she wanted. And above all, he wanted her to be happy, even if the cost was his own misery.

The curse of love.

"I will sit right here while you get ready."

"For God's sake, Xavier, I'm not going to try to escape you."

"Well that would be foolish on your part, Landon. However, I do not trust you one iota. So I shall wait here in your sitting area while you dress in your best garments. Then I shall escort you to my townhome where you will propose marriage to Lady Alexandra."

"Fine. As you wish it." Landon sighed and disappeared into his bedchamber.

★ ★ ★ ★

Ally's hands shook. Woods had entered the parlor looking for Evan. He had a parchment for him. Ally had grabbed it out of the butler's hands and run to her chamber. Before she opened it, she pulled a novel off of the shelf, opened it, and grabbed the parchment she had received previously.

I know your secret.

She tore open the new parchment, and her heart nearly stopped.

We have your stepsister Lady Alexandra. If you want to see her alive, be at 32 Chilton Place at midnight tonight. Come alone.

Chills enveloped her body. Someone thought they had *her*? It was obviously a hoax. Where was Evan? He would know what to do. He was brave and strong. He stood up to any man, even those wielding weapons.

But would he help her, after...

A knock on the door startled her. She opened it to see Woods.

"My lady, I must insist that you return the message for Lord Evan. It is highly irregular—"

"Yes, yes, I know. I apologize, Woods. But I need to find Evan. Do you know where he is? I promise I will give him the parchment."

"He left a while ago, my lady."

"Do you know where he went? It's a situation of utmost importance."

"I'm afraid I do not, my lady."

"Drat." Ally clenched her fists at her sides. What to do now?

"Woods!" Evan's voice boomed from downstairs.

Woods left Alexandra, and she followed at his heels. Swiftly down the stairs they flew.

Evan stood in the foyer with Mr. Landon. Ally reddened. What must she look like?

"Alexandra, good, there you are. Landon has something to say to you."

So he had done it. Evan had gone to Mr. Landon and forced him to do right by her. Oddly, she didn't much care at the moment. These notes had consumed her. Her nerves were rattled. Whoever had written them did not have her, obviously. Did they have someone else? Or were they trying to trap Evan?

She had to speak to him alone to determine what course of action to take. And she'd have to tell him the secret he didn't know.

"Mr. Landon, it is lovely to see you as always, but I need to speak to Lord Evan alone for a moment."

Evan strode forward. "Not until Landon has a word with you."

"Evan, please, this is very important." Alexandra bit her lip.

"Nothing is more important than what Landon has to say to you, trust me. Get on with it, Landon."

"My lord," Landon said, "could I have a moment alone with the lady?"

"No," Evan said, his lips pursed. "I shall be witness to your proposal."

"Proposal?" Ally nearly shrieked.

"Yes, my lady." Mr. Landon cleared his throat. "I would be greatly honored, Lady Alexandra, if you—"

"Stop this instant!" Alexandra balled her hands into fists.

"This is what you wanted," Evan said, "is it not?"

At any other time, Evan's words would have filled her with embarrassment. At this moment, the only thing Ally wanted was to know who had sent these notes and what they meant. The one about the secret unnerved her. She hadn't known which secret it referred to—her tormented childhood, or... The arrival of the second note made clear it was the other.

She wasn't doing anything wrong, per se—nothing that others before her hadn't done. And she certainly wasn't hurting anyone. She enjoyed what she did, and she made some money. What was wrong with writing erotic stories for *The Ruby*?

And what did all of this have to do with Evan?

She had to come clean with him. She would tell him what she had been doing. It was the only way.

She grabbed his arm, and another knock pounded on the door. Woods walked around them and opened the door.

An errand boy stood outside. "I have a message from the

Brighton estate for Lord Evan."

Woods gave the boy a few coins and took the message. "Thank you." He handed the envelope to Evan.

Evan tore it open, and his eyes went wide.

Ally's heart dropped. Probably another ominous message... But no, the errand boy had said it was from the Brighton estate.

"What is it?" she asked.

Evan's face paled. Ally had never seen him like this. He was worried. His lips trembled.

"Please, Evan, what is it?"

"It's Sophie." He swallowed. "She hasn't been seen since yesterday morning."

★ ★ ★ ★

Sophie had lost track of time. She'd been abducted early in the morning, but the room where she was being kept had no windows, and without a timepiece, she had no way of knowing what time it was, or even what day it was. She'd been fed three times now, and the lady in grey had come in several other times to empty her chamber pot. No one had allowed her to speak yet, and she still had no idea what was going on.

Her immediate fear had abated a bit. She could handle the sparse meals, her body and mind remembering such smaller repasts. Since her father had died, and she, her mother, and Ally had been taken care of by their mother's sister, the Countess of Ashford, they no longer had to go to bed with their bellies only half-full. She'd gotten used to having enough to eat. It was a luxury so many took for granted.

No, what she couldn't handle was not knowing what was

happening. She'd stopped worrying so much for safety. They hadn't hurt her yet and probably would not. But why had they taken her? She was nobody. Truly.

She looked up as the grey woman entered once again. An older gentleman accompanied her, also dressed in grey. His beard and mustache were grey. His countenance was grey. He was simply grey, inside and out.

She didn't dare speak, although they had removed the gag.

"My lady," the grey woman said, "this is Nigel Ryland."

Ryland nodded. "My lady," he said, his voice low and toneless.

Sophie nodded in return.

Ryland sat down in a chair next to Sophie's table. "I suppose you're wondering what you're doing here."

Sophie nodded again.

"We are members of a group crusading against the publication and distribution of obscene literature."

Sophie widened her eyes. What would they want with her then? She knew nothing about obscene literature. She certainly wouldn't go anywhere near it.

"So I'm sure you can guess why we've brought you here."

She opened her mouth and dropped her jaw. What was he talking about?

The grey woman stepped forward. "I have told her not to speak."

Ryland's lips twitched. "She certainly is an obedient little thing, isn't she?"

"Yes," the grey woman agreed. "I've not had a speck of trouble with her. It's been surprising, to say the least."

"Well, my lady," Ryland said, "I give you permission to speak."

Sophie opened her mouth, but no words came out. After a few seconds, she finally said, "You have no right to hold me here. I have done nothing wrong."

"You are aware that the distribution of obscene literature is against the law, are you not?" Ryland said.

"I don't pretend to be an expert in any of our laws," Sophie said. "But whether or not this literature you speak of is against the law has nothing to do with me."

"Really, my lady, why must you lie to us?"

Sophie trembled. "I am not lying. I have nothing to do with any of it."

"I'm afraid that we have proof of your association with an underground publication entitled *The Ruby*."

Sophie gasped. *The Ruby*? The name sounded familiar. Of course, she had heard Ally speak of it. How Ally knew was a mystery to Sophie. She loved her sister dearly, but there were some things sisters did not need to know about each other. She couldn't say anything about Ally, though, and risk these people going after her. She sealed her lips shut.

"So you have nothing to say for yourself?" Ryland said.

Sophie shook her head. The less said the better at this point. Soon one of the servants would notice she was gone from the estate, and they would begin searching. At least, she hoped they would. With both Evan and Ally gone, and her mother and the earl gone, it was quite possible no one would even notice she was missing. She spent most of her time stealing around the house quiet as a mouse. She was never a bother to anyone, or at least she tried not to be.

Then a thought struck her, quick as a bolt of lightning. Perhaps they had mistaken her for Ally. Perhaps Ally had something to do with that underground paper. She had always loved writing, and she did seem to do a lot of it lately...locked in her bedchamber...

No. It couldn't possibly be. Ally would never write anything like that, though she did read a lot. She knew so much about things she couldn't possibly have experienced herself. Although, the liberties she'd allowed Mr. Landon to take... *Oh, Ally, how could you get yourself into such a mess?*

There was only one thing to do. Sophie had to protect Ally, so she would continue this charade. And because she knew nothing of whatever Ally was involved in, she could tell them nothing. They didn't look like the kind of people who would physically harm her, although she might be wrong about that. She shuddered.

Sophie let out a sigh and resigned herself to her fate. Van Arden had jilted her, and no other gentlemen had come calling. She wasn't beautiful and vivacious like Ally. Though she'd tried to deny it, she had surrendered to spinsterhood long ago. Now she could do something worthwhile. She could protect Ally. Her destiny was no longer meaningless.

It was no less than Ally deserved. Though two years younger, Ally was stronger and braver than Sophie could ever be. So many times Ally had taken beatings from their father to protect Sophie. And she had allowed it to happen. She had been too weak to protect her baby sister.

This was her chance to make it up to Ally. For now, she *was* Ally, and if these people had any intention of harming Ally, the harm would come to Sophie. Though filled with fright, a calm peacefulness settled over her. She could finally turn the tables and protect her strong and beautiful sister. To be able to do so saturated her with a tranquil joy.

★ ★ ★ ★

Ally's heart nearly stopped. "What?"

Evan's face went even whiter. He was truly frightened. Ally had never seen him this way.

"I have no idea. It's not like Sophie to run off—not like some other people I could mention."

"My goodness, Evan, you can insult me later. We must figure out what has happened to Sophie."

"And of course all of my resources will be at your disposal," Mr. Landon said.

Evan clenched his fists. "We have no need of your resources, Landon."

Ally tugged at Evan's elbow. "We should let him help. No expense can be spared to find Sophie. We must find her!"

"I have every intention of finding Sophie." Evan shoved Mr. Landon toward the door. "Your business here is ended."

"You mean I—"

"I don't mean anything except that we do not need you right now. I will be in touch with you later." Evan pushed him out the door.

At this particular moment, Ally didn't care whether she ever saw Mr. Landon again. All she cared about was Sophie. And then a horrible thought struck her.

She pulled the parchments out of her skirt pocket. *We have your stepsister Lady Alexandra.* Oh, no. They had mistaken Sophie for her. The time had come to tell Evan everything.

So she enjoyed erotica. She certainly wasn't the first woman who appreciated it, or erotic novels would not exist. Her maid, Millicent, who'd introduced her to *The Ruby*, certainly did. So she made a few pounds writing it. What was so bad about that? She didn't want to be a disappointment to Evan. He had come to mean so much to her.

But none of that mattered. Sophie was more important than what Evan thought of her.

"Evan," she said quietly, "I need to speak with you."

"Yes?"

She showed him the parchments. "I received this one yesterday." She handed him the first one. "And this one came earlier today for you. I intercepted it, and yes, I know I was wrong to do so. Please do not berate me about that now. I am interested only in Sophie's well-being."

"As am I." He wrinkled his forehead and rubbed his jawline as he read the second parchment. "How can this be? You are right here."

"Whoever has Sophie has obviously mistaken her for me. And I'm so sorry to tell you, Evan, but I know what this is about."

"Oh?"

"Yes." Ally gathered all her courage. "Remember I told you that my maid, Millicent, who was with me at my father's estate—if it could be called an estate—had a large collection of erotic literature?"

"Yes. But what does that have to do with—"

"She introduced me to some underground papers. One of them was called *The Ruby*."

"Yes, I have heard of it." Evan pursed his lips into a thin line. "In fact, Woods found a couple of issues on the doorstep. I figured they probably belonged to you."

Evan did not look pleased. It broke her heart to disappoint him. If he did indeed love her, he would no longer love her after this conversation.

"The only secret I have, Evan, that they could be referring to in that note, is that I do some...writing. For *The Ruby*."

Evan shook his head, his complexion regaining its color. "Then you are the one... Oh my God, I never thought you could do anything so despicable!"

"Evan! I've been writing for the paper for little over a year. It gives me a few pounds in my reticule, something I've never had of my own before. I enjoy it, and I'm good at it."

"I don't give a bloody rat's arse if you write erotica, or if you are paid for it." He stomped toward her. "But you've involved me in this."

What was he talking about? This had nothing to do with him, other than the fact that they were threatening him now.

"I certainly have not. Other than this...extortion attempt, and I had no idea they'd come after you. And Evan, you know I'd never put Sophie in harm's—"

"How did you find out I owned a printing business, anyway?"

What was he talking about? Confusion muddled her brain. He owned a printing business?

"I assure you I had no idea you owned anything. You're a second son. Nothing in the estate belongs to you."

Evan shook his head. "We will deal with this later. Right now, we need to find your sister and get her home."

At least he was talking sense now.

He continued, "I will go to this address now and find her."

"She won't be there. It says to go at midnight. Who knows where they are now? But at least we know she's safe until midnight."

Evan stalked around the foyer, clearly restless, his hands clenched. "How in the world were you able to begin writing for this thing?"

"I told you. Millicent. She got the papers from a servant friend of hers who knew the person who started it. They move around a lot, and the papers aren't printed regularly. One of the servants at our townhome in Mayfair dropped my stories off at an undisclosed location for me and brought back payment. Since we've been in Wiltshire, I've had the stories messengered to the servant back in Mayfair."

"You have no idea with whom you're dealing." Evan sank into a chair and raked his fingers through his unruly hair. "Do you have any idea how dangerous this is? They have kidnapped your sister, for God's sake."

Ally shuddered, her stomach sinking. He was right, of course. Sophie had been taken because of Ally's involvement with the paper. How could she ever forgive herself? Poor, timid Sophie must be scared to death.

"Evan, you must believe me. I had no idea anything dangerous could come of my involvement."

"Alexandra, you're a lady of the peerage. How can you be so stupid? There are laws against this."

Yes, she knew. She was aware of the Vagrancy Act of 1824. The publication of obscene material was a common misdemeanor. But she was not publishing it. She was simply writing it, and she personally did not consider it obscene, nor did many so-called ladies of the peerage, nor gentlemen either.

Her dander rose. "I suppose it's no different than the laws against prostitution. And I'd bet my arse you've visited a brothel."

Evan reddened. "Goddamn it, this is not about me!"

True enough, though he was evading the subject. Sophie needed to be their priority right now. Ally had acted without thinking. Never had she considered that someone she loved could be put in danger.

"Evan," she said, "please promise me you will find Sophie. Please, and I will never ask you for another thing."

"Just hours ago, I would have promised you the world, Alexandra. But now..." He shook his head. "I will find your sister. But I'm not doing it for you. I'm doing it for her, and for your mother and my father."

CONFESSIONS OF LADY PRUDENCE

by Madame O

Dearest Amelia,

I did not have to wait until my next art lesson for a frolic. Lars came to my bedchamber door the very next evening. I can't tell you how aroused I got just seeing him at my door, so handsome is he. Though it was hardly proper, I of course invited him in. I had already removed my dinner gown and corset and was lounging in my chemise and drawers with only a silk robe covering them.

"What brings you up here, Lars?" I asked innocently.

"I was hoping you would allow me entrance, my lady."

"It hardly seems necessary to stand on ceremony when you have spanked my bottom, Lars." I winked at him, and my whole body tensed. Oh, how my bum wanted another spanking.

"I have a surprise for you tonight."

Excitement surged through me. "Oh, what might that be?"

He took two silk scarves out of his pocket. "I wonder what kind of fun we could have with these, my lady."

My heart sped up. I believed, Amelia, that he meant to restrain me. My nipples hardened as I thought of what might be in store.

"Strip for me, my lady."

Slowly, I peeled off my silk robe. I then brushed my chemise off my shoulders and let it drop to the floor. With great care, I untied my drawers and let them drop into a white puddle at my feet. I stepped out of them.

Lars smiled, his tongue slithering over his lips. "Yes, very good. Now, lie on your back on the bed, my lady. And then reach up and grab the bars on your headboard."

Amelia, it never occurred to me to say no. So aroused was I, I did as he bid, no questions asked. I lay down on the bed, my breasts jutting out, my nipples hard and poking upward.

I grabbed two bars of my headboard.

Lars walked toward me, his eyes glazed over with lust. He bound first one wrist and then the other to the headboard. I tested my restraints. He had tied them securely.

"And now, my lady, you are mine, to do with as I please."

His words lit a fire within me, Amelia. I quaked, waiting, wanting, desiring his touch. He pressed his hands lightly over my cheeks, my shoulders, over the top of my bosom, and then cupped each breast and found my nipples.

"What beautiful titties you have, my lady."

I convulsed, my pussy quivering.

He climbed atop me and pressed his lips to mine. We kissed fervently for precious moments while he continued to play with my nipples.

Then he broke the kiss and slid his tongue all the way down my belly. He spread my legs and began to feast on me.

CHAPTER EIGHTEEN

Ally's heart plummeted to her stomach. She had never dreamed that Evan would be so disgusted by her interest in erotica. He was conventional, yes, but he clearly enjoyed the pleasures of the flesh as much as anyone else. He had all but admitted to visiting brothels, and he definitely knew his way around a woman.

Well, so be it. Right now, the only important thing was Sophie.

"When do we leave?" she asked.

"*We* don't," he said. "I do. I will make the rendezvous at midnight tonight. You will be here, under lock and key."

Anger rushed through her veins. "You will not cut me out of this! She is my sister, not yours. I love her more than anything. And as you have reminded me, she is in this mess because of me. Clearly, they think they have me. She has either not told them who she truly is, or they don't care at this point. You cannot keep me from her."

"Oh, yes, I can, and I will."

Ally whipped her hands to her hips. "Yes, you've done such a good job of controlling me up until now, haven't you?"

Evan's face trembled. Oh, she had hit a nerve. No man would control her—not the way her father had controlled her mother.

"You will do as I say this time. Your sister's safety depends on it."

"I am the person who loves my sister the most. You cannot keep me out of this. She needs me."

"She needs you here, where you are safe. That is what she would want."

Yes, he was right about that. But Ally was not one to sit still, especially not when Sophie might be in peril. She would simply sneak out like she always did. And no one would stop her.

"Fine. But please, Evan, bring her back safely. I promise I will no longer be a thorn in your side. If you bring Sophie back to me, I will never bother you again."

As much as she loved Evan and as much as the words broke her heart, she truly meant them. Sophie's safety was paramount.

★ ★ ★ ★

Evan's heart pounded. He should have known Alexandra was behind all this. What would her mother say? Or his father? One thing was certain—he had to get Sophie home. His father would never forgive him if something happened to one of Iris's daughters.

He wasn't upset that Alexandra wrote erotica. He enjoyed such literature as much as anyone else. She had obviously written about Prudence Spofford and then used that name for her fictitious friend. The writing didn't require his forgiveness. But she'd involved his business...

He sighed and retired to his office to think. Alexandra was wrong about no good coming from going to the address now. True, Sophie wouldn't be there, but he could investigate, get to know the area. He would go. First, however, he pulled out the papers Woods had found near the front entrance.

The Ruby. And there it was. *Confessions of Lady Prudence.* He began to read.

My Dearest Amelia,

Forgive me for not having written in several weeks, but I had terrible sickness on the ship home. I miss you so, and I especially miss all the fun and frolic we shared whilst I visited you on holiday in the Americas.

I was no sooner back in our London townhome when Auntie Beatrice insisted that I begin art lessons. Amelia, I can't draw a straight line to save my own soul. Art lessons? Truly? I dreaded the very thought. An hour several times per week listening to some old codger preach the virtues of light and dark hardly excited me, and I possess the artistic talent of a tomato. But Auntie would not be swayed. So yesterday, I began...

When Evan had finished, he was not only impressed, but also aroused. Alexandra had true talent as a writer. If only she had come to him first. But what would he have done? He would have refused to publish her stories. It was against the law.

No more against the law than prostitution...

He let Alexandra's words fade from his mind. He'd deal with his own hypocrisy later. Besides, she had gone behind his back to use his business for the publication of the underground paper. He could not forgive her for that.

He erased Alexandra from his mind. Sophie had to be his main concern. He and a servant would go to the address now, before darkness fell, to see what lay ahead.

He summoned Woods and asked him to arrange for a coach and someone to accompany him. He then went to his bedchamber and changed clothing to something nondescript. He pulled his blond hair back in a queue so it would be less noticeable.

He stole down the back stairway to avoid Alexandra and made his way to the coach. One of his most trusted servants, James Lafleur, was already seated inside. Evan nodded to him.

"Thirty-two Chilton Place, please," Evan said to the coachman.

Within an hour, they arrived in a poverty-stricken area of London. The coachman stopped, and Evan and James alighted.

"Gardyloo!" a woman shouted from several stories above.

James pushed Evan out of the way just in time. A splash of urine hit the ground.

Was this how Alexandra had grown up? Streets lined with garbage? Air scented with waste? Of course not. Longarry may have been a pauper, but he did at least have an estate. Or had they been so poorly off that they had lived in a similar area in Scotland? Longarry's coffers had been dry for some time. He was no doubt attracted to Iris's dowry.

Evan's heart broke at the thought of Alexandra living like this.

Evan led James to 32 Chilton Place. It appeared abandoned. The steps were dirty and covered in refuse. A couple of stray dogs sniffed around. The poor animals were bony and starving, and Evan wished he had some scraps from the kitchen to feed them. Instead, he shooed them away and approached the door. He knocked. Nothing, of course. He hadn't expected anyone to be there. They would not arrive until midnight or a little before.

He tried the door, but it was locked. He turned to James.

"Let's go around back and see what we find. There's probably another entrance."

James nodded, but Evan put up a hand to stop him.

"I'm going to have the coachman move to a safer area. I'll tell him to be back in a half hour."

After Evan took care of the coach, he and James trudged through to the back alley. Sure enough, there was a back entrance, but it was also locked. Evan inhaled. The smell was thick—human and animal waste, filth.

"Go back around front," he said to James. "Check the windows. See if any are loose or open. Maybe check the adjacent buildings."

"Yes, my lord."

Evan continued to search the grounds. One window in the back was broken, but the glass was jagged, and he didn't dare try to break it further and enter. Perhaps he would return later with some leather gloves to protect his hands. It hadn't occurred to him to bring a weapon during the daylight, though in this neighborhood, it would not have been a bad idea.

He walked down the alley a bit, looking around. Debris littered the small path. More stray dogs and alley cats nosed around. Muffled voices yelled from within the adjacent dwellings. Then a woman shrieked.

Why would whoever took Sophie bring her here? It was not safe. If only he could figure out where she was and get to her before her captors brought her here. But that would be impossible. All he had was the parchment her captors had sent.

This was all Alexandra's doing. Somehow she had found out about his business and corrupted one of his employees. He didn't doubt that she could have persuaded one of them to do the deed. The woman was a siren. She could most likely persuade anyone to do anything.

Even as his anger bubbled, his heart still yearned for her. He still loved her.

How could he have misjudged her? Yes, her childhood had been miserable. Could he excuse her behavior on those grounds? No, Alexandra was a grown woman. The time had come to leave her childhood behind and exist as a good person should.

Evan shook his head. He had wanted so much to fall in love with Lady Rose Jameson. She had personified what he thought he always wanted in a woman—adherence to convention, social grace, a good family line, intelligence, and beauty.

The heart wanted what it wanted.

He would have to get over it. While the erotica writing didn't bother him, the fact that she had pirated his printing house did. Damn, he should have stayed in Bath and taken care of the problem when he found out about it, rather than following Alexandra to London. He knew damned well that the publication of obscene material was against the law.

"Your purse, mate."

Evan jerked. A dull knife poked into his back.

"I'm afraid you won't get much if you're depending on that blade," Evan said, rolling his eyes. He'd gotten out of way worse jams. "It won't even go through the fabric of my coat."

His attacker poked harder. "I said, your purse. I assure you I've done much damage with this knife."

Quick as a flash, Evan turned, knocked the knife to the ground, and grabbed the young man in a headlock. "You were saying?"

The young man, not much older than a boy, struggled

within Evan's grasp. "Please, sir, let me go."

"The constable will decide what to do with you."

"Please, I only needed some food for my ill mother. I'm all she has. Neither of us has eaten in days."

Evan softened a bit. The lad could very well be lying, but something within him wanted to give the boy the benefit of the doubt.

"Take me to your mother, lad. If things are as you say they are, I will make sure you are both fed."

The boy nodded and led Evan down the alley to a ramshackle flat. Evan followed him in. A sickly old woman lay on a cot in the only room. A small table and a chair occupied the rest of the dwelling.

"Mum," the boy said, "this nice lord is going to bring us some food."

"Madam," Evan said, "how long have you been ill?"

The woman opened her mouth to speak but no words came out.

"She's too weak," the boy said. "She had the consumption, and she never fully recovered. We couldn't afford to have the doctor come."

"How have you been taking care of her?"

"Stealing mostly. I don't like to do it, but I've had no other choice. There's no work to be had, and the landlord comes around every week or so wanting his rent."

"I will find my servant and coachman and see that the two of you are taken care of for the next few months. Are you able to work, lad? I can give you a job at my townhome."

"I cannot leave Mum."

Evan nodded. He couldn't very well take responsibility for the sickly woman. "Is she able to travel? My family has an estate in Wiltshire, and we have tenant homes available. If you are willing to work, we could probably find a solution."

The boy shook his head. "I'm sorry, sir. I cannot see how that will work."

Evan nodded. If the boy was willing to work, Evan would find a way to move his mother and him and get them the help they needed. "I can arrange for transport for you both."

"We cannot take advantage."

"I am giving you the advantage," Evan said. "Don't be a fool."

"No, sir. If you could just give us the food you promised..."

"Lad, I'm offering you more than a few meals—"

Evan stopped as his eye caught a glint of glass on the floor. A whiskey bottle. And another. At least a dozen were scattered in the corner of the room.

These people didn't really want his help. They wanted his charity. They were not going to change.

"Very well, then." Evan took out his purse and retrieved several coins. "Buy some food. This will last you a couple of weeks. Make sure your mother gets fed decently." He met the boy's gaze. "And do *not* spend the money on the drink."

"Yes, sir."

"And give me your blade."

"But sir..."

"Consider it payment for the food."

The boy reluctantly handed over the knife.

Evan shook his head as he left the humble dwelling. The boy wanted to take the easy way out. It was so very clear.

Was Alexandra any different? She wanted to marry Nathan Landon for his money. Granted, it was difficult for a woman to make it on her own in this world, but she'd obviously found a way to make a little bit of money selling her stories.

Evan's dander rose again. She'd probably made more from using his business to publish *The Ruby*.

He sighed. He had done all he could for the lad and his mother, and he had done all he could for Alexandra. He had given her his love, willingly, but she did not want it.

Right now his priority was Sophie. He would return here at midnight.

★ ★ ★ ★

"Here you are, Lady Alexandra," the grey woman said, bringing in another sparse meal.

Sophie shot her eyebrows up. This was the first time they had called her something other than my lady. She had been right. They had mistaken her for Ally. She did nothing to correct the error.

She simply nodded as the grey woman set the small meal on the table. The woman then took her chamber pot and left the room. A few minutes later, she returned it.

"Aren't you going to eat, my lady?"

Sophie was not hungry. She had not been hungry since they took her. What she really wanted was a basin and pitcher to wash the grime off her face and hands. But she wouldn't ask. She was at their mercy now, and if they wanted her clean, they would bring her a basin and pitcher. "Yes, of course." Sophie picked up the sandwich and took a bite out of the dry bread. She took a gulp of the water that had been brought with it. Maybe she could get some answers from the woman. "I'm sorry, but who are you again?"

"It's like Mr. Ryland told you. We are members of a group

against the publication and distribution of obscene literature. We seek to punish those involved with it."

"Why not let the legal system take care of that?" Sophie said.

"The legal system is a joke, my lady. Publication of such material is a common misdemeanor. The constables look the other way, just like they do with the whorehouses."

"Why do you care so much about it?"

"Because it is obscene, my lady."

Who gives you the right to decide what is obscene and what is not? The question sat on Sophie's tongue, but she did not ask it. They had not hurt her so far, but they were clearly fanatics who thought they were above the law. She could not trust that they would not do her harm. After all, they had kidnapped her.

If only Ally had not gotten involved with this. Well, Ally was Ally. Sophie would protect her, with her life if necessary.

★ ★ ★ ★

Darkness had fallen when Evan returned. Woods met him at the door, his expression unreadable.

"My lord, I'm not sure how to tell you this."

"What is it, Woods?"

"I have heard from your father. He and the countess will be returning in a few days' time. They will be stopping here in London first before going on to Wiltshire to the estate."

Evan rubbed his jawline. Just what he needed—his father home, and he had managed to lose one of his stepsisters. "Lord," he said.

"I'm afraid that's not all," Woods said.

What could be worse? Then he realized he already knew.

"She's gone, isn't she?"

CONFESSIONS OF LADY PRUDENCE
by Madame O

Amelia, I cannot even begin to tell you the pleasure I felt. Not being able to move my arms, not being able to sift my fingers through his glorious tresses, heightened the sensation. I tugged at my restraints, willing them to release me so that I could touch him. To no avail. Yet he continued to plunder me, licking my pussy until I screamed.

"Lars! Release me, please! I must touch you!"

He only chuckled, his voice sending further tremors through me as it vibrated off of my folds. He pushed my thighs forward, baring me further to his view. He forced his tongue in and out of my entrance, and he sucked on my nether lips. His tongue slithered farther now, to my most secret opening. He licked it, teasing it, and Amelia, such shocks quivered through me.

"Release me!" I begged again.

And again he only chuckled, teasing my anus, and then breaching it with a finger.

I nearly jerked off the bed, so intense was the pain of the breach. He continued eating my pussy while he fingered me, the pain slowly subsiding. In and out, in and out, and Amelia, it began to feel absolutely amazing. He sucked my folds into his mouth again and then he teased at my clitoris, licking, sucking, until I exploded in an earth-shattering climax.

"Oh, Lars, how wonderful! Now, please release me, and I

shall do the same for you."

Lars only chuckled again and moved forward on top of me, straddling me. At some point he had disrobed, and oh, was he a sight to behold! Lighter skin than Christophe or Mr. Peck, and lean muscles and a nearly hairless chest! His sculpted cock sprang from a triangle of copper.

He nudged my lips with his erection. He had no intention of releasing me, Amelia. He was going to fuck my mouth just like this. And I found, to my utter surprise, that I was thrilled.

He said nothing, only inched his cock past my lips, which I opened for him obediently. He placed his hand behind my neck and raised my head off the pillow, bringing my mouth into closer contact with his cock. He held my head fast, controlling the movement. I had never sucked cock before where I was not the one in control, Amelia, and it was something splendid indeed. He forced himself into my mouth, moaning, groaning.

"My lady, that is so good," he said.

I, of course, could say nothing in return as his cock filled my mouth. However, his pleasure coursed through me, giving me greater pleasure myself. I wanted him to climax, yet I didn't, because if he climaxed now in my mouth, he would not be able to fuck me. I yearned for that big cock in my pussy.

As if reading my mind, he left my mouth and slid downward. He forced my thighs forward, my feet resting on his shoulders, and he entered me with one swift thrust.

Oh, the ecstasy! He filled me so deeply, so completely, that I nearly shattered at first contact.

He plunged and he plunged, and I was just on the verge of my climax, when the door to my bedchamber opened.

CHAPTER NINETEEN

Evan stood, immobilized. No good would come of berating Woods or any of the other servants. Alexandra possessed magical powers when it came to getting what she wanted. Putting her under house arrest was futile. He'd tried it before, to no avail, and obviously it wasn't working any better today.

What would he say to his father and his new stepmother? Now he had lost both of their daughters.

"I've questioned some of the servants," Woods said. "None of them know where she went."

"How could she have escaped the manor undetected?"

"Your guess is as good as mine, my lord. She is a very smart young lady—fair of face, strong of will, and crafty of mind. I'm afraid that's a lethal combination."

Evan drew in a breath. All things he admired greatly about Alexandra—and what might become his undoing.

He should call his brother, but Jacob was at the other Brighton London residence, the larger one, of course, in full enjoyment of the end of the season with Marvella. Evan definitely didn't want one of Jacob's big brother talks.

How had he come to this? He'd managed not only to fall in love with one of his new stepsisters but also to lose track of both of them. And his father and new stepmother were on their way home at the moment and would be back, stopping in London, in two to three days. Could he have blundered this any worse?

He would fix this tonight, for he knew exactly where Alexandra had gone—32 Chilton Place. He shuddered at the thought of either her or Sophie in that vile neighborhood.

He pulled his timepiece out of his pocket. A few more hours until midnight. He didn't know what to expect, so he prepared for the worst. He'd been told to come alone, but he wasn't that stupid. He would bring a few loyal servants and leave them in the coach a few blocks away, just in case.

His stomach growled. He didn't feel the slightest bit hungry, but he had not eaten since lunch. He strode quickly to the kitchen and bid a servant to quickly fix him something.

★ ★ ★ ★

Ally fished several coins out of her reticule to pay the hansom cabbie.

"This ain't the greatest area, milady," the cabbie said. "You sure you want me leaving you here?"

"I will be quite fine, thank you." Ally, a dark cloak covering her, handed him the coins, hoping the words she spoke were true. The area was poverty-stricken, not unlike where she had grown up. They had lived in town during her teens, rather than on the Longarry estate, which her father couldn't afford to keep in repair. Ally had hoped never to see areas like this again in her lifetime. She wouldn't have to, if she got through tonight. After she saved Sophie, she would marry Mr. Landon, and they would both be taken care of forever.

To be legal, the marriage would have to be consummated. She had looked forward to sleeping with Mr. Landon...until she had slept with Evan. She couldn't imagine that the two would compare. Although she enjoyed her kisses with Mr. Landon, comparing his kisses to Evan's was like comparing a coddled egg to the most decadent cheese soufflé.

Nothing to be done about that. She had made a decision, and she intended to see it through.

There were still a few hours until midnight. She would go to the address, look around, and find a good hiding place. She fingered the kitchen knife in her pocket. It wasn't much, but it gave her a bit of confidence. Evan would show up at midnight or a bit before, and she would be here to help him if he needed her.

The cobbled street was littered with refuse and waste. Ally held a handkerchief to her face and breathed through her mouth. Rats scattered away from her, and tomcats strode the alley mewling and looking for females in season.

Yes, this was all too familiar to Ally. After tonight, though, this type of life would truly be in her past.

None of the doors of the building were open, though one window was broken. She walked toward it and touched the jagged glass. "Ouch!" She had not expected it to be quite so sharp. A bead of blood pearled on her fingertip.

Why would anyone bring her sister to such a godforsaken place? Who had Sophie?

Darkness surrounded Ally. Even if she had come here at high noon, she still would have felt the darkness. Neighborhoods like this were just dark.

Quick as lightning, a blur ran past her and grabbed her reticule.

"Wait!" Her feet started to move, but she rethought the action. She would never catch the perpetrator. She hadn't brought much money with her, but how would she get back? She hadn't really thought this out. Evan was right. She was impulsive. All she knew was that she had to rescue Sophie.

After all, this was her fault.

She found a spot on the side of the building where she was out of sight of the moonlight. She sat and waited.

★ ★ ★ ★

Sophie was blindfolded and gagged again. They had placed her in a rickety old coach and they were now driving who knew where. Her heart thudded as fear barreled through her. If these people were part of a group against the publication and distribution of obscene literature, what did they plan to do with her?

Kidnapping her wouldn't gain them anything. Perhaps they were just eliminating people who were associated with what they called obscene literature.

She gulped, refusing to let the fear overtake her. She would protect Ally at all costs. After all, she owed her.

The horses stopped, and Sophie was forced from the carriage. Her hands were bound, and she was still blindfolded and gagged. She was pulled and pushed forward into what she assumed was a dwelling.

★ ★ ★ ★

Ally's ears perked up at the low voices. She stole toward the front of the building, taking care to stay out of the light. A broken-down coach stopped, and two people—no, three people—emerged, one woman blindfolded and gagged.

Sophie!

Ally resisted the urge to cry out her sister's name. A woman unlocked the door, and the two forced Sophie in.

Now what? Ally's feet were glued to the ground. She had no idea what to do. What had she been thinking, coming here? Evan was right. She would just be in the way. Her eyes misted with tears.

Ally, don't cry like a ninny. This is all your fault!

She readied to knock on the door and demand that they let Sophie go, to tell them that *she* was Alexandra. She again resisted her impulses. That would just give them two hostages instead of one. They would not let either of them go, and Evan would have to save them both. She could not do that to Evan, and she might end up putting Sophie in even more danger. She bit her lip. What to do?

She stood, hidden, until a large dark figure approached the dwelling. She cowered, fear coursing through her, until— *Evan!* He was all in black, his hair pulled back, a black hat upon his head. Had he truly come alone? Without even a horse and coach?

Against the side of the building, she felt the vibrations when he knocked on the door.

The door opened and Evan was ushered in. If words were exchanged, Ally could not hear them.

★ ★ ★ ★

"All right, I've come alone, as you asked." And Evan had. At the last minute, he'd decided not to ask servants to accompany him. The fewer people who knew about this dratted situation, the better. He would trade himself for Sophie and then deal with the aftermath. If he died, what would it matter? The woman he loved had betrayed him. What was there to live for anyway? "Where is Lady Alexandra?"

"Mr. Ryland, bring her in," the lady who had answered the door said. "Evan Xavier is here."

A man pushed a bound and gagged Sophie before him. He pushed her at the woman and then frisked Evan.

Evan shoved Ryland away and moved quickly toward Sophie. "My God, are you all right?"

She nodded.

"For God's sake, take that gag off of her!"

"In good time," the man called Ryland said. "It is not every day that I meet a pornographer."

Evan clenched his hands into fists, and raw anger surged into him. "How dare you? I am no more a pornographer than you are a prize citizen of London. Release her. Whatever argument you may have with me, she has nothing to do with it."

"You must really think me a fool, Xavier. She is one of your prized writers of that little gem you call *The Ruby*."

"Let her go," Evan said through clenched teeth.

"Why should we?" Ryland stood his ground. "She's as guilty as you are."

"So that's your modus operandi. You kidnap everyone associated with what you feel is obscene literature. What do you expect that to prove?"

"We took her to draw you out as the publisher," Ryland said. "We're going to get rid of both of you tonight."

"Oh my God, you are insane." Evan stepped back a bit. He hadn't come unarmed, as bid. As he had hoped, they hadn't checked his stockings. A sharp blade sat snugly against his skin. He could get to it quickly if need be.

"Me, insane? You dare say such when you are the person who is flooding our society with such rubbish?"

Evan would punish Alexandra for this. If he ever found

her, that was. How could she possibly rationalize using his business to distribute that paper?

His heart sped up at the thought of her. God, he hoped she was safe. He'd half expected to find her here. Thankfully, she had stayed away.

He held his anger in check. Right now, he had to do what was best for Sophie. He had to get her out of here.

"The woman you are holding is innocent. She is not Lady Alexandra MacIntyre. She is her sister, Lady Sophie, and I can assure you she has nothing to do with any kind of erotic literature."

Sophie's eyes widened and she shook her head, her voice straining against the gag. What was she trying to say?

"You're lying."

"Take the blessed gag off of her. Let her tell you in her own voice. She's clearly no threat to you. She's trying to say something."

"She has already told us that she is Lady Alexandra," Ryland said. "Your little game won't work, Xavier."

What was Sophie up to? Evan didn't have time to figure it out. He lunged toward Ryland, tackling him to the ground. "Run, Sophie. Run!"

But the woman held Sophie fast. "Mr. Ryland, are you all right?"

Evan held Ryland down, covering his mouth.

Once Evan had subdued the other man, he punched his face once, twice, three times, until blood spurted from his nose. Sophie's muffled sobs formed a haze around him. He punched Ryland again, and then again...until an excruciating pain lanced through his thigh.

He cried out, rolling off of Ryland and gripping his leg.

"Hurry, come on," the woman said.

"Let me get the girl," Ryland said.

"There's no time," the woman said. "Some vagrants are outside, lurking. They'll run to the constable if they see us. The back way. Come on, we must get out of here!"

Evan grasped at his leg. He needed to help Sophie. She floated above him, her hands bound, her mouth gagged. Her voice, muffled, seeped into his thoughts.

"Evan... Evan... Evan..."

Sophie's image metamorphosed into Alexandra. His beautiful Alexandra, hovering over him, pulling him toward something.

And then...the curtain fell.

CONFESSIONS OF LADY PRUDENCE

by Madame O

Amelia, I turned toward the door of my bedchamber. Who could be entering without knocking? I nearly fainted when I saw who it was. Hattie, followed by Christophe. What in the good Lord's name could be going on?

Hattie's cheeks turned pink when she saw us naked on the bed, entwined with each other, Lars pumping in and out of me.

"I beg pardon, my lady."

"It is my fault, my lady," Christophe said. "I insisted that I see you straightaway. Hattie was kind enough to show me to your bedchamber door."

"No matter," said I. "You two shall join us, of course, and we shall have a high time indeed."

"Oh, my lady, I couldn't..." Hattie looked at the floor.

Lars continued pumping, and at last groaned and withdrew, climaxing on my belly.

I smiled, a wonderful idea forming in my head.

"Hattie," I asked, "have you ever had the joy of two men pleasuring you?"

Her cheeks still pink, Hattie replied, "No, my lady."

"Then it shall be my pleasure to give you this extraordinary gift."

"But, my lady..."

"You must accept, Hattie dear. I shall consider it an insult if you do not."

"I do not wish to insult you, my lady."

"It would be our pleasure, my dear," Christophe said. "I do believe I can speak for you, Lars?"

Lars nodded, a mischievous grin forming on his mouth. "Absolutely." He untied the scarves from my wrists. He walked toward Hattie, still naked, and trailed the silk over her cheek. "Would you like me to tie you to the bed, as I did Lady Prudence?"

Hattie trembled, nodding.

"Does the thought of being bound excite you?" Lars asked.

Again, Hattie nodded.

Amelia, my loins throbbed at the thought of watching these two spectacular men seduce and pleasure Hattie. I rose from the bed, walked to my chair where my silk robe was strewn, and draped it over my shoulders, sitting down.

The two men, one dressed and one not, undressed Hattie provocatively, and with every new inch of porcelain skin they exposed, I grew hotter and wetter.

When she stood before them naked, Christophe turned to me.

"And what shall be your pleasure, my lady?"

I licked my lips. "I shall watch."

CHAPTER TWENTY

Ally quickly unbound and ungagged Sophie, and then cradled Evan's head in her arms.

"Where did you come from?" Sophie cried.

"I came earlier in a hansom cab. I've been hiding in the shadows, waiting for you to arrive... And it's a damn good thing I did. One of us can go for help."

"How? He's... He's been shot... We don't even know if... Oh, so horrible. Too horrible for words!"

Ally shuddered. Evan was *not* dead. Evan could *never* be dead. She could not entertain the thought. His chest rose and fell. He still breathed. *Thank God!* He had been shot in the leg, not through the heart.

His heart. She willed herself to be calm. Evan was all that mattered right now. Evan, and getting help.

"Sophie, I need to go for help."

"It's not safe. I have no idea where we are, but I can tell by the condition of this place."

Oh, her sister had no idea. How would she hail a cab at this time of night? She would have to walk until she found someone who could help.

She looked down at Evan, his breathing labored. Blood from his thigh wound seeped through his britches, leaving a dark wet mark.

His eyelids fluttered.

Ally's heart lurched. "Evan, can you hear me?"

"Alexandra..." His voice was hoarse and raspy.

"Yes, Evan, I'm here. You've been shot. I will get help for you. I promise you."

He opened his mouth but nothing more emerged.

"Don't try to talk. I will help you."

"Too dangerous... I must...keep you safe..."

Ally's heart nearly broke. Here he was, bleeding profusely, in pain, and he was concerned about *her* safety. Oh, she truly was in love with this man. She would never love another.

Had money really been so important to her that she had been ready to marry someone other than the man she loved more than her own life? What a self-centered imbecile she had been. She had to save Evan, one way or another. She had no medical training, and she had no idea where to even go for help at this time of night and in this area. But she *would* save him. Failure was not an option.

"Sophie, we have to get the bullet out."

"Ally, you and I have a lot to talk about. Those people who took me, they thought I was you. They said you were writing for a—"

"I know. And I'm so very sorry, Sophie. But right now I can't think about that, and I can't talk to you about it. All that matters is Evan, don't you understand?" Tears formed in her eyes and fell down her cheeks. "We can't lose him, Sophie. We just can't."

"Of course. Of course I understand."

"Dear Lord, I'll do anything if only he'll be all right." Ally sobbed, her nose running, her voice cracking and choking. "This is all my fault, Sophie. You were taken because of me, and he was coming to save you. And now..." She gulped. "I may lose him. I may lose the man I love."

Sophie gasped. "You love him?"

"I love him more than anything." Ally laid her head on Evan's chest, his heartbeat faint against her ear.

"Oh, Ally, I had no idea. You've always said how useless he is, and—"

"I was wrong." Emotion flooded her. "He is everything. He is all I'll ever want."

"I will hold you to telling me all about this later. Right now we need to see to his needs." Sophie stood. "I have no idea how to get the bullet out."

"Nor do I." Ally sniffed and willed herself to regain her composure. Losing it was not going to help Evan. "I need to go for help."

"I'm sorry, Ally, but it's just not safe. We've already got one person injured. I cannot risk losing you as well."

"I fear if we try to remove the bullet we may cause further damage. Let's just try to stop the bleeding before he bleeds out. Unfasten me, will you?" Ally turned her back to Sophie.

"Unfasten you? What for?"

"I want to tear my dress into strips to help stop the bleeding."

"You're not thinking clearly. Use your petticoats. We can use mine too."

Ally shook her head. Of course, the petticoats. She had to think clearly or she would be no help to anyone, especially Evan. Her reticule was gone, but she did have a handkerchief in her pocket. She grabbed it, fitfully blew her nose, and gulped. "Of course, you're right." Ally pulled the petticoats out from under her skirt and began ripping them into strips. She took a fistful of the fabric and pressed it against Evan's wound.

"We could use a tourniquet to stop the bleeding," Sophie

said.

Ally hated the idea. Evan could lose his leg, but at this point they had no choice. "Yes, you're right. Tie this off while I continue to put pressure on the wound."

If only morning would come.

"All we need to do is get him comfortable and stop the bleeding," Sophie said. "If we can do that, he will survive until we can get help."

Then, damn it, that is exactly what Ally would do. She leaned forward and kissed Evan's cheek. *I swear to you, Evan, I will not let anything happen to you. I will get you help. I will take care of you. Always.*

A half hour later, Ally and Sophie had stopped the bleeding. Evan's breath was shallow, but at least it was present.

"Ally," Sophie said, "you should try to get a little bit of sleep."

Ally shook her head. "I will not go to sleep until I know he is all right. I'm so very sorry, Sophie, for all that I've put you through. Please, you try to get some sleep."

Sophie nodded and lay down on the floor. Soon her soft snore wafted to Ally's ears. Though she tried not to, Ally wept. She sat next to Evan, keeping vigil, waiting for the elusive dawn.

Many hours later, sunlight finally filtered through the dirty window of the dank room.

Evan still breathed, but had not awakened. Ally nudged her sister.

"Sophie, wake up. It's finally light, and I must go for help."

"I will go with you."

"No, someone must stay with Evan. I will go." Ally couldn't bear to leave Evan's side, but she would be more able to get help than Sophie. Though they had both come here in the dark, Sophie had been blindfolded and would have no idea where she was. Ally at least had a small idea of what she was dealing with.

She jerked and looked up as the door was forced open. Two constables entered.

"What is going on here? You do know you're trespassing."

Ally sucked in a relieved breath. "Oh, thank God! This man needs help. He was shot. We managed to stop the bleeding a few hours ago, but there's a bullet inside his thigh. He has been unconscious for the most part since the shooting. Is there a doctor anywhere nearby?"

"Yes, madam," one of the constables said. "I shall fetch the doctor." He left quickly.

"How did you know we were here?" Ally asked.

"We received an anonymous message that someone might need help here."

"Who on earth? Sophie, it must've been your kidnappers." Ally widened her eyes. "Kidnappers with a conscience. That's a new one."

"You were kidnapped, madam?"

Sophie nodded. "Yes, I was taken from the Brighton estate in Wiltshire. I'm not sure how long ago—maybe two days? Three? They kept me in a dark room and I lost track of time."

"We received a note telling us to come here at midnight last night," Ally said. "This is Lord Evan Xavier, second son of the Earl of Brighton."

"My God. Well, with any luck, the doctor will be here soon. You ladies have obviously taken very good care of him. If I had to wager a guess, I would say he will recover. Of course, I am no medical professional."

Ally let out a sigh of relief. The constable might not be a doctor, but hearing someone—anyone—say those words helped.

"And who might you ladies be?" the constable asked.

"I am Lady Sophie MacIntyre," Sophie said, "and this is my sister, Lady Alexandra. We are Lord Brighton's stepdaughters."

Ally's heart nearly stopped. This man was a constable, sworn to uphold the law. Whoever had kidnapped Sophie had done so because of Alexandra's involvement with *The Ruby*. Though she was not involved in the publication and distribution of the paper, she did write stories for it. Was that against the law? Would Evan somehow get in trouble for this?

She could not risk that happening. Once Evan got the help he needed, she and Sophie would have to decline to speak to the constables any more about the matter. If only she hadn't mentioned Sophie's kidnappers.

Nothing to be done now.

What seemed like hours later, the other constable arrived with the doctor. "I'm sorry it took so long," he said. "I had to go several blocks over. I also had to promise that he would be paid double for coming into this area."

Double? Triple, quadruple, Ally didn't care, as long as the man helped Evan. "Of course. This man is Lord Brighton's son. You will be paid adequately, Doctor."

The doctor, a stout man with grey hair and spectacles, set down his black bag and knelt to examine Evan.

"It's very good that you got the bleeding stopped. I would like to be able to remove the bullet, but at this point I cannot tell exactly where it is lodged. We will need to transfer him to my office. Let's get him into your coach, Constables."

★ ★ ★ ★

Ally wrung her hands as she sat in the waiting area at the doctor's office. Evan had been taken into the back for surgery.

"Ally," Sophie said, taking her hand, "we have a lot to talk about. I know you must be worried sick about Evan, as am I, so we will save our talk for later."

Ally nodded. "I am so sorry that you got dragged into this. If anything had happened to you..." Ally's heart wrenched.

Sophie's touch soothed her.

"I am fine, and Evan will be fine too, God willing."

"Oh, Sophie, he just has to be."

A few moments later, a nurse joined them.

"My ladies, Lord Evan is out of surgery. The doctor wishes to speak to you. Please follow me."

Ally sucked in a breath. "How is Evan? Will he be all right?"

The nurse smiled. "The doctor will explain everything."

The nurse wouldn't have smiled if anything had gone wrong, right? At least that's what Ally hoped. They followed the nurse to a small office. Dr. Stanton sat behind a desk.

"My ladies, do come in and have a seat."

Ally sat in a leather chair, and Sophie sat next to her.

"You'll be happy to know that Lord Evan came through surgery brilliantly. He is strong and healthy. I was able to remove the bullet, and he is stitched up. Right now he is sedated and on morphine for the pain. I've already made arrangements to transport him back to the Brighton townhome in London."

Ally let out a huge sigh of relief. "Thank God."

"It was rough for a little while, but everything worked out fine," the doctor said.

"Thank you so much, Doctor," Sophie said. "We will see that you are paid handsomely for your services."

"Thank you," he said.

The nurse opened the door. "Excuse me, Doctor, but the transport has arrived for Lord Evan."

"Excellent," the doctor said. "My ladies, you will go with Lord Evan in the transport. We will put him aboard on a stretcher. Two attendants will travel with you and get him safely to his chamber."

Sophie politely thanked the doctor, but all Ally could do was nod her head and cry. She had never been so thankful in all her life—more thankful even than when her father had passed away and freed her, Sophie, and her mother from the prison of their home. Never in a million years could she have imagined that any person would mean as much to her as Evan did. His life meant everything to her.

Once he had regained his strength, she would accept his marriage proposal.

Sophie had been right all along. Some things were more important than money.

Once in the transport, Ally asked Sophie whether her kidnappers had harmed her.

"I was frightened more than anything else," Sophie said. "They were not unkind to me, and they did feed me regularly. They did not hurt me, though they did say they were going to get rid of both Evan and me last night. I don't know exactly what they meant, and I'm glad I didn't find out."

"As am I. Something spooked the woman. I don't know who or what it was, but I thank God for it. I could never have forgiven myself if any harm had come to you," Ally said.

"But what is it all about, Ally? I don't understand. Have

you truly been writing erotica?"

Ally's cheeks warmed. "I have. But please believe me that I never would've done it if I had thought any harm could come to anyone I loved."

"I know you would never let anyone harm me," Sophie said. "You've proved that many times." She cast her gaze downward.

"That is all in the past, dear sister."

"I'll never forget how you took on Father for me." Sophie wrung her hands. "I should have been stronger."

"Please, Sophie." Ally didn't like to think about those times. "As I said, it is in the past."

"But I can never repay you—"

"I never asked for repayment, did I? And truly, I never thought any harm could come from my writing. I do get paid a small amount for it, and having any money of my own is such a treat after our childhood."

Sophie nodded. "I am not judging you. If you enjoy erotica, you're certainly not alone in the world. I just don't understand how it could have come to all of this."

"I don't understand either, Sophie, but we will figure it out, I promise you."

"No." Sophie shook her head. "I just want to forget this ever happened. Mother and the earl need know nothing about it. I couldn't bear the thought of you getting in trouble."

"I'm not concerned about me."

"I am. After all those years of you protecting me, please, let me protect you just this once."

Ally smiled and squeezed her sister's hand. "As I said, I'm not concerned about me. But I *am* concerned about Evan. So if you are willing, I agree. Let's not tell anyone. If the constables come to call, asking questions, we will just explain that we would rather forget the whole thing. But I'm not asking you to do this for me. I'm asking for Evan."

Sophie's lips trembled. "I agree, but I do have one condition."

Ally arched her eyebrows. "And what would that be?"

"Tell me, dear sister, how you came to fall in love with Evan."

Ally warmed as she relived their love affair through words to her sister. "I never expected it," she said. "It sneaked up on me, you know? I've always found him attractive, but we are so different. There's this fire between us, this passion. At first I thought it was only lust, but I was wrong, Sophie, so very wrong. It is love of the highest degree. Lily and Rose were right. When you fall in love, you will know it with all your heart. I can no longer imagine my life without him. When I thought he might be..." She closed her eyes, and a tear slid down her cheek.

Sophie squeezed her hand. "He will recover. The doctor said so himself. You will be with your love."

"Yes, I will be." Ally smiled as she said the words.

Marrying for money seemed foreign to her now. She didn't care if Evan was a second son with no inheritance. She didn't care if he was a pauper. She loved him, and she would be his wife.

She had lived without before. She could do it again.

She would do anything to be with her love.

★ ★ ★ ★

Evan was still asleep several hours later, lying in his own bed in his own bedchamber in the townhome. Ally sat next to the bed, his hand clasped between both of hers. She had not left his side since they got home, and she would not. Dr. Stanton had said that Evan would awaken eventually this evening, and Ally was determined to be here to see it. She wanted her face to be the first thing Evan saw and for her "I love you" to be the first words he heard.

When Evan's eyelids fluttered open, Ally smiled.

"I love you. Welcome back, my love. You had us all very worried."

"Alexandra?" Evan's voice was hoarse and raspy.

"Yes, Evan, I am here. And I love you."

His face taut, he said nothing.

"I'm so sorry for everything that has happened. But I love you, Evan, and I want to marry you."

His face showed no reaction to her words. "What happened? Why am I here in bed?"

"You were shot, my love. In the thigh, last night." Ally squeezed her eyes shut, trying to stop the tears, to no avail. "But you're going to be all right. The doctor got the bullet out, and you will be good as new in no time at all. Then we can be married, as you asked. I love you so much, Evan. I was wrong to refuse you. I was wrong about so many things. If you'll have me, I promise to love you until the day I die and to devote my life to you and the children we will have."

Evan wrinkled his forehead, a slight frown marring his beautiful face.

"I'm sorry, Alexandra, but it is over between us."

CONFESSIONS OF LADY PRUDENCE

by Madame O

Christophe and Lars laid Hattie on my bed.

"Grasp the posts on the headboard, Hattie," Lars commanded.

Hattie obeyed, her body trembling.

Lars fastened one silk scarf around Hattie's right wrist while Christophe secured the left. My whole body throbbed as images of what they might do to her swirled through my mind. My nipples tightened, Amelia, and I'm not sure I could've been more excited if I'd been the one lying supine on the bed.

Christophe pushed Hattie's thighs forward and swiped his tongue along the crease of her arse. I quivered as Hattie did. Meanwhile, Lars went to work on Hattie's cherry nipples, plucking one with his fingers and licking and kissing the other. Hattie gasped, arching her back. The sight was so beautiful, Amelia. Part of me wanted to strip off my silk robe and jump on the bed and join the fun while the other part of me was enraptured by the vision before me. I never knew how erotic being a voyeur could be.

For now, I decided to watch and let Hattie have her fun.

Lars ripped his mouth from Hattie's nipple and clamped it down onto her lips, kissing her. As I caught a glimpse of their tongues entwining, I became so aroused that I reached for my clitoris and began massaging it. Christophe worked on Hattie's pussy, licking and slurping, as Hattie arched off the bed. When

Lars broke the kiss, Hattie squealed.

"Oh, kind sirs, it all feels so good!"

Christophe continued to lick Hattie's sweet cunny, and I moved my other hand to my breast, cupping, teasing my hard nipple. Dear Amelia, I was so hot from watching the scene unfold that I was about to burst on the spot.

When Christophe thrust two fingers into Hattie's pussy, and she came, screaming, I climaxed as well, squirming in my chair, moaning, groaning, wanting so badly a hard cock to fill me.

Christophe quickly freed his cock from the confines of his trousers and plunged it into Hattie's cunt. Lars went back to Hattie's nipples, kissing, sucking, plucking.

I could wait no longer. I stood, brushed the robe off my shoulders into a silky puddle on the rug, and walked slowly to my bed.

CHAPTER TWENTY-ONE

Ally's heart sank. "Evan, you can't mean that."

Evan turned his head away from her. "Leave me, Alexandra. I do not wish you to be here in my bedchamber."

Ally leaned over and kissed Evan's cheek. She turned his face back to her and pressed her lips to his.

"My love, only days ago you confessed your love to me and said you wanted to marry me. I was an idiot to say no. I loved you then, and I love you even more now. You are all I want in this world. I will not leave your side."

"You are not the woman I—" Evan coughed.

"Easy, my love. Don't try to talk too much. The doctor will come to see you tomorrow. What do you have need of right now? Are you hungry? I can get you a tray."

Evan let out another dry cough. "All I need at the moment is for you to leave."

"But—"

"I said leave." He turned away again, closing his eyes.

Ally sat back down in the chair. She was not going anywhere. She was made of stronger stuff. Evan was in pain. He was hurting. He didn't know what he was saying. Ally would not leave his side. She would prove her loyalty to him, her love to him.

When Evan's breathing became softer, she knew he had fallen back to sleep.

"Yes, sleep, my love. Everything will be better tomorrow."

Surely he would be back to his senses by then.

★ ★ ★ ★

Ally paced in the parlor while the doctor examined Evan. She had tried to see him earlier, but his valet insisted that she not be allowed in the room. The only information she had now had come from his valet. According to Redmond, Evan was faring well. But Ally longed to see him to make sure for herself.

"Ally, do sit down. Let me fix you a cup of tea or something." Sophie patted the divan next to her.

"I can't possibly, Sophie. I need to see Evan. I need to see with my own eyes that he's doing better."

"The doctor will be down soon, and he will let us know what is going on. You're not helping anything by pacing around the room."

"I can't sit still. I'm sorry."

"Don't be sorry. Just calm down. You won't be any use to him in this agitated state."

"That is my fear, Sophie. I fear he doesn't wish me to be any use to him at all. I don't know why he is closing me out like this. It can't possibly be because of my writing for *The Ruby*, can it?"

Sophie shook her head. "I declare, I do not know, Ally. Evan is very conventional. I suppose that could be the problem."

"But Evan knows me. He knows me like no other man does. And knowing me as he does, the little tidbit about *The Ruby* should come as no shock to him."

Sophie's cheeks pinked. "Please, go into no further detail. There are some things about my sister I do not wish to know."

"I'm still the same person I always was. I am still the sister who protected you all those years ago, and I would do so again if I had to. Why do you think I went after you two nights past?"

"That is a good question. You knew Evan was going, so you knew I would be in capable hands. Why did you go?"

"It's certainly not that I didn't trust Evan to take care of you, but as it turns out, it was a good thing I was there. Evan got shot. I was worried about both of you. I had to make sure you were both all right."

Sophie shook her head. "I shall always love you as my sister and also as my closest friend, but you don't always think. Your impulsiveness is going to get you into trouble someday, I fear. You're a gifted writer, and your interest in erotica does not disturb me overly much. But did you think about what you were doing when you tried to sell it to the paper? You do know that the distribution and publication of erotica is illegal."

"A common misdemeanor, Sophie. And it is enjoyed by many. Most law enforcers look the other way."

"They don't all look the other way, Ally. And law enforcement aside, you seem to have caught the attention of a group of people who do not look the other way. Who knows how many other zealots are in the group with Ryland and the woman? I'm just glad they left."

Ally opened her mouth to respond, but was interrupted by the doctor coming to the parlor door.

"My ladies," he said, "Lord Evan is doing well. He's a bit feverish, which is common after a surgery. We need to watch for signs of infection. So far, everything looks good. He will be bedridden for the next few days. His movement is good, but his thigh can't take his weight. In a few days, he will be able to get up and walk around the house with assistance."

"Thank you, Doctor," Sophie said. "What should we be doing for him?"

"Just arrange for the servants to see to his needs. I understand his father and your mother will be returning soon, within a day or two. There is no need to send word to them and worry them unnecessarily. Lord Evan will be fine, barring any infection or other unforeseen circumstances."

"I must see him." Ally strode quickly toward the door.

"Ally..." Sophie hedged.

The doctor bowed politely. "I will leave this to you at this time. Send word to me if you have any concerns. Otherwise, I shall return in two days' time to check on Lord Evan."

Ally followed Dr. Stanton out of the parlor.

"Ally..." Sophie said again.

"Do not try to stop me. I am going to see the man I love."

Ally briskly marched up the stairs, her nerves skittering, and stopped when she reached the door to Evan's chamber. She hesitated and then boldly knocked.

Redmond opened the door. "Lady Alexandra, I'm sorry, but Lord Evan does not wish to see you."

"Yes, yes, I know. But I have never let what Lord Evan says stop me from doing what I want." She brushed past Redmond and entered.

Evan sat up in bed, a tray of food in front of him.

"My lord," Redmond said, "I tried to stop her—"

"It's all right, Redmond," Evan said. "Normal people seem to be defenseless against Lady Alexandra. You may leave us."

Once Redmond had shut the door behind him, Ally turned to Evan. She opened her mouth to speak, but he held up his hand to stop her.

"Alexandra, I have not changed my mind. I do not wish to

see you."

"Then you owe me an explanation. Only days ago you wished to marry me."

"And only days ago, you wished to marry Landon. I do believe he has proposed marriage, has he not?"

"I am not in love with Mr. Landon. I'm in love with you, Evan."

"So you have said. But again, only days ago that fact did not seem to matter to you."

"I know, and I'm so sorry about that. I was wrong. I was interested only in Mr. Landon's money. I wanted to make sure that Sophie, my mother, and I were taken care of, and that we would never ever have to live in near poverty again."

"I see, and now you're willing to live in near poverty with me?"

"Oh, Evan, I nearly lost you. It was a jolt to me. I always knew I was in love with you, but facing losing you... I realized how wrong I was to be focusing only on marrying for money. I want only to marry you."

"Well, unfortunately, my offer is no longer on the table."

Ally's heart fell. Sadness rivered through her. "Are you saying you no longer love me?"

Evan cleared his throat. "I'm saying I no longer wish to marry you."

"But you still love me?"

Evan did not answer.

"So I take that as a yes?"

"Take it however you want it. It does not change anything."

Ally leaned over and pressed her mouth to Evan's. She traced her tongue along the seam of his lips, which were tightly closed. She nibbled across his upper lip and then his lower. She could be patient if she had to be. She rained tiny kisses around his mouth, and then tried again to open his lips. This time he parted them, and she slid her tongue into his mouth. Oh, sweet warmth, sweet love. This was far from their first kiss, but it was the sweetest, because she knew now, without a shadow of a doubt, that this was the man she was meant to be with—her true love.

Evan responded and tangled his tongue with hers, his breathing growing more rapid. The kiss turned frantic. Ally didn't want to stop, but Evan was weak. With all her might, she withdrew her mouth from his.

"You responded to my kiss, Evan."

"That means nothing. You are beautiful. A man would have to be dead not to respond to you."

Ally smiled. She turned her head. His cockstand was apparent beneath the blanket. Perhaps she could still reach him.

"Evan, I nearly lost you, and I realized how important it was to be with a man I was in love with. If you are truly in love with me, how can you not see things the same way?"

"Because, Alexandra, there are more important things in life than love."

Her own words, hurled back at her, and they cut into her like a sword. She flinched. "Like money? You're wrong, Evan. I was wrong. Please, can't you see—"

"Damn it, I'm not talking about money. Not everything is about money."

"Then what are you talking about? What on earth is more important than love?"

"Trust, Alexandra."

"Trust? Are you saying you don't trust me, Evan? How

can you not? I took care of you. If I hadn't been there the night you got shot—"

"If you hadn't been there the night I got shot, you would've been doing what I asked of you. I told you to stay away for your own safety."

"But Evan—"

"Damn it, do not interrupt me!" Evan sucked in a breath.

Ally cupped his cheeks. "Don't exert yourself. Please."

He swallowed. "I am fine. Please allow me to say my piece, and do not interrupt me again."

Ally nodded. She owed him that.

"I asked you to stay away. I've asked you many things since our parents left on their wedding trip, and you have continually disobeyed me."

Ally opened her mouth to disagree, but Evan shot daggers at her with his eyes.

"However, those are not the reasons for my lack of trust. You are impulsive and strong-willed. I accept that about you. It's part of your charm. However, you have done something that I cannot forgive."

"If you're talking about my writing erotica for *The Ruby* "

"No, Alexandra, that is not what I'm talking about. I have no problem with your enjoyment of erotica. Clearly I've enjoyed your knowledge of the art of pleasure. Whether you learned from reading erotica or by any of the ways men learn it—of which there are more than a few—really doesn't make a difference to me."

"Then what—"

"I think you exercised poor judgment in selling your writing to *The Ruby*. The distribution of such literature is illegal, as you well know."

Ally opened her mouth.

"Stop right there. I am not finished. You're going to tell me it is a common misdemeanor and that most close their eyes to it. And you would be right. Yes, you exercised poor judgment in selling it. I stand by that point, but that is not the reason for my mistrust."

"Then what in the world are you upset about?"

His face reddened. "Are you really going to stand there and make me spell it out for you?"

Confusion muddled Ally's head. If he wasn't upset about her writing for *The Ruby*, what was going on?

"I'm afraid you'll have to, Evan. I don't mean to be ignorant, but I haven't the faintest idea what you could be talking about."

"Damn it, Alexandra! You brought my business into this."

Ally dropped her mouth into an O. "Evan, I don't know what you mean."

"Somehow you managed to get my business to print *The Ruby*. I don't know how you did it, but do you realize I could be arrested for publishing obscene literature?"

Ally's heart fell to her stomach. Evan owned a printing business? Yes, he had said something like that before... Here, in London? Or at home, in Bath?

"I don't understand..."

"Do not act so innocent. Who else could be behind it? You are my new stepsister, and you write for *The Ruby*. Who else would have taken it to my business?"

She shook her head, confounded. "You need to back up a few steps. How is your business involved?"

"You really are something. My business is printing that rag—for free, no less. And it's all your doing."

"It's not. I swear. You know of my involvement. It's a

servant at our home in Mayfair. I know nothing else, I swear to you!"

"Please, spare me the sinless act. Who else could have taken *The Ruby* to my printing house?"

"Why, I have no idea, but I promise you I will find out."

"No!" Evan pounded his fist on the mattress. "You will stay out of this from now on. Once I am able, I will take care of it. In the meantime, I will have some trusted employees look into the matter. I should have taken care of this days ago. Instead, I had to follow you here to London. If I had known you were behind this from the beginning, I would have let you come to London alone and get into all the trouble you wanted. I would not have cared."

Ally looked down, swallowing, and then up to meet Evan's gaze. His eyes were misty as though he wanted to cry. Her heart shattered.

"Evan, I love you. I would never do anything to harm you."

"I do not wish to hear it, Alexandra. Leave my chamber now, please."

"But—"

"I said now!"

She looked down the length of his bed. His arousal was still apparent. He was not as immune to her as he would have liked her to believe. He could not make love to her. He wouldn't want to. Even if he did, he wouldn't have the strength. But she had the strength...

She grasped him through the coverlet.

He winced, a small groan escaping his throat. "Alexandra..."

"Please, let me." She removed the cover and unbuttoned his night shirt. His cock stood proudly from its golden nest. So beautiful he was, perfectly sculpted. A pearl of clear liquid emerged from the tip. She leaned down and licked it off.

He trembled. "Alexandra," he said again.

"I love you, Evan," she said, and sank her mouth onto his hardness.

"Ah, God..." His body stiffened.

His cock was warm against her tongue, the skin soft as velvet. He tasted of salt and cinnamon, with a touch of musk. Delicious. His low moans wafted to her ears, and she wanted more than anything to give him this. Though her nipples were tight and her loins aching, she only wanted his pleasure. Her own was unimportant, inconsequential.

She twirled her tongue around his cockhead, sucking and licking, his soft groans fueling her desire to please him. When his shaft was nicely lubricated, she grasped the base and moved her fist up and down along with her lips, finding his rhythm.

He jerked his hips and let out a small cry.

She pulled her mouth away. "No, my love. Don't move. Your thigh can't take it. Let me do the work. Please. I want to do this for you."

He closed his eyes, and a tear squeezed out from one. Ally's lips trembled as she descended onto his cock once again. Emotion overwhelmed her—love, tenderness, soul-wrenching desire to give him everything. She sucked him slowly, gripping him and moving with him, loving him in the most intimate way she could.

When the tiny convulsions started at the base of his cock, she took him deep, to the back of her throat, drinking in his seed as though it were the nectar of life.

"Alexandra...my God."

She let his cock drop from her mouth and slid forward, kissing him, letting him taste his own essence on her tongue.

He responded, sweetly returning her kiss, moaning into her mouth, grasping her upper arms.

Until he pushed her away, breaking the suction of their mouths with a loud smack.

"Damn it! I cannot!" He turned away from her.

She cupped his cheeks and forced his gaze back to her. "I love you, Evan, my dearest Evan. Please don't turn me away."

"Without trust, we have nothing."

"I swear to you, I had nothing to do with your business printing the paper." Tears streaked down her cheeks.

"I'm sorry, Alexandra." Evan cleared his throat, his own tears pooling in his beautiful eyes. "I don't believe you."

Ally turned, her body nearly immobile. Sadness clogged her throat. She willed her muscles to move and left the bedchamber, closing the door quietly behind her.

She should be angry at Evan for not believing her, and she was, but she hadn't proven herself the most trustworthy during the past weeks. Damn it! How could she have been so ignorant?

Who could be behind this?

Whoever it was would not cost her true love. She would find a way out of this mess.

★ ★ ★ ★

After a good cry, she swallowed back her tears and raced downstairs to the first story of the townhome and into the office. No help. Most of Evan's important papers would be in his office on the estate in Wiltshire. She had to get back there, but how? It would be easy enough to escape Evan, he being bedridden for the next few days, but the earl and her mother were due to come through London first before going home to the estate. And what of Sophie? Sophie would not let Ally out of her sight right now.

And she was tired of running. She had run off to London twice now and hadn't gotten what she wanted either time. But she had found something so much more wonderful. She had fallen in love with Evan, and she would not let him go without a fight.

She riffled through the papers on the desk. If Evan owned a printing business, perhaps he owned other businesses. She knew precious little about the man she loved. She had thought he was a second son with nothing to his name. She should have known better. Evan was much smarter than that. He would have seen to his own financial well-being, just as she had tried to. Evan and Ally were cut from the same cloth. She warmed at the thought.

As much as she enjoyed it, Ally would no longer write for *The Ruby*. She couldn't risk anyone she loved paying for her actions. Evan had been right. She had not used good judgment.

She sighed. Nothing on the desk. She would have to check the drawers and the cabinets. She would find something, even if it took her all day.

After nearly an hour of investigating, she stumbled upon the address of a printing house in London. Printing houses of the same name were located in both Bath and Edinburgh. She scribbled the London address on a piece of parchment and headed to the parlor to tell Sophie she would be leaving on an errand.

Before she left the office, she caught a glimpse of a corner of parchment sticking out from under the desk blotter. Curious, she removed it. She dropped her mouth open. It was a poem, written in Evan's hand.

Her hair the color of roasted chestnuts, silky against my fingers,

Her eyes of liquid gold, sparkling as she gazes into mine,

Her skin of rosy porcelain, soft as a feather beneath my touch,

Her voice like a delicate claret, so sweet as she says my name,

Her breasts, scarlet-tipped peaks, velvet against my tongue,

Her pussy, pink and swollen, slick as she moves against me,

Her hands, peachy and delicate, nestled in mine,

Her lips, ruby red and supple, so perfect as we kiss,

Her beauty, her strength, her will...like a storm on the roaring sea.

She is my love,

She is...

Alexandra

Ally's heart melted. Evan wrote poetry? Erotic poetry? No wonder he didn't have any issues with her writing for *The Ruby*. And this had been written for her.

Her eyes misted with tears. He was a writer. Evan. Her Evan.

And yes, damn it, he would still be her Evan. He still loved her, and she would prove she was worthy of his love. She would get to the bottom of whatever was going on at his business.

She walked quickly to the front entrance, looking around to make sure no one saw her. Sophie was in the conservatory playing the pianoforte and singing.

She opened the door and—

"Good afternoon, my lady." Nathan Landon bowed.

Goodness, was it afternoon already? What was Mr.

Landon doing here?

"Mr. Landon, I'm afraid I was just leaving..."

"My lady, I was so relieved to hear of Lady Sophie's safe return. I have been worried sick about both of you."

Ally forced a smile. "I do thank you for your concern. However, I'm afraid I do not have the time to visit."

"But my lady, I was so hoping to finish our conversation. I would consider it a great honor if you would consent to be my wife."

Mere weeks ago, Ally would have been delighted. Right now, all she could think of was her true love, Evan, who currently wanted nothing to do with her. The old Ally would have jumped at this proposal. Not today's Ally. She was done with Mr. Landon. She intended to marry only one man, and he was in his bedchamber upstairs.

"Mr. Landon, I am indeed flattered by your offer, but I'm afraid that the sun has set on our time together."

"You mean, you don't wish to marry me?"

Ally shook her head. "No, and I'm truly sorry. I have enjoyed our time together."

Mr. Landon returned her smile, and was that actually a look of relief on his handsome features?

"I am disappointed, my lady, but I do wish you well." He bowed again.

"And I you, Mr. Landon." An idea came to her. "Might I ask you a quick favor?"

"Of course, my lady, anything."

"Could you give me a ride in your coach a couple of blocks into town where I might hail a hansom cab?"

"I can do better than that, my lady. It would be my honor to escort you to wherever you're going myself."

What would be the harm? He probably knew Evan owned the printing business, and it would not be unusual for Ally to go there. "Mr. Landon, I would be most appreciative. Thank you."

When they arrived, Mr. Landon helped Alexandra alight.

"I thank you for the lift, Mr. Landon. And I do hope there will not be any awkwardness between us as we both go about our lives."

"Of course not, my lady. I hope to see you at many events in the future. Please always save a dance for me."

Ally smiled and blew him a kiss as he left. Then she turned and walked forward.

She drew in a deep breath, opened the door to the printing house, and strode in confidently.

CONFESSIONS OF LADY PRUDENCE

by Madame O

Amelia, all the licking and sucking, cocks and pussies everywhere. It was pure heaven, I tell you. Christophe grabbed me first and pressed his lips to mine. We kissed with fervor, our tongues whirling, twirling, dueling, my skin tingling all over, my pussy wet and hot.

Hattie was still bound to the bed. Lars unfastened her and turned her over, entering her swiftly from behind. She shrieked as he pounded her.

Christophe released me and positioned me in front of Hattie. "Lick Lady Prudence's pussy, Hattie."

I'd dreamed of this moment since I first seduced Hattie, Amelia, but she shied away.

"Don't be timid, dear Hattie," said I. "We shall both enjoy this. I promise you."

She smiled and bent to her work. Her tongue was silken, Amelia. I'm not sure I'd ever felt any sensation quite like it. She licked my folds gently, so unlike Lars or Christophe. Tingles shot through me, and I nearly shattered.

Christophe straddled me, the tip of his cock nudging my lips. I opened for him gladly, taking him into my mouth. We were all joined, Amelia. Lars pounding Hattie, Hattie eating me, and me sucking Christophe. It was pure hedonistic pleasure.

I wanted to cry out, to scream all their names and tell them of the wonderful pleasure they were giving me, but my mouth was full of Christophe's cock. I sucked him to the back of my throat, his knob nudging my tonsils. I grabbed his buttocks, kneading his muscular arse as he pounded into my mouth.

Hattie continued to eat me, her silky tongue pleasuring me like no other. When she forced a finger into my wet cunt, I nearly climaxed then and there. Such a slender little finger, Amelia, but the feeling was indescribable. She continued to fuck me with her finger as she sucked on my clitoris. I moaned, groaned, Christophe's cock still filling my mouth. As much as I adored sucking his cock, I wanted to be able to see Hattie eating me and Lars behind her, fucking her. But imagination is almost as good, dear Amelia, and the images in my head made me so hot.

I brought my hands to Christophe's cock and added them to the pleasure I was giving him. Soon he groaned and pumped into my mouth, spilling his seed down my throat. No sooner had I swallowed than my own climax came to me, and I shattered over Hattie's silky tongue and finger. Behind her, Lars grunted loudly, withdrawing his cock and spurting over the lovely globes of her arse.

We all collapsed in a heap of quivering flesh, absolutely sated.

Amelia, I must part for now. Just thinking about our romp has me wet, and I am going to retire to my bedchamber and pleasure myself. Until next we write, I am affectionately yours,

Prudence

CHAPTER TWENTY–TWO

A young man stood behind the counter. "May I be of assistance, madam?"

Ally gathered her courage. "Yes, please. My name is Lady Alexandra MacIntyre. I am stepsister to Lord Evan Xavier, who owns this establishment."

The young man extended his hand. "It is a pleasure to meet you, my lady. My name is Frank Osborne. What may I help you with today?"

"It has come to my attention that certain erotic literature is being printed here."

Osborne arched his eyebrows. "Excuse me?"

"I believe you heard me. Do you wish me to repeat myself?"

"No, of course not, my lady. But I can assure you that—"

"You may not be aware of it, but Lord Evan is currently recovering from a gunshot wound."

"I'm so sorry to hear that. What happened?"

"He was shot by a member of a group that crusades against obscene literature. Evidently, they believe Lord Evan is publishing it at one of his printing houses. I am here to find out who is behind this."

"You should probably check with the night staff, my lady. I can assure you nothing like that is done during the day on my watch."

Yes, the night staff. That did make sense. No one would

be stupid enough to print erotica during the day, especially without Evan's knowledge.

She would have to return after dark. But how could she? Her mother and the earl were due home any day now, and she needed to be at home. She breathed in and once again steeled herself for bravery.

"I will have a look around back myself."

"My lady, I'm sorry but that is quite impossible."

"This is my stepbrother's establishment. You would be wise to do as I ask." She walked behind the counter.

"My lady, please..."

Ally ignored him and headed toward the back. The sound of the presses whirred, the pungent scent of ink and newsprint wafted to her nose. The workers stared at her, their mouths open.

Osborne ran behind her. "My lady, please..." he said again.

And then, staring her in the face, at the end of one of the lines, sat a stack of papers.

The Ruby.

Ice formed in her veins. She turned to Osborne. "You lied to me. You *did* know that this was going on. Do you have any idea how much trouble Lord Evan could be in because of you?"

Osborne curved his thin lips into a nasty smile and moved his jacket aside to expose a handgun in his waistband. "You would do well to come with me."

Alexandra shivered. The frigid fingers of fear lynched her. Not again. Hadn't she endured enough?

Osborne took her arm and led her to the back and up a narrow flight of stairs. A chair sat in the middle of a dark room.

"I will have to keep you here until I can figure out what to do with you," Osborne said. "I'll have to gag you, though any noise you make wouldn't matter anyway. No one would hear you over the sound of the presses."

"Why are you doing this?"

Osborne pushed her into the chair and bound her ankles to the wooden legs. "Why do you think? For the money, of course. Not everyone is born into finery like you are, my lady."

Ally gulped and said nothing. This man had no way of knowing she had been far from born into finery. Her mother had only recently married into it.

Money. Always the money. She had been no better than this man only a short time ago. She grimaced at how shallow she'd allowed herself to be.

"You do understand that what you're doing is against the law."

"Yes, yes, it's a lousy misdemeanor. I am not worried."

Ally saw red. "No, you don't have to be because it is Evan who will take the blame if you are exposed."

"Yes, that is a bit of a benefit. But I honestly never thought he would be exposed. We are only printing the papers here and at the facility in Bath."

"Why didn't you just ask Evan if you could print papers here?"

"Are you completely mad? First of all, he would want the house to be paid. But more importantly, he's an uptight peer. He would never have consented. He would never do anything against the law."

"No, he wouldn't. He is a good man—more of a man than you will ever be."

"Easy, my lady. I can show you exactly what kind of man I am right here. And no one would hear you scream." He licked his lips lasciviously. "You are a beautiful woman. Beautiful...

and that body..." His tongue snaked over his thin lips again.

Ally squirmed, nausea overwhelming her. No one would ever touch her again, other than Evan. Certainly not this lowlife. "Don't you dare touch me."

He chuckled. "What exactly would you do about it if I did? As I said, who would hear you? And if you went running to the constables, I would expose you for the little harpy you really are."

"You don't know anything about me."

"Oh, don't I...*Madame O?*"

Ally swallowed. Her pseudonym for her erotica. Oh, that she could go back in time and end this before it began!

"No one would believe I had violated you. I will simply tell them that you begged for it. And when I expose the fact that you are a writer for this lovely little paper, no one will believe that I did anything to you without your consent. Unfortunately, though, now is not the time. I must get back downstairs. The business doesn't run without me." He grinned.

Ally sat while he bound her hands behind her. "Why are you printing the paper now, in broad daylight?"

"Not that it's any of your business, lovely lady, but we have a deadline, and we got behind a few days ago printing some useless rubble for his lordship. Something he deemed important, and everything had to be put on hold for it. A book of drivel."

What had Evan deemed so important to stop the presses? Ally didn't know, and right now she couldn't dwell on it anyway.

"You'll be quite comfortable here, my lady. We close at six p.m. At that time, I will come up and figure out what to do with you."

"That's hours away."

"Yes, it is. It's too bad I have to bind your hands, otherwise I could bring you some parchment and you could do some writing of your feisty Lady Prudence."

She seethed. "There is nothing wrong with what I write."

"I couldn't agree more, my lady. There is nothing wrong with what I print."

"Except that it is not your printing house, and not your decision to make."

"I'm bored with this conversation, I fear." Osborne placed a gag in Ally's mouth. "No need to blindfold you. You know where you are. I shall see you in a few hours."

He left.

Ally struggled against the bindings, to no avail. Once again, she had managed to get herself stranded without a paddle. She did seem to have a penchant for it.

Evan wouldn't come for her. He was physically incapable. And at this point, he probably wouldn't want to anyway. How had she made such a mess of this? She had finally come to understand what was important in life, only for it to be too late.

The minutes crept by slowly. At least she had fulfilled her goal. She'd found out who was behind the printing of *The Ruby*. However, it wouldn't do any good when she couldn't get to Evan.

It was past time for luncheon, but she wouldn't have been able to eat anyway. Her empty stomach gnawed at her. She fought back the ever-present nausea.

Sweat beaded on her forehead. The presses and the workers downstairs created more heat, and it rose to the second floor where she was. Her clothing stuck to her skin. She fought back tears. She wouldn't be able to wipe them anyway. Nothing to do but sit—sit and await her fate.

Wait! Mr. Landon knew where she was. But no one knew he had come calling earlier, and because she had rejected his proposal, he would not come back. Most likely no one would think to ask him where she might have gone.

She was truly out of luck.

* * * *

Evan drifted in and out of slumber. His thigh ached, but it was nothing he couldn't handle, thanks to the morphine that a servant gave him every six hours. Unfortunately, the morphine couldn't touch the pain in his heart.

Thoughts of Alexandra tormented him. He'd used every bit of strength he possessed to send her away this morning, and it had weakened him even more. He would always love her. No one else would satisfy him now. So he had resigned himself to bachelorhood. Hell, who needed an heir, anyway? He was only a second son.

But a child...born of Alexandra's womb... He'd dreamed of holding his son or daughter as he gazed at his beautiful wife...

Alexandra was everything to him. But he had to be strong and leave her be. He could no longer protect her. She was too impulsive, too strong-willed. She would always want to be doing something contrary to her best interests. What kind of life would that be for him, constantly keeping her out of trouble?

He couldn't help smiling to himself. It would be an amazing life. A challenging life. A life of surprises.

The life he wanted.

But if he couldn't trust her, no future existed for them. He could live with the fact that she wasn't a soft-willed woman who acquiesced to all of her husband's demands. That was the kind of woman his mother had been, and she had been a good wife to his father. But his father had never loved her. Instead, he had fallen for Alexandra's mother. Iris was beautiful, tall, and regal, like Alexandra. She no doubt possessed some of her daughter's fire—what hadn't been burned out by her first husband—and that is what had drawn his father to her. She was a woman of strength and character who had sacrificed everything to protect her daughters.

His father could not have done better for himself.

Evan finally understood. It was Alexandra's fire that drew him. Her passion. Her strength. She was nothing like Evan's mother.

If only she hadn't violated his trust. He would have to learn to live without her. But how could he live when half of his heart—his soul—was missing?

★ ★ ★ ★

Ally had sunk down in the chair as much as the bindings would allow. Dear Lord, the heat! The muskiness of her own body odor wafted to her nose. It hadn't become unpleasant yet, but it was well on its way. Her hair felt like it was plastered to her scalp.

Her heart hammered as heavy footsteps clomped up the stairs. Osborne walked in.

"Good evening, my lady. I trust you have not been too uncomfortable."

Ally strained against her gag. How dare he come in here so nonchalantly after kidnapping her and tying her up.

"And now, I must decide what to do with you. The night

crew will be in before long, so I need to get rid of you before then." He tapped his foot, rubbing his chin. "What to do?"

Ally's stomach threatened to empty. She willed it back. Getting sick through the gag would not be pleasant.

Osborne strode forward, his eyes glazed over. He stroked her cheek, his bony fingers clammy against her skin. She winced.

"Do not shy away from my touch, my lady."

Ally let out a scream, muffled through the gag.

"You are a beauty." He leaned toward her and slithered his tongue up her cheek.

Ally nearly vomited. Her skin tightened against the gooey disgustingness of his saliva. This man oozed creepiness. He was a vile creature, and he would not violate her.

"Leave me alone!" The words did not make it past her gag.

"Such lovely lips." Osborne traced them with his index finger. "If I remove this gag, will you kiss me?"

Ally violently shook her head.

"Oh, I think you will." He ripped the gag from her and clamped his mouth onto hers.

The dreaded invisible worms crawled over her skin. She wanted to vomit. She pressed her lips shut, even as his tongue tried to force its way in. She would not allow it.

He withdrew. "So you want to make this rough, do you? I can't say that will be unpleasant for me." He chuckled and leered at her.

She cringed.

"I'll have to get you out of that chair as your legs are no use to me now. I want them spread apart. I want to see the treasures you hide between them."

Ally gagged and spat in his face. "You will not touch me!"

He laughed as he wiped her spittle from his cheek. "I think you've mistaken who is in control here. I will do what I please with you. After all, I have to dispose of you anyway. Why not have some fun before I do? What is the harm?"

"Lord Evan will come for me," Ally said. "He is probably on his way right now with the constables."

"Lord Evan is recovering from a gunshot wound. You said so yourself. I somehow doubt he is coming anywhere for you. And if anyone knew you were gone, the authorities would be here by now. I call your bluff, my lady."

Ally wilted against the chair. He was right. No one was coming for her—certainly not Evan, who could barely walk.

So this was truly to be her fate. A result of poor judgment, Evan would say.

And he would be right.

She could only pray that it passed quickly.

Osborne unbound her feet from the chair. Quick as a jackrabbit, she landed a swift kick on his hand.

"Ouch! You filthy little bitch!" He slapped her across the face.

The strike stung, but it was nothing compared to the kind of punishment her father had doled out. "Is that all you have?"

He slapped her again. "You will not speak to me like that."

Ally held back a sarcastic laugh. Osborne had no idea with whom he was dealing. Ally was no limp violet. She could take a beating, and a beating by this revolting creature would be far preferable to any sexual act with him. Make him angry enough, and he would beat her senseless instead of raping her.

And when he was done, she would somehow keep her vow—to kill any man who ever laid a hand on her again.

"Try to stop me, why don't you? You're weak. You can't

even hit a woman properly. Unbind my hands, and I'll show you who is stronger between the two of us."

"The only thing your hands will be doing is pumping my cock, you little whore, before I force it into your pretty mouth."

She nearly retched, but she caught herself, continuing to play her part. "Suck you? You can't be serious. Why, your tiny thing would get lost between my lips."

"Shut up, bitch." He slapped her across the face again.

Oh, the blow stung. Her cheek was probably red as an apple by now. She held fast, bracing her resolve, determined that he would not see her pain.

"You like hitting girls do you? Compensating for your tiny little cock, I'd wager."

This time he punched her in the gut. His fist landed on her stomach with a dull thud. Had her hands not been bound behind her, she would have doubled over in pain. Still, she held her head high.

"You seem convinced of the size of my cock, my lady. Perhaps I should show you. It will prove to you its worth."

Lord, she didn't want to see that or any other part of him. *Keep him angry, Ally. Make him hit you. Don't let him bring his cock into this.*

"Anything of yours that comes near me, you're going to lose," she said, clenching her teeth.

Whomp! He whacked her face again, this time hitting her eye. She'd have a shiner tomorrow.

If she saw tomorrow...

"You talk big, don't you? I get the feeling this isn't the first time a man has taken a fist to you. I can see why. Some women just need a good beating."

The words slammed into her like a thunderbolt. Images

whirled in her head—her father above her, taunting her, smacking her, turning her over and caning her...

Some girls just need a good beatin', lassie. Like your mother. And you. Teach you respect for your father. Respect for your betters. You're nothin' but a little harlot, you and your sister both. Aye, your arse is good and red now...

Her father's voice. The devil's voice. That sadistic gleam in his eye as...

Stay strong, Ally.

"Unbind my hands, and we'll see who beats whom," Ally said. "I promise you I'll see you dead. My face will be the last thing you see when I plunge a dagger into your heart."

"You're feisty, I'll give you that." He licked his lips. "I bet you're a tomcat in bed."

"Tomcat?" Ally grinned slyly. "That's a male cat. Are you saying you prefer bedding males?"

Thud! His fist hit her stomach again. She retched, dry heaving. She hated showing weakness, but she couldn't help it. At least she hadn't eaten since breakfast, so there was nothing in her to vomit.

He hit her again, and then again. She might die from the beating, but it would be better than being raped by this lunatic.

Besides, death no longer seemed so horrible. Why go on living? The earl would take care of Mother and Sophie. Evan no longer wanted Ally, and she would never love another. Money was no longer important to her. Now, in this moment, all she wanted was to keep this maniac from raping her.

Whatever it took, she would do. She'd die before she let this creep into her body.

"Coward!" She spat out blood. "You won't unbind my hands. You're afraid of me. Of a lowly woman!"

Still he pummeled her. Blood flowed from her nose, and her body weakened and throbbed. She couldn't take much more. She was on the verge of losing consciousness. Just as well. Sleep would give her peace.

Evan. She could dream of Evan...

"Move away from the lady, now!"

Not a voice she recognized... Images were all grey. Eyes... wanted...to close...

Had Osborne stopped punching her? Her body had gone numb. Her eyes were slits. Darkness had fallen. No light.

Again the voice. "Move away from the lady, or I will shoot."

CONFESSIONS OF LADY PRUDENCE
by Madame O

Dearest Amelia,

I must confess that neither I nor Christophe pretend to have art lessons anymore. I guess he got over his need to give me what my auntie is paying for. In fact, at our last lesson, he suggested that we have an orgy. Can you even imagine? He asked me to arrange for Hattie and Lars to be available and he would bring himself and Mr. Peck, and perhaps one other if he could arrange it. Does that not sound absolutely delicious?

So I have that in the works.

In the meantime, during our last "lesson," which took place in my chamber, Christophe educated me on the "back door."

As you know, Lars had already breached me there, and the sensation, while painful at first, turned out to be something different and amazing. It's a wonder that you and I never experimented in that way with Broderick and Miles. I think we all would have enjoyed it.

"You will enjoy this kind of fucking, my lady," Christophe said to me with a wicked smile. "I've found that the only ladies who don't enjoy it are those who haven't tried it."

I confess, Amelia, that I was quite frightened. A finger is one thing...but a cock? Good mercy, and Christophe, Lars, and Mr. Peck are all quite large!

We undressed, and Christophe turned me over so I was on

my hands and knees on my bed. I jerked when he slid his tongue between my arse cheeks. It caused no pain, of course, and I expected it, but still I lurched. The sensation overwhelmed me—such a private, forbidden place, yet I quivered with elation.

"Do you trust me, my lady?"

"Of course I do," I said.

"Good. We must have trust for this to work. Relax, my lady. Let me soften you. We will go slowly. That will ensure your enjoyment."

I breathed in calmly and let it out on a sigh. Slow was good. But fast was better. I wanted to experience all the pleasure that life had to offer...and he wanted to go slowly!

I gritted my teeth and nodded. He knew best, of course.

"Your arsehole is nice and wet now, my lady. Relax, and I will get it ready for penetration."

I breathed in deeply again, as he rubbed my opening with his finger.

"Yes, my lady, such a lovely arse. Relax."

He breached me.

And I jolted again. The agony of the penetration surged through me, but Christophe eased my tension with soothing words and a lovely massage to my buttocks.

Oh, the burn, Amelia! But as I relaxed my muscles and he glided his finger in and out of my hole, my cunny began to respond.

I wish I could describe it, Amelia. It's different than a finger in your pussy. The fact that it's so naughty makes it all the more enticing, but the feeling, the sensation...there's nothing like it. It's an alien feeling, intensely delicate, unnatural yet amazingly natural.

I wanted more, Amelia, but when I opened my mouth to voice my need, he began playing with my cunny with his other hand.

And I exploded.

CHAPTER TWENTY-THREE

Someone had come for her. Who could it be? She lifted her eyelids as much as she could. Everything was blurry, but four figures emerged in her sight—Osborne and three other men. One looked vaguely familiar.

Osborne lifted his hand. "Hey, mate, I don't want any trouble."

"Any man who hits a woman deserves trouble," the man with the gun said.

"Who the fuck are you?"

"Move away from the lady, and I'll tell you."

Osborne edged away from Ally.

The man nodded to the others. "Take care of her. Get her some help."

Two men unbound Ally.

"Are you all right, madam?" one asked.

Ally couldn't answer. She could barely nod her head.

"We need to get you home. Can you tell us where you live?"

Ally tried to form the words, but she couldn't.

"Ryland! She can't talk. We'll have to take care of her."

Ryland? The man who'd taken Sophie had been named Ryland. Sophie had told her. Ally tried to scream, but still, nothing came out.

"All right. Give me a minute to take care of this pornographer." Ryland held the gun to Osborne's head.

"No!"

Was that her voice?

The men all turned to her.

"No shooting." The words came out slurred.

"Madam, this man is producing obscene material."

"Is that really any of your business? Let the law take care of him."

"The law won't. It falls to me." Ryland shot Osborne in the head.

Ally gasped. Agony threaded throughout her body. Good riddance, but seeing someone killed unnerved her even more. Evan and Sophie could have met a similar fate previously if Ryland and the woman hadn't gotten spooked and left the scene. Ally's skin chilled.

The man called Ryland paced around the room while the other two helped Ally to her feet. Ryland might feel that violence against women was wrong, but he had arranged Sophie's kidnapping. Granted, he had not hurt Sophie in any way, and someone—perhaps the woman?—had alerted the constables. Still, Ryland had scared the hell out of Sophie and the rest of them. Ally had best not reveal her true identity, or he would take her.

What to do? She was badly battered. She had been beaten this badly and worse by her father and survived. She would survive this time. All she needed were some headache powders and her bed. In a few days, she would be good as new.

Ryland was clearly crazy. She didn't know about the other two, but if they were in league with him, she didn't hold out much hope for them. She had to find a way to get away from them. Right now they seemed concerned with helping her, and oddly, she wasn't sure whether that was good or bad.

The whirring of the presses below still buzzed in her ears. No one would come for her. Likely no one had heard the shot fired by Ryland.

"Find a cabbie and get her home," Ryland said. "I need to stay here and take care of this body."

The two men helped Ally descend the narrow staircase and took her out the back way.

Darkness had fallen, and now that her fear and adrenaline had subsided, the pain permeated her body. Her strong will had kept her numb during the beating. She hadn't endured punishment of this magnitude in several years.

However, it had been a small price to pay to keep Osborne from raping her.

And what of Ryland, her unlikely savior? He had probably saved her life. Osborne might have beaten her to death. Should she be grateful? Bewilderment cluttered her mind. The images in front of her appeared normal, distorted, and then normal again.

The two men deposited Ally into a hansom cab. Ally managed to give the cabbie the address of the Brighton townhome, and then she lay back, each bump in the road jarring her body, pain radiating through her.

After only a few moments, the cabbie nudged her. "My lady, we have arrived."

She must have dozed off. The cabbie helped her to the door and knocked.

Woods opened the door and gasped. "Lady Alexandra! What happened?"

"She's in pretty bad shape, I'm afraid," the cabbie said. "Two men got her in my cab."

Ally opened her mouth, but couldn't speak.

"Thank you," Woods said. "Wait a moment please, and I'll see that you're compensated."

"Not to worry, mate. The men paid me for my services. Just take care of the young lady. Good night."

Woods helped Ally up the stairs and to her chamber.

"I'll find a maid to attend to you, my lady."

Alexandra fell onto her bed.

★ ★ ★ ★

Ally woke, shivering. Sunlight streamed through her window. Her whole body throbbed. She groaned.

"Ally?"

Ally turned her head, each minute change of position excruciating. Sophie sat in a chair next to her bed, holding her hand.

"Sophie?" Ally's voice cracked.

"Oh, Ally, I've been so worried. Don't try to talk too much."

"Evan..."

"Evan is fine. He is resting comfortably."

"Does he...?"

Sophie shook her head. "No. We didn't want to worry him unnecessarily. He needs to sleep right now. I will go to him later today and tell him what happened to you."

Ally tried to shake her head but wasn't sure if she managed to. "No. Don't tell him."

"Of course I must tell him."

"He won't care, Sophie."

"That's ridiculous. Of course he will. He loves you."

"He no longer wants me." Ally let out a raspy cough.

"Let me get you some water." Sophie stood and fetched

a dipper of water from the basin. "Here, can you sit up a bit to drink?"

Ally rose on her elbows enough to get some of the water in her mouth. The rest dribbled down her chin.

"The doctor will be here soon to see Evan. We will have him examine you as well."

"I don't need a doctor. This is no worse than when—"

"Yes, I know." Sophie nodded. "But we have a doctor now. We have money for your care, and you will damned well see him."

Ally couldn't help grinning at her sister's curse. Sophie must be serious. "Oh, don't make me smile, Sophie. It hurts."

"You need to rest. Perhaps in a few hours, if you are feeling a little better, you can tell me what happened."

Ally nodded. Might as well give Sophie some solace. Of course, she had no intention of telling anyone what had transpired.

She drifted off again.

★ ★ ★ ★

"Well, my lord, I'd say everything is looking good." Dr. Stanton snapped his black medical bag shut.

"That is good news," Evan said. "When will I be up and around, other than to use the convenience?"

"It's only been a few days, my lord. You're strong and healthy and are healing very quickly. However, you must use caution. I recommend nothing strenuous. In other words, do not leave the house... In fact, do not leave the bedchamber unless you absolutely must."

Damn. He really needed to get back to work and find

out who was behind the printing of *The Ruby*. Other than Alexandra, of course.

"You'll be pleased to know that your stepsister should fully recover as well."

Evan jolted and sat straight up in bed. "Excuse me?"

"Yes, Lady Alexandra. I examined her just before I came to see you."

His heart fired rapid beats. "What are you talking about? What happened to Alexandra?"

"You mean, you didn't know?"

"Do I look like I have any clue what you're talking about?"

"I'm so sorry. Lady Alexandra was beaten badly. However, she is strong and healthy like you. She will be fine."

Rage surged through Evan. Who had laid a hand on Alexandra? He'd kill whoever was responsible. He winced as he swung his legs over the side of the bed.

"And just where do you think you're going?" the doctor asked.

"I'm going to see Alexandra, of course."

"Lady Alexandra is resting comfortably. She's asleep right now. She should not be disturbed. I assure you she is fine and will recover."

"No one will keep me from her!"

"I don't think anyone is going to keep you from her, my lord. However, your visit with Lady Alexandra will have to wait until later, perhaps when you are both fully awake."

Evan stood and grimaced. A pain shot through his thigh. "I don't care if she's not awake. I need to see her. Where's that blasted cane you brought me last time?" He looked around and spied the walking stick in the corner.

"I can see no one will talk you out of this." Dr. Stanton

retrieved the cane and handed it to Evan. "Please do not disturb her, and please get back here as soon as possible and continue resting."

Evan left his bedchamber, pain lancing through his leg, and walked down the hall to Alexandra's room. He knocked quietly. A few seconds later, Sophie came to the door.

"Evan! What are you doing here? You should be resting."

"I assure you, I am fine. Why was I not informed of Alexandra's condition?"

"We didn't want to disturb you."

"Disturb me? Are you daft? I love this woman."

Sophie smiled. "The doctor assures us she will be fine. Trust me, Evan, I have seen her in...*worse* condition."

Evan's heart nearly broke at Sophie's words. "Please, I must see her. I need to know for myself that she is all right."

Sophie opened the door wider. "Come in, then. But be quiet. She is sleeping, and I don't want her woken."

Evan stumbled past Sophie to Alexandra's bed. She lay, breathing rapidly, her beautiful face marred with blue and purple contusions. Her eyes were swollen. He shuddered. Those bruises might as well have been on his own body. He felt the agony of every single one of them.

"Who did this to her?" Evan said through clenched teeth.

"I'm afraid we don't know. She hasn't been awake long enough to tell me or anyone."

"I don't accept that. We must know something."

"Only that she was brought home last night in a hansom cab. Woods said that two men had paid the cabbie."

"Where had she come from?"

"The cabbie didn't say. It probably didn't occur to Woods to ask."

"Goddamn it! I'll have him removed from service."

"No, Evan, please don't. It's not Woods's fault."

Evan breathed in and let out a long sigh. Woods had been with the family for years. But God, he should have thought...

"When I find out who did this to her—"

A knock on the door interrupted Evan's words.

Sophie opened it. Woods stood there.

"I beg pardon, my lady. I'm looking for... Oh, there you are, my lord. There's a constable here to see you."

"A constable?"

"Yes, my lord. He says it's quite an urgent matter."

Evan sighed. He was going to be arrested for the publication and distribution of obscene material. "Fine. Bring him up here then. I am not leaving Lady Alexandra's side."

"Evan," Sophie said, "you're supposed to be in bed yourself."

"For God's sake, doesn't anyone listen to me around here anymore? I am not leaving her side. That is final. If the constable needs to speak to me that badly, send him up here."

Woods bowed. "Yes, my lord."

A few moments later, Woods returned with the constable.

"I'm very sorry to disturb you, my lord," the constable said.

At least he was being polite before placing Evan under arrest. "Yes, you are disturbing me. What is it that I can do for you?"

"There was a disturbance at your business last night."

Evan arched his eyebrows. "There was?"

"The desk clerk at your printing house, Frank Osborne, was shot and killed. We attempted to arrest the man responsible—a Nigel Ryland."

Ryland? Could it be? "Indeed. How did you find him?"

"Two of his men turned canary. Told us he's the head of some anti-pornography group. They say he's gone off his nut. We questioned a few of the employees at the printing house this morning, and they corroborated that Osborne had been printing an underground paper at the press without your knowledge."

"He had?" So Alexandra had been in league with Osborne... Or had she? Was it possible she'd been telling him the truth? That she knew nothing about his printing business? And who had beaten her?

"Yes."

"What of this Ryland fellow?"

"He resisted arrest and was shot dead by a constable."

Evan opened his mouth to speak but shut it abruptly. If Ryland was dead, there was no need to inform the constable that he had kidnapped Sophie and shot Evan. Nothing could be done about it now anyway, and Alexandra might be incriminated if he said anything. Sophie had been returned unharmed, and Evan would recover.

"There's something else you may want to know. The two men who turned him in mentioned that Osborne severely beat a woman matching Lady Alexandra's description."

Fire rose within Evan. That fucking bastard. He was damned lucky he was already dead.

What had Alexandra been doing there? Well, it didn't rightly matter. The man was gone, and now Evan knew who had been behind the printing disaster. Why hadn't he believed Alexandra? His love?

None of it mattered now. All that mattered was Alexandra. The doctor had sworn she would recover. Evan prayed to God that Dr. Stanton spoke the truth.

He gazed at the woman he loved. Her swollen face and battered body pained him more than his gunshot wound—more than any wound to his own body ever could.

"Is there anything else I can do for you, Constable?"

"Not at this time. I'm sorry to have to give you the bad news about one of your employees."

"Good riddance, it would seem."

"Yes."

"What of the two men who gave you the information about Ryland?"

"They both turned themselves in and have agreed to give us information on Ryland's group. Evidently it was simply an anti-obscenity group that Ryland took leadership of and turned guerrilla. Most of the people involved are not crazy killers."

Evan nodded. Alexandra was out of danger. Thank God.

"Thank you. Please leave your calling card with my butler in case I have further questions."

"I certainly will. We've shut down production of *The Ruby*, so that particular paper won't be haunting you anymore. At least not for a while. These things have a way of resurfacing." He tipped his hat. "Good healing to the both of you." He left.

Evan stumbled over to Alexandra's bedside and began to sit down in a chair, when yet another dratted knock came on the bedchamber door.

"My lord," Woods said, "your father and stepmother have returned."

CONFESSIONS OF LADY PRUDENCE

by Madame O

When I came down from my explosive climax, Christophe had replaced his finger with his tongue. He licked and sucked at my swollen cunt lips. My arse yearned for his cock.

As if reading my mind, he said, "My lady, you need more preparation. Next time I will use two fingers, and then three. After that, you will be ready."

He flipped me over and lay down next to me. "Come sit on my face, sweet Lady Prudence."

I wasn't going to turn that down! I positioned myself above his lips.

"Now you can lean down and suck my cock whilst I pleasure you," he said.

How exciting! He began to kiss my slit, and I did as he bid, taking his glorious erection between my lips. I sucked him hard, wanting to milk every last drop of essence from him, to bring him at least a bit of the pleasure he had bestowed upon me.

Meanwhile, he sucked at my pussy. I shivered, my whole body trembling with need as I continued to lick and kiss his beautiful cock.

And then a shock coursed through me, followed by the intense delicate pleasure I had come to know. He was fingering my arsehole whilst he ate my cunny. Oh, Amelia, such rapture! I knew I couldn't hold out for long, but I did so love when we climaxed together.

I increased my suction on his cock, sucked him hard until my cheeks and jaw ached. I pushed harder, determined to milk him to the limit, yet still he tortured me with his lips, tongue, and finger.

Amelia, the man has a will of steel! But I can give as good as I get. I summoned all the strength I possessed and held back my climax, even lifting my hips a little to escape his tormenting mouth.

Within seconds, though, he had yanked me back down to his mouth, his tongue tantalizing me once more.

I writhed. I ground against his probing tongue, so wanting to scream his name but unable to with my mouth so full of hard cock. I braced myself and circled one hand around his member, twisting my wrist as I pumped him, still sucking him.

That did it. His hips tensed beneath me, and I knew he was ready. I ground against his face to my heart's content, Amelia, my whole body quivering, my veins bubbling with boiling nectar.

When the convulsions began at the base of his cock, I let myself go, flying, soaring, shimmering, traveling to places unknown. He filled my mouth with his seed, and I flew higher and higher still.

When I finally drifted back down, he gave my pussy a smacking kiss and released me. I crawled off of him and lay down next to him, in his arms.

"My lady," said he, his voice shaking, "I am spent beyond recognition. You are magnificent. I do believe that was the most brilliant orgasm I have ever known."

I smiled into his chest. "For me too, good sir."

And I eagerly await the next one. Until then, dear Amelia,

I am yours, affectionately,
    Prudence

CHAPTER TWENTY-FOUR

Evan groaned. What was he going to say to his father and new stepmother? He'd gotten one of her daughters kidnapped, the other beaten. They'd never trust him again.

"In a moment please, Woods," Sophie said.

"Of course, my lady. I haven't told them anything yet." Woods left.

"Look, Evan," Sophie said. "I don't want to worry our parents, and I don't want to violate Ally's confidence. I don't know how they would feel about her writing...well, you know."

Evan agreed. He would do nothing to hurt Alexandra. She'd been through enough.

Sophie continued, "I hate dishonesty, so I think we should tell them the truth—minus Ally's involvement. I need to protect her."

Evan nodded. "Yes, that seems prudent. I truly had no idea that my business was publishing the material, and the culprit is now dead. We'll tell them of your kidnapping and my being shot."

"Do you suppose Ally went to your establishment to exonerate herself? To find out who was behind this?"

He nodded. "That's exactly what I'm thinking. Why didn't I believe her? This is all my fault." He cupped his head in his hands, his heart threatening to break.

"It's not your fault, Evan. We both know Ally has her own mind."

He looked up at Alexandra's sister. Sophie was quietly brave in her own way. Nothing like Alexandra's passionate strength, but still courageous despite what she'd been through. He had newfound respect for his—he hoped—future sister-in-law.

"We can't tell them why Ally went to your business," Sophie continued.

Evan nodded. "We'll just say she went to the shop to check on something for me while I was laid up, and she found evidence— Oh, I hate lying."

"As do I," Sophie said. "But I don't think we have a choice until we're able to get the truth out of Ally."

★ ★ ★ ★

After several hours of talking, Iris had calmed down enough to take to her chamber for a few hours.

"We're fine, Mama, I assure you," Sophie said again and again.

"I'm so sorry I couldn't take care of the girls better, Father," Evan said, his head bowed.

"It doesn't sound like any of it was your fault, Evan," the earl said. "I'm just glad everyone is all right. I must see to my wife." He strode up the stairs.

Evan stood with his cane. He was exhausted and filled with disappointment in himself. He had strived to look after Iris's daughters, and he had failed miserably. And he'd fallen in love with one of them. Once Alexandra was able, he would speak to her and beg her forgiveness. Even if she wouldn't take him back, at least she would recover. That was the most important thing.

He took to his own chamber and slept for the rest of the day and well into the night.

★ ★ ★ ★

Ally woke the next day to find her mother at her side.

"Mama?"

"Yes, my darling. We returned yesterday. My God, what did that barbarian do to you?"

"It's all right," she choked out. "I've endured...worse."

Iris nodded. "I know you have, Ally, and I'm so sorry."

"There was nothing you could do, Mama."

"I did what I could. Please believe that."

Ally's heart filled with love. For once, she truly did understand what her mother had endured to keep her and Sophie as safe as possible. "I do believe you. Truly."

Iris's eyes filled with tears. "I thought these days were over. I thought..."

"I'm going to be fine."

She nodded. "Yes, I know." She let out a yawn.

"Mother, when is the last time you slept?"

"For a few hours yesterday afternoon. I've been with you most of the night."

"Please, go. I'll be fine. Get some rest. Spend some time with your new husband."

"I've spent the last month with him. Now is for you."

"Please. I just need to rest."

"If you insist." Iris kissed Ally's forehead. "I'll be back to check on you in a few hours."

Ally yawned as her mother left. She hadn't dared say anything. She wasn't sure what Sophie had told their mother.

Before she could ring for a maid to summon Sophie, a knock sounded on the door, and in walked Evan, limping with a cane and holding a leather-bound book in his other hand. He set the book on her bed table.

Oh, no. Well, she'd have to deal with this sooner or later. Lord, surely she looked a fright.

He strode quickly to her bedside. "My love, I'm so sorry."

My love? Had she heard correctly? She opened her mouth, but he stopped her.

"Please, this is all my fault."

His fault? "What?"

"You went there because...because I didn't believe you, didn't you?"

She nodded shakily. "I'm sorry, Evan."

"You have nothing to be sorry for. I should have believed you when you professed your innocence. If I could, I'd kill the man who did this to you."

"He's already dead."

"Lucky for him."

"Evan—"

"No, please let me finish."

She wanted to hear what he had to say more than anything, but first she needed to know what he and Sophie had told their parents.

"Please, Evan. Just tell me what our parents know. Do they know about my...writing?"

Evan shook his head. "No. We told them everything except why you went to the print shop that day. We said you had gone on an errand for me, to pick up some documents."

She heaved a sigh of relief. "Thank you."

"They're terribly worried about you."

She nodded. "I know."

"As am I."

"I'll be fine, Evan. I've been through worse."

Evan frowned, his eyes sunken and sad. "That doesn't make me feel any better. This is truly my fault, Alexandra."

"How in the world could it be your fault?"

"If I had believed you, trusted in you, I would have known you had nothing to do with publishing *The Ruby*. You swore you didn't, yet I didn't believe you."

"It's still not your fault. My actions these past few weeks haven't inspired a lot of trust."

"But if I had trusted you, you wouldn't have gone there."

Ally's heart warmed. "I might have anyway, to find out who was behind this. After all, Sophie was kidnapped and you were shot. You didn't expect me to just sit idly by and let that happen."

Evan let out a chuckle. "No. I do know you better than that."

Ally smiled, and then grimaced. "Ouch."

"My love?"

"Sorry, it just hurts to smile."

"You poor thing. And your smile is so beautiful too."

She tried again...and failed.

"Alexandra..."

"Yes?"

"I don't deserve your forgiveness, and I'm completely unworthy of you, but if you'll forgive me..."

"I forgive you, Evan, if you'll forgive me."

"For what?"

"For being such a pain. I was truly horrible. And then insisting upon marrying Mr. Landon when I was in love with you. I was a ninny. A true idiot. Can you forgive me that?"

"I'll forgive you anything, love. And if you'll have me, I promise to spend the rest of my life making you and our children happy."

Warmth bubbled through Alexandra. "Then you mean...?"

"Yes, my beautiful love. Will you marry me, Alexandra MacIntyre?"

"Oh, Evan"—she blinked back tears—"I would be proud and honored to be your wife."

Evan leaned over and kissed her gently on the lips. A tiny spark exploded inside her.

"Mmm," she said. "I wish..."

"What, sweet?"

She smiled again...and winced. "I wish we could do more."

Evan laughed. "In a few weeks, we'll be able to do everything we want to do."

Ally spied the book Evan had set on the bed table. "You came in carrying a book. What is it?"

"Oh, I almost forgot. I just had this published. The printers had to rush to keep deadlines on other projects, but I'm the boss." He smiled and handed her the book.

It was covered in embossed leather. She opened it.

Leaves in the Wind, A Collection of Poetry by Evan Xavier

Tears welled in her eyes. "You're a writer."

"You don't sound surprised."

"Well"—her cheeks warmed—"I found a poem in the bureau downstairs when I was looking for— Oh, never mind. Anyway, it was about me. It was lovely, and quite...erotic."

Evan's handsome face reddened. "You saw that?"

"I did."

"I'm sorry to tell you, but that particular poem won't be

in the book."

"Why not? It was beautiful."

"Because of its nature. And the Vagrancy Act..."

Ally looked away. "Oh."

He cupped her cheek and turned her back to face him. "Listen to me. I love your writing. You're a natural, but let's both cease trying to publish our more...*arousing* works until the law is changed."

Ally nodded sadly. He was right, of course.

"That doesn't mean we have to stop writing. We can write erotica solely for our own pleasure, and we can write mainstream work for publication. Write a novel, my love, and it will be my privilege and utter joy to publish it for you."

Ally nodded. "Of course. Whatever you want."

"It's whatever *we* want from now on. I do love you so, Alexandra."

The warmth of love consumed her heart. "And I love you, my Evan."

EPILOGUE

A month later, Evan and Ally retired to their suite after being married via special license. It had been a small ceremony at the Brighton estate, attended only by family and a few close friends. Although they had both been cleared for pleasure a week earlier by the doctor, they had chosen to wait until their wedding night.

Ally bathed with Millicent's help and dressed in a sheer pink night rail. She sat down at her dressing table, dabbed a bit of lavender on her pulse points, and pinched her cheeks and bit her lips to pink them. Her face was back to normal, the only remnant of her beating a small scar next to her right eye. It wasn't her first scar, but it would be her last. She smiled in gratitude for her new husband and life she had been given.

Perhaps she was not as broken as she'd thought. Perhaps she was worthy after all.

She lay down on the bed and waited for her new husband to come to her. A few moments later, he walked through the door, breathtaking in a burgundy silk robe.

"Alexandra, my love. You are stunning."

"As are you, my Evan."

He slid the robe off his shoulders and hung it over the back of the chair, striding forward, his nakedness mesmerizing her. She would never tire of looking at his magnificence.

"I've missed you so much," he said, pressing his lips to hers. "The last month has been torture, not being able to touch you, to love you."

"I assure you it has been no less torturous for me."

They crushed their lips together in a primal and drugging kiss. Oh, how she had missed his kisses, those kisses that were not kisses at all, really. They were another form of lovemaking. When Evan broke the kiss, they both took a deep breath. He rained tiny pecks over her cheeks, her neck, her earlobe.

"My God, I love you."

"And I love you, Evan. Only you. Forever."

He sank his teeth into her shoulder. She shivered. She was so ready for this man, this night. Her wedding night.

Evan pulled back slightly, lifted her night rail over her head, and let it fall to the floor.

"Tonight, my Alexandra, I shall claim *all* of you."

CONFESSIONS OF LADY PRUDENCE

by Madame O

Dearest Amelia,

You won't believe the adventures I've had this week. Let me begin...

THE END

*Continue The Sex and the Season Series
with Book Four*

SOPHIE'S VOICE
THE STORY OF SOPHIE AND ZACH

AVAILABLE NOW!

AUTHOR'S NOTE

The Vagrancy Act of 1824 was an act of Parliament in the United Kingdom. The wide definition of vagrancy included prostitution. In 1838, the act was amended to include the exposure for sale of obscene books and prints. The publication of obscene material was a common law misdemeanor at that time. Crusading groups against such material did exist, and although Mr. Ryland is a fictional character, perhaps some were as zealous as he.

Lady Alexandra's Lover takes place in 1853. Four years later, The Obscene Publications Act of 1857 was enacted, making the sale of obscene material a statutory offense and giving the courts power to seize and destroy offending material.

Despite the new law, erotica continued to thrive during Victorian times. Underground magazines surfaced, most notably *The Pearl*, after which I modeled the fictional Ruby.

The Pearl was issued from July 1879 to December 1880, when it was shut down by the authorities. Its publisher, William Lazenby, followed with several other erotic papers.

The Pearl pushed boundaries far beyond where I was willing to go with The Ruby. Still, it's a worthy relic of an era thought to be ruled by uptight morals and tight corsets. That these papers continued to flourish despite being repeatedly shut down speaks to the demand for them.

MESSAGE FROM HELEN

Dear Reader,

Thank you for reading *Lady Alexandra's Lover*. If you want to find out about my current backlist and future releases, please like my Facebook page: **www.facebook.com/HelenHardt** and join my mailing list: **www.helenhardt.com/signup/**. I often do giveaways. If you're a fan and would like to join my street team to help spread the word about my books, you can do so here: **www.facebook.com/groups/hardtandsoul/**. I regularly do awesome giveaways for my street team members.

  If you enjoyed the story, please take the time to leave a review on a site like Amazon or Goodreads. I welcome all feedback.

  I wish you all the best!

  Helen

ALSO BY HELEN HARDT

The Sex and the Season Series:
Lily and the Duke
Rose in Bloom
Lady Alexandra's Lover
Sophie's Voice
The Perils of Patricia (Coming Soon)

The Temptation Saga:
Tempting Dusty
Teasing Annie
Taking Catie
Taming Angelina
Treasuring Amber
Trusting Sydney
Tantalizing Maria

The Steel Brothers Saga:
Craving
Obsession
Possession
Melt (Coming December 20th, 2016)
Burn (Coming February 14th, 2017)
Surrender (Coming May 16th, 2017)

Daughters of the Prairie:
The Outlaw's Angel
Lessons of the Heart
Song of the Raven

DISCUSSION QUESTIONS

1. The theme of a story is its central idea or ideas. To put it simply, it's what the story means. How would you characterize the theme of *Lady Alexandra's Lover*?

2. It's clear from the first two books that Alexandra is more like Lily than like Rose. Compare and contrast Ally and Lily. How are they alike, and how are they different?

3. Alexandra and Evan are both children of an earl, yet they had vastly different childhoods. Do you think any of their characteristics stem from their respective childhoods? How so?

4. How might Alexandra's life have been different if her father hadn't died? Do you think she and Evan would have still found each other? Why or why not?

5. Discuss Alexandra's strength. Why do you think she preferred to take her father's beatings rather than witness him beat Sophie? Does this make Sophie a weak person? Why or why not?

6. Evan takes his responsibility toward the girls very seriously, yet they both end up in precarious situations. Did

Evan fail to protect them? Why or why not?

7.   Nigel Ryland is an interesting character. He feels he has the right to dole out punishment to those who publish what he considers to be obscene, yet he is against men abusing women. Are these two views contradictory? Why or why not? How did you feel about his demise?

8.   Did you enjoy Ally's stories that she wrote for *The Ruby*? Why do you think Victorian women enjoyed erotica?

9.   What do you think will become of Mr. Landon? Will he eventually marry? What type of woman do you suppose he'll end up with?

10. What do you think of groups that take the law into their own hands? Today, this can lead to terrorism, and it can be deadly. What motivates people to do these things?

11. Did Ally use poor judgment in selling her stories to *The Ruby*? Why or why not?

12. What might the future hold for Ally and Evan? Will their marriage be successful? Why or why not?

13. Why do you suppose Ally's father was so abusive? How might the abuse have affected Ally, Sophie, and Iris in the longterm? Are they capable of having happy relationships? Why or why not?

14. This book is full of colorful supporting characters: Mr.

Nathan Landon, the Earl of St. Clair, Viscount John Brooks, and Nigel Ryland, to name a few. Discuss the roles of these characters. What is their purpose in the story?

15. Who do you think Sophie's hero will be? Or have we yet to meet him?

ACKNOWLEDGEMENTS

While *Lily* and *Rose* were both written in 2007, *Alexandra* is brand new. I had a lot of fun going back into their world, and I'm already hard at work on ideas for Sophie's story. My wonderful publisher, Waterhouse Press, wants a fifth story too. I have an idea of whose story it should be, but I'd love to entertain ideas from my readers, as well. Keep your eyes posted on Facebook to cast your vote for your favorite characters!

As always, thank you to my brilliant editor, Michele Hamner Moore, my proofreaders, Lauren Dawes, Scott Saunders, and Lia Fairchild, and to all the great people at Waterhouse—David, Kurt, Shayla, Yvonne, Robyn, and Jon. You guys work marketing magic. And thank you to Meredith Wild for your continued support and encouragement.

Thank you to the members of Hardt and Soul, my new street team! HS members got the first look at *Alexandra*, and I appreciate all your support, reviews, and general good vibes. You ladies rock!

And thanks to all of you who read *Lily* and *Rose* and looked forward to Ally's story. I hope you enjoyed it. Sophie is up next. Look for our timid little heroine to heat up the pages!

ABOUT THE AUTHOR

New York Times and *USA Today* Bestselling author Helen Hardt's passion for the written word began with the books her mother read to her at bedtime. She wrote her first story at age six and hasn't stopped since. In addition to being an award winning author of contemporary and historical romance and erotica, she's a mother, a black belt in Taekwondo, a grammar geek, an appreciator of fine red wine, and a lover of Ben and Jerry's ice cream. She writes from her home in Colorado, where she lives with her family. Helen loves to hear from readers.

Visit her here:
www.facebook.com/HelenHardt

ALSO AVAILABLE FROM
HELEN HARDT

After being left at the altar, Jade Roberts seeks solace at her best friend's ranch on the Colorado western slope. Her humiliation still ripe, she doesn't expect to be attracted to her friend's reticent brother, but when the gorgeous cowboy kisses her, all bets are off.

Talon Steel is broken. Having never fully healed from a horrific childhood trauma, he simply exists, taking from women what is offered and giving nothing in return...until Jade Roberts catapults into his life. She is beautiful, sweet, and giving, and his desire for her becomes a craving he fears he'll never be able to satisfy.

Passion sizzles between the two lovers...but long-buried secrets haunt them both and may eventually tear them apart.

ALSO AVAILABLE FROM

HELEN HARDT

El Diablo strikes no fear in the heart of Dusty O'Donovan. The accomplished rider knows life holds much greater fears than a feisty stud bull. Diablo's owner, Zach McCray, is offering half a million dollars to anyone who can stay on him for a full eight seconds. That purse would go a long way helping rebuild Dusty and her brother's nearly bankrupt ranch.

Let a woman ride his bull? Not likely. Still, the headstrong Dusty intrigues Zach. Her father worked on the McCray ranch years ago, and Zach remembers her as a little girl when he was a cocky teen. Times change, and now she's a beautiful and desirable young woman. A few passionate kisses leave Zach wanting more, but will Dusty's secrets tear them apart?